Glory Shone

Lollie

ISBN:1500127248

ISBN-13:9781500127244

"Christopher, I will be back in a few minutes," his sister was saying.

He put his arm around her and patted her shoulder compassionately. "Okay Shella Esther, I will hold down the fort. Are you okay?"

"I just need some air," Shella smiled weakly, as she disappeared in the crowd.

His poor little sister. He knew this was hard on her. He was grieving, but he had lived away from home longer, besides, he was a guy. He could take things in stride, but Shella was a girl, and girls were not able to hide their emotions like boys. This was no longer the age where women swooned, waiting on their handsome prince to catch them, but Shella was still young and little. Everything was happening way too fast for both of them. She looked like she needed a break from the shaking hands, sympathetic comments, and people grabbing her neck.

He did not get a chance to watch her, for the next person in line was speaking to him, requiring his attention. These friends and acquaintances of his mom and dad had come this evening to show respect for them. He knew some of the people as church members, some as coworkers of his dad's, but many, he never met. He plastered a generic smile for each visitor to display appreciation for the honor.

He wished Amber was standing beside him, but she was not able to leave until the morning. He had gotten so caught up in his own life in Maine, that he procrastinated in bringing her down to meet his folks, and now, it was too late. His mom would have loved her too. He was confident that both parents would have put a seal of approval on this marriage, had he brought her home to meet them. As it were, they would not meet his bride-to-be in this life, and that saddened him as well as made him feel guilty.

This tragic turn of events would change Shella's life and his impending plans. He would be responsible for his baby sister, his grandmother, and soon a wife; that is, if she would have him after the new responsibilities. Would Amber still want to marry him, if he had to move back home and take care of his family? Shella had two semesters left at college to graduate. Grandmother was in her sixth year of Alzheimer's, with no delusions of ever recovering, and the weight of his dad had suddenly fallen on his shoulders. Mom and Dad left some pretty big shoes to fill.

Shella was making her way from the ladies' room slowly. If she had to pretend to be strong much longer, she thought she would burst. Her head was aching profusely and her eyes were beginning to puff from tears. It seemed that everyone passing through the line said something that made her start crying again. All she could think of was how badly she wanted her Mom.

She smacked into someone accidentally, but kept her eyes toward the floor. "Excuse me," she discharged generically.

"Shella! How in the world are you?"

When long strong arms reached around her, lifting her feet from the ground, she quickly became irritated and embarrassed at her next-door neighbor. Tyler and she had grown up spending time together both at home and school. They had been next door neighbors ever since Shella and Tyler were born.

Tyler had an older brother, Teddy, who always teamed up with Christopher to play mean tricks on the two younger siblings for the entirety of their childhood, which made them all very close. It was okay for Christopher and Teddy to pick on her, but no one else dared. Teddy, as much as Christopher, would pommel them good, if they had. It was as if she had three brothers, instead of one.

"Tyler, you are embarrassing her," scolded his mother.

"Your mother is right, Son." His dad had a somber tone.

Tyler's eyes seemed to mock Shella as they laughed merrily. Tyler Gordon was a charismatic young man who had no problem in the women department. He was tall and thin, but not too thin. His light brown hair parted and combed to perfection. Actually, it was almost as if even every eyelash was positioned to perfection. His outgoing and chameleon like personality caused him to rarely go out with the same girl twice. His charming good looks won him the attention of many beautiful girls.

"Aw Dad. It's just little Shella. Hey Shella, remember the t…"

His mother insisted, "Tyler, she is not a little girl anymore. You just don't go around hugging young ladies that way."

"You're right, Mom. I am sorry. Shella, when did you grow up? You were not supposed to grow up," he sported wickedly.

"Tyler, it is good to see you again." She could feel the heat of her blushing cheeks. "Mr. and Mrs. Gordon, thank you so much for coming. It is good to see you."

Tyler was awkward at such an event as this and reverted to the merry making. "Is that any way to greet your future husband?" He threw his arm around Shella and kept it there, after she hugged his mom and dad.

"Excuse me?" Both parents and Shella looked puzzled.

"Don't you remember our pact?"

Her cheeks brightened again from the embarrassment of so much attention, as some of the other guests were drawn to look at the spectacle. "What pact was that, Tyler? We made so many."

"We promised to hitch up, if neither of us were married, when we were twenty-five. Don't you remember?" Shella briefly looked into his hazel eyes. He noticed her discontent. "Don't worry, Shella, I won't hold you to it. How about when we are thirty, instead?" he laughed.

Shella wanted to laugh hysterically. She was getting ready to bury her beloved parents, and here was this immature childhood friend making foolish converse about getting married. "Tyler, when we were kids, we thought twenty-five was old and hopeless. Surely you do not expect us to keep some silly oath we made in childish ignorance."

Tyler still held his arm tight around her shoulder. Shella looked to her brother as a means of escape, but Christopher was smiling proudly at her as if he were clueless to her misery. She would get him good for this.

"Shella Esther," her cousin tapped her arm, "Momma sent me to fetch you. She's in the office with some man that wants to talk to you."

"Thank you Cory." She was grateful for the interruption. She had already stopped listening to Tyler's insane conversation with his parents a few seconds before. "Will you excuse me?"

ဖာ

Her Aunt Carolyn was with the funeral director, who had some legal questions to settle. Shella was glad to be away from the Gordons, and when the two hours were over, relief rushed over her entire body that the whole evening was over. No more fake smile, no more pretenses from family members who had not spoken to her mom and dad in years.

Yes, after the funeral tomorrow, this would all be over. Maybe then, she could catch her breath.

Immediately upon arriving at her lovely home, Shella removed her shoes and released her hair from the pins that held it up. She went to the kitchen for a cold glass of water. This empty old house would never be the same. Her momma's sweet hands would never wash this glass again. Oh, how she wanted to cry.

"I am going to hit the shower, Shella Esther," Christopher informed, while striding up the stairs.

They had not had much time to talk, since she had picked Christopher up from the airport a couple hours before the visitation. It seemed as if they hardly knew each other any more. Christopher had been away at college, and then she went. They had not talked in a long time. She missed that in him right now. Her mom and dad's death put her sibling relationship in a whole new perspective. Christopher may not always be around. He was so grown up now, so mature and responsible.

"It is time to make some decisions," she spoke audibly to herself, after her brother was gone. When she received the call that her mom and dad had been killed in an automobile accident, Shella left her college life in ten minutes to come home. Her Aunt Carolyn helped her make the arrangements for the funeral, since Christopher was not able to get there any sooner. Christopher was a man of few words, like his dad. Shella knew he was hurting, but her brother would put up a front to grieve alone.

Christopher had his own life somewhere else. He had been up north for three years. It was quite obvious that he had no plans to move back here. She could not ask him to give it up to come back here to take care of their grandmother. That is why she sadly made her phone call to the dean of her school, after Christopher was safely out of earshot. With great regret, she withdrew from college only two semesters away from obtaining her Bachelor's Degrees in physical therapy and in music. Her responsibility lay with her grandmother, just as it had with her mother. Taking her parents from her was God's choice, and if this was what He chose for her life, then she must not grieve the Holy Spirit.

"Well, maybe you can come back next semester, or the one after, to finish," the dean suggested hopefully, "I hate to lose you Shella. Is there any way you can come up for a couple of days next week or the week after to take your finals? You should not have to lose this whole semester this close to the end."

"I can probably manage that at some point in the next couple of weeks."

"Wonderful. I will speak to your professors about your absence in class. Considering the circumstances, we will be able to excuse you for the time. We will keep you registered as a student, until you can get back to finish the last six months."

"Thank you, sir."

"You are welcome. Again, I am sorry about your parents. If you need anything else, please don't hesitate to call me."

"I will and goodbye."

She hastened her goodbye, because the doorbell rang throughout the house at that moment. She replaced the receiver and looked to see if Christopher was coming yet. When he was not, she went to open the door with a saddened countenance. This had been a difficult choice for her, but a necessary choice, nonetheless.

"Shella! It has been a long time. I don't know if you recognize me, b..."

"Teddy! How are you? It is good to see you. Why are you knocking?" She proceeded with a sisterly hug and peck on his tanned cheek, leading him in the house. This brother was a bright spot in her weary day.

He grinned at her remembrance of him. "Mom sent me over with some food. She said you and Christopher would be hungry," he lied. Truthfully, his mother had sent Tyler over, but Tyler had other plans and asked Teddy to do it.

"How nice! Are you doing well, Teddy? It has been a long time." She took his arm and led him to the kitchen, where he deposited the dishes.

Teddy was handsome in his own right. He was bashful and quiet, which made him less memorable than his younger brother. Sometimes he would have to repeat his name several times to whomever he was speaking, but not Shella. He knew she would remember him. They had spent almost two inseparable decades together. She better know him!

He smiled to himself. Whereas most girls thought Teddy to be awkward, Shella didn't. She had climbed trees, dug worms, fished, and played ball with him. They even shared the chicken pox together. She hadn't changed that much. Teddy was at ease around Shella, too, because she treated him just like she did Christopher. She made it easy for him to talk to her. She was not a *girl*, she was a kid sister. They had been in trouble with each other and for each other many times. His folks looked at her and Christopher as part of the extended family.

"How long has it been?" he laughed, "I was gone for four years at college and have been back two. I have seen you at holidays from across the yard, but I never realized how much you have grown up. You are not the same knobby knee bag of bones anymore."

"What are you talking about? She will always be that little punk sister of mine," Christopher accused, coming upon them.

"And you will always be my cootie head brother," she returned defiantly.

Teddy thrust out his hand to Christopher, "Buddy, how in the world are you?"

"Just fine. How about you?"

"I apologize for not getting a chance to speak to either of you at the visitation. You were both quite busy with other people, and I didn't want to interrupt."

"Thank you for coming. I know it is almost like losing your mom and dad too. You guys spent as much time over here growing up, as you did at home."

"I will miss them. They were wonderful people." Teddy lowered his voice respectfully. "I have not seen much of them, since I left for college. We have not been getting together for Thanksgiving and Christmas, like we did when we were little."

Shella lightened the spirits with a perky voice. "What have you been up to, Teddy?"

Teddy grinned wryly, "I have been working over at the paper mill about two years now. Of course, I am still living with the folks right now, although I plan on moving out within a year." He turned to the young woman again. "Boy Shella, I can't believe how grown up you are. You are so different."

Christopher nudged her arm, "Yeah, remember when she used to be in love with Tyler?"

Teddy laughed, "You should have seen them tonight at the visitation. I declare they make a handsome couple." He ignored the withering glare and open mouth of his victim. "Do you remember those love letters she gave him in grade school?"

Christopher grinned, "I remember them well."

Teddy had gone too far to stop now. "By the way Shella, thanks a lot. That's what gave Tyler the big head. You gave him the ego of a maniac. Now, he thinks he is God's gift to women."

She held up her head proudly, "That just goes to show you two bums what you know, which is nothing. I never was in love with that arrogant brother of yours. He was always crazy over Missy Staton, besides boys were gross, especially Tyler Gordon!"

Teddy continued the banter, "Then why did you write him all those love letters?"

"What letters? I never wrote that hound dog any letter!" she maintained.

Christopher threw her his mischievous grin, "Yes you did. I remember. It said, 'Tyler, you are so cute. I love you. The next time we are in the tree house, I want to kiss you," he mocked in a girlish voice.

"Christopher Aaron Evans! I cannot believe you did that! Do you know he did try to kiss me in the tree house one time? I had to punch him in the nose. You are a horrid brother, and if Mom and Dad knew about it, they would have blistered you good and proper, and you would have deserved it, and for your information, if I had known you wrote him those letters, I would have told on you." She ran her thoughts together without pausing.

Christopher threw his arm around Teddy, who was enjoying the sport of watching the kid squirm. They laughed as Christopher continued, "Dear Tyler, you are the man of my dreams. Will you hold my hand on the bus to the field trip?"

By now, the two men were laughing uncontrollably, but Shella wanted to cry. She remembered that field trip, when Tyler tried to hold her hand. She punched him in the nose. That poor boy went home with a bloody nose so many times, his mother took him to the doctor, thinking something terrible was wrong with him.

"Laugh at my expense, will you? How many letters did you write? It doesn't matter, because you are going to tell Tyler you wrote those stupid letters and not me! And I have a witness." She stepped beside Teddy and put an elbow on his shoulder.

"Why Shella, why would I say Christopher wrote those letters? You know you wrote them, because you were, and still are, crazy about my brother."

Shella quickly removed her arm from the enemy. "I see how you two stick together. You are just as bad as Christopher. Shame on both of you. God is going to punish you both for lying through your teeth. You may be my brothers, but you are not my friends. I hate you both. Get out of my house Teddy Gordon."

Still laughing, Christopher enveloped her in his arms, "You do not hate us. You love us, 'cause we *love* you."

"No, I don't. I hate you," she struggled to free herself, exhibiting funny faces in her struggle.

Christopher wrestled her to the couch, tickling her. "Tell me you love me."

"No. Ahh!" she did not want to laugh.

"Say it."

"No." He tickled her mercilessly until finally she gave in, "Okay, okay. I love you."

"And Teddy?"

"No. He lied too." Christopher went to tickle her again, as she slid to the floor. "Okay fine! And Teddy, too. Now, let me up, you big bully." She would have added the, "I hate both of you," aloud, but she knew Christopher would start again, so she mumbled quietly.

The neighbor watched all the horse playing in amusement. It was just like old times again. This was nice. Shella picked her mussed self from the floor and straightened out her skirt, dusting off the lint. She threw an intentional snarled face at her brother and then stuck her tongue out at Teddy.

"I love you too, Shella," he defended.

"I am sure you do. I am no longer speaking to you or your friend over there. Just go home and leave me alone. I am going to my room now, and the next time I see your momma, I am telling on you." She shook her head in an exaggerated gesture of pride and started up the stairs.

Christopher sobered. "Seriously Shella Esther, about tomorrow, I can drop you off at the nursing home in the morning, but I can't pick you up before the funeral. I have to pick someone up at the airport about a half hour before we have to be at the church."

Teddy threw in another sarcasm, "Her boyfriend could pick her up."

"You are so funny, Teddy Gordon. Your brother needs no encouragement."

"Shella, I think it is a great idea. Do you think he would do it?" Christopher asked Teddy, seriously.

"I am sure he would be glad to."

Deliberately not looking at Teddy, Shella returned the sarcasm,

"Well Christopher, I do not need anybody to pick me up. I am perfectly fine on my own." Having said that, she shook her long curls, and with head held high, ascended out of sight.

ℰ◦ℰ

Shella rose early for the long day ahead. She was going to spend the morning with her grandma at the home, and if she was mentally able, Shella was going to take the woman to her daughter's funeral.

She was not hungry, yet she forced something down, when Christopher appeared disheveled and yawning. "Morning."

"I ought not speak to you, after what you did to me, you wretched brother."

"Come on Shella. I'm sorry. Will you forgive me?"

"It may take some time, because I know you are not really sorry, but yes, I will forgive you."

He poured a cup of the coffee Shella had made and continued. "I talked to Tyler last night. He is going to pick you up at twelve thirty. That should give you plenty of time to get to the church."

"Christopher, why did you do that? I told you I could find my own way to the church."

"Please don't fight with me or get mad at me this morning. It was no problem for him. He said he would be glad to do it. This will help us out a lot."

"Fine, but from now on, let me make my own plans, please."

He drew her to his embrace, "Okay Shella Esther, I will not presume to do it again." He kissed her hair. "I love you."

"I love you too, you big lug." She slapped her hand softly against his broad chest. "Do you think Grandma will be able to come to the funeral?"

"Beats me. Mom said she doesn't even know who she was. She was living back in her twenties, the last time I talked to Mom."

"I will not bring her, if she is like that. It would serve no purpose at all."

Christopher released his embrace. "Use your good judgment, Shella Esther."

୬ଡ଼୧

The nursing home was the best around, but no nursing home was good enough for any loved one, but her mother had no choice. With the Alzheimer's, grandmother could wander off, or worse. This was the best place for her.

Shella's big eyes scrutinized every detail. She passed one room that emitted a foul odor. Her nose wrinkled against her will. Cautiously, she stepped down the hallway to her grandmother's room, not knowing what to expect.

Grandmother seemed to have shrunk, since the last time Shella had seen her. She was petite to begin with, but she looked so small sitting in the chair, looking out the window. She wondered what thoughts might be going through grandma's mind. Did she know her baby girl was killed in that awful car wreck? Did she even realize she had a baby girl? Would she remember her granddaughter?

The old woman sensed Shella's presence and turned with a smile.

"Hello Mother. Can I come out of my room now?"

Shella, thinking it would be better to go along with her, put her gentle touch on her grandmother. "You certainly may. I thought we might take a walk outside. It is a beautiful day outside."

"I don't know. It looks windy out. I'll get an ear ache, if it's windy."

"They have put some pretty flowers in the garden," she coaxed.

The old woman became agitated, "Mom, I don't want to go outside."

"Okay Sweetie, we do not have to go outside. Would you like to take a walk down the hall? We could go to the kitchen and get something to eat."

"I'm not hungry." She shot Shella down with a curt response.

For the next several hours the grandmother contradicted almost everything the granddaughter suggested, as she envisioned Shella as her mother. A few times, grandmother snapped cruelly and ordered her to leave.

Once, when the nurse came in, she yelled at Shella and told the nurse that Shella was abusing her. The nurse explained to Shella that with Alzheimer's, the patients often acted that way. It was normal and Shella shouldn't take it personal, but she almost ended in tears two or three times.

She tried to help her grandmother with the crafts that the activities director planned for them, but received a slap for her efforts. Shella turned red with embarrassment, but the director encouraged her by telling her that sometimes they had good days, and sometimes they had bad days. On the downside, her grandmother, unfortunately, was beginning to have more bad days than good.

She caressed the old woman's fragile back and shoulders carefully, as she read John chapter fourteen to her and softly sang *Amazing Grace*. The precious little creature was eighty-three years old and sweet and innocent, "God touch her, I pray. Give her a perfect and complete healing, according to Your will." It was during this time of reading God's Word that the grandmother quieted, becoming serene and bearable. That is the effect God's Word has on one.

However, as the hour drew near that she must leave, the old lady became agitated again. Maybe she sensed Shella's nervousness over the ceremony about to take place, but she was no longer seeing her mother in Shella. It seemed that now, she had become some horrid memory to grandmother; a horrid memory she couldn't seem to escape from. She began screaming angrily and threw her brush at Shella, barely missing her head. She was trapped in her own level of hell.

The young woman ran from the room with her grandmother's words ringing through the hall, "Get out of here! Help! Help! She's gonna kill me! Help!"

Tears blinded her vision so that Shella could not see as she cut the corner of the door quickly. She came to an immediate halt, when an object would not move out of her way. She knew her grandmother could not help it, but the pressures of the last few days had peaked. Everything was devastating. Her mom and dad gone, quitting college, dealing with a loved one that hated her, and now, her nose hurt from her run in.

Before she could apologize, two strong arms drew her close in comfort. The cologne soothed her senses, and the voice soothed her soul, "Shella, what is the matter?"

"Oh Teddy! I don't know how Mother did it. I cannot control Grandmother. She hates me. Everything is so wrong. Oh, how I wish Mother was here now."

"It is going to be okay," he soothed, kissing her hair. He could feel the tears fall onto his arm. His heart swelled with compassion. "Shella," he lifted her tear-streaked face with both hands, "You do know I love you and am here for you, don't you?"

"I know you do, Teddy. I love you for always being right where I need you, when I need you. It is not fair. I miss Mom and Daddy so much. They are gone, and I didn't even say goodbye to them."

"I know, little one," his thumbs pushed the tears from her cheeks, while his long fingers reached around her jaw bones to hold her face securely, "I am so sorry, Shella. I wish I could make everything right again."

"I am so glad you are here, Teddy. I don't think I am strong enough to handle this alone."

The tears, the empathy, and the sweet soft fragrance of her hair made

Teddy react completely out of character. What was this that was overwhelming him? He had never imagined this in a million years. In the heat of the moment, Teddy Gordon had reached down without forethought and touched her lips with his.

He had never thought about kissing a girl before. Even when he dated Elizabeth Marsh for nine months, he made a point to not kiss her. He chose to wait until he was sure she was to be his wife, and when she turned out not to be the one, he was thankful for his reserve.

Shella found comfort in the moment. His touch, his friendship, his kiss, this tender Teddy was complimentary compared to the old Teddy. For the brevity of that kiss, all else was forgotten, as Shella closed her eyes and returned his gesture. All the worries and sorrows of lost parents and ailing grandmothers were removed. The act took her by surprise, but delighted her, nonetheless.

The taste of the salt from her tears brought the man to his senses. *Then*, it dawned on Teddy what he was doing. His actions had taken him by surprise, also. What was he doing? "You stupid fool!" he chided himself. "You are taking advantage of this poor girl at her weakest moment."

He quickly pulled away shamefacedly almost pushing her away. "I am so sorry, Shella. I shouldn't have done that. That was very stupid of me. Please forgive me."

She blushed red at his repentance, "It is okay, Teddy, really."

"Some brother I am! I wait till you are vulnerable, and what do I do? I start kissing my brother's girl," he stammered, shoving his hands in his pockets. "I cannot apologize enough."

Shella became angry at his assumption about Tyler. "I am no one's girl." She threw her head up with indignation, tossing her hair across her shoulder. She angrily finished wiping the tears from her face that Teddy's fingers had missed. As usual, her pride crept in. "Why are you here, Teddy?"

"Something came up at the last minute, and Tyler wasn't able to come, so he asked me to."

That was not exactly the whole truth. Tyler, had made a date days earlier with some girl he worked with, and was not willing to pass it up so quickly, so he asked Teddy to run interference. Tyler would meet up with them at the funeral, and all would be happy.

"We should go, then," Shella announced coolly, so Teddy would know that she was angry with him.

The ride to the church was silent with Teddy nervously biting his fingernails, knowing the ramifications of this error in judgment he had made. Shella had his horrible words burning in her ears, which fueled her pride. She had not experienced the practice of kissing before, but was she *that* bad? By the way, how dare he call her Tyler's girl? His audacity to kiss her in the first place was bad enough, but for him to recoil as if she was some horrible ugly creature was just adding insult to injury.

She must refuse such anger, because these thoughts could not remain forefront in her mind. Her darling mom and dad were about to be submerged into the cold uncaring earth, until Christ raised them again to be with Him. Of course, their souls were already with Him, because to be absent of the flesh is to be present with the Lord.

Teddy tried to offer a brotherly arm of support around Shella, as he opened the door to the church, but she curtly sidestepped his touch. Inside, they went their separate ways. She wanted no misunderstanding with Teddy. He was cruel and she hated him!

She found Christopher at the front of the church accepting condolences from their second cousin. She approached him with the intentions of fussing about sending Teddy *or* Tyler to pick her up.

"There you are Shella Esther. I was beginning to wonder if Tyler was going to get you here on time," he greeted.

"Well, I am here, no thanks to you, Christopher." She took a breath to continue.

Christopher interpolated, "Shella Esther, I have someone I want you to meet. I was going to bring her down to meet Mom and Dad, but I guess I waited too long. This is my fiancé, Amber."

Shella watched in amusement, forgetting her anger, as her brother put his arm around the pretty young girl beside him to push her toward Shella. He *was* joking, right? "Your fiancé? Christopher, we didn't even know you were dating someone."

"You know how Momma is. She would have us married two years ago, if she knew."

"But Christopher…" She stopped on her own as she was tongue-tied.

"I have been wanting to meet you so much, Shella Esther. Christopher talks about you all the time. He wanted to visit you at college to tell you, so we could meet, but we were never able to catch up with you." She hugged Shella. "Is it Shella or Shella Esther?" The young bride to be seemed to be nice.

Shella smiled politely, "I will answer to either. My family calls me Shella Esther, but I go by Shella at school and around my friends. Since you are going to be in the family, I will answer to either."

Christopher could not help but throw in some more brotherly banter, "She will answer to Barky too."

A young man approached them at that time, saving Christopher from a contemptuous look from his sister. "Hello Shella Esther," he said with smiling eyes. Turning to her brother, "Christopher, we are about ready to begin, if you want to go outside to walk in."

"Hey Steve." Christopher shook the young preacher's hand. "Do we have to walk in? Do you want to, Shella Esther?" She shook her head. "I didn't think so. Steve, we would rather not go through all those formalities. We can just stay in here, right?"

"Sure, I'll tell the pastor." He turned a big grin toward the sister. "Shella, it is good to see you, again."

"Likewise, Steve."

"Did you know I am a preacher, now?"

"Yes, Mother told me a while back that you were called to preach. That is wonderful. I hope to get to hear you soon."

He looked at his hands and asked nervously, "Do you think we could get together sometime and maybe go to prayer meeting together, or something?"

Before she could answer, Tyler was standing too close to her with his arm falling dominantly on her shoulder. He kissed her hair quickly with a veiled warning in his glance at the preacher. "You ready Shella?" He claimed authority over her.

She gave him a disparaging look as he directed her away from Steve. Shella stood steadfast contrary to Tyler's urge.

"We are not walking in, Tyler." Christopher told him with an appreciative handshake. He was glad his sister had Tyler to lean on during this time. "Come on brother, we will go ahead and sit down. They are about to begin."

Shella became irritated that Tyler had put his claim on her. She was NOT his girl! She was NOT, NOT, NOT! He moved his arm from around her shoulder to her lap, where he took her hand in his, but Shella quickly made a point of removing her hand. She dared not look at him, because she could feel his eyes on her. As a matter of fact, she felt like the focus of several eyes, as her cheeks burned.

The pastor spoke kind words about their mom and dad. There was no doubt that he loved them very much. Then, Steve sung "The Old Rugged Cross", because that was Mrs. Evans's favorite song. He, Christopher, and Shella formed a trio years ago, and the three had grown up singing in front of the church. However, today he was singing solo. Then, there was preaching.

After the preaching, the two caskets were rolled down the aisle, followed by two sets of pallbearers. Neither Shella nor Christopher could look in the direction of the coffins. A sad gasp escaped Shella's lips against her will. They could not take her mommy and daddy away like this! The brother took the sister's hand as the pastor directed them to stand and follow the procession to sit under the tent at the graveside.

Shella almost cried and Christopher must have sensed this. The brother wrapped his arm around her in comfort, allowing her to rest her weary head on his shoulder.

The preacher read some comforting scripture before finishing the ceremony with a prayer. The pastor and Steve went through the chairs under the tent shaking the family's hands.

The crowd dissipated after a while, and as soon as she could, Shella slipped away by herself to say her goodbyes. She softly touched her fingers to her lips, and then each coffin. "Goodbye Momma. Goodbye Daddy. I love you so much." One tear surfaced, falling slowly down her cheek. "I am going to miss you."

"Shella, I'll take you home now, if you are ready." Tyler was getting good at intruding on her personal moments.

"I can ride with Christopher, thank you Tyler. I don't want to put anyone out."

"You are not putting me out. I *want* to take you home. May I?"

Shella heard a genuine kindness, like the old Tyler, in his question. "Okay Tyler. I would appreciate it, but it will be a few minutes."

Stragglers were coming to her now to offer final condolences, and Christopher invited the entire crowd back to their house, because, according to the Baptist custom, too much food had been prepared, and he knew that they could not eat it all by themselves in a week. Christopher and Amber left ahead of everyone to set everything out for the guests, so Shella was left alone to accept the respecters.

∽✑

The ride home with Tyler was more pleasant than Shella had anticipated. When they were alone, he was not so egotistical. He questioned her comfort several times and ecumenically tried to please her. He was more like the old brother from years ago.

"I am sorry about your mom and dad, Shella. They were good to

Teddy and me. Your mom treated me like one of hers. I hate like the dickens that they are gone."

"She was a good mother."

Tyler laughed to himself, "Remember that time we snuck off to go swimming?"

"Oh yes, and Mom lined all four of us up on the porch, wet and all."

"I know." Teddy rubbed his leg as if remembering, "I didn't think she would really use that hickory on Teddy and me, but she sure laid it to us."

That was a happy memory that put a smile on Shella's lips. Her mother was precious. Dad was normally the one that delivered earned whippings, but on rare occasion, when it was required, her mother had to, and when she distributed punishment, Christopher and Shella avoided getting another. They hated displeasing their mother.

Tyler pulled the car into his own driveway, which allowed them a short walk across the yard, but before he would emerge from the car to open Shella's door for her, he turned to face her.

"I am glad to see you Shella. It's been so long. I want you to know that you have always been my closest friend and I love you. I hope it is not the last I see of you."

"Tyler, I have always felt the same way about you. We *are* such good friends. I would never want to lose that friendship." She touched his arm in hopes he would understand her meaning.

He responded by putting his hand over hers. "Can I get anything for you?"

"No, thank you anyway."

"I am driving over to the lake tomorrow after church. Wanna come?"

Shella replied gleefully, "That would be quite lovely. We could bring some bread to feed the ducks."

"Can you still bait a hook?" he asked, as a thought came to him.

"You know it!"

"We could get some fishing in."

Shella curled her nose while shaking her head. "Not tomorrow, Tyler. I don't have my fishing license, plus, it *is* Sunday. I will take a rain check, though."

Tyler looked like a boy that just had parental reprimand. "We can still go to the lake, can't we?" he asked repentantly.

"Yes."

Tyler quickly gave her a kiss on the cheek, before getting out. "I love you."

It was not odd for that phrase to be thrown around between these two families, because they truly did love one another. It was something they always said.

"I love you," she replied as he opened the door.

As he walked her across the yard, he fidgeted, "I have to go. I have a prior engagement."

"Thank you, my friend. Go, you shouldn't break a commitment."

He gave her cheek another kiss, "Thanks, I will see you tomorrow."

"Okay"

ↁ◠◡

Shella entered her old home, where Christopher and Amber had already begun preparing for the other family members and well-wishers. Many people were in and out, eating, consoling, and celebrating the life of her parents.

She went in through the kitchen door at the back of the house to sneak up the back stairs. She did not want to mingle with all those people, so she decided to change her clothes and find somewhere else to be.

"Shella Esther can you open this jar for me?" her second cousin, Brenda, asked before she managed to escape.

"I can try." She took the jar and strained to turn the lid. "Goodness. Brenda, I don't know that I can."

A familiar masculine arm reached around her and took hold of the jar. "Do you want me to try?" The cologne that pacified her earlier, now made her sick.

"Thanks." She released the jar to him, before trying to slip out the door. She wanted to escape, before Teddy opened the jar, but he caught up with her on the third step of the porch. Although she quickened her pace, he placed a hand on her shoulder."

"Shella, can we talk?"

She replied curtly as she turned to continue leaving, "We have nothing to talk about, Teddy. We said everything we needed to earlier."

"Come on, can we take a walk?" he pressed.

"No thank you, Teddy. I would rather not."

Over his shoulder, another voice interrupted to her fortune, "Hey Shella!"

"Hey Steve. Would you like to go for a walk?" She gave Teddy a spiteful, triumphant last look, as she pushed past him.

Christopher arranged to stay over at the Gordon house with his old best friend, so that Amber could stay with Shella. It would be improper and scandalous for them to stay under the same roof. At the Gordon house, though, it was just like old times, when they were thirteen and practically lived together between both houses. Teddy rolled out two sleeping bags in the basement den for them to sleep in.

Christopher hadn't had much time to think of his mom and dad. On the other hand, Shella thought of nothing but her parents. Like the night before, Shella slipped down the back stairs with an extra blanket and pillow to ascend the old rope ladder to the tree house and make a bed. She couldn't sleep in that house, for the memories it held haunted her, so that she could not fall asleep.

As she lay beneath the stars of the open window, the tears fell silently, until she fell asleep. Her mom and dad were gone from this earth for good. Never again could she call her mom up from school and wish her a happy birthday. Never again would she open her mail to find a hundred dollar bill with a love note from her daddy in it. They had been such good parents. They had loved her and Christopher so much. Unlike most of the broken families around, they were blessed to have a mom and a dad living in marriage, together. She cried, until her eyes burned to the point she had to close them for comfort, when she fell into her slumber.

She woke up early Sunday morning, slipped back into her room, made her bed, and fixed herself a bowl of cereal. No one would be the wiser of where she slept, because Amber was still asleep in Christopher's room. Shella felt childish and silly for not being able to sleep in the house. Mom and Dad would think she was being childish. Maybe she was, but she didn't care.

Christopher called a little later from the neighbor's. Mrs. Gordon invited Amber and Shella to come over for breakfast before church, but Shella gracefully declined, promising to send Amber over as soon as she was ready for church. Christopher questioned Shella's reasons for not wanting to join them, and gave her a little argument about it, but Shella conceded to 'think about it', stating she had already eaten. Instead, she quickly readied for church, waited for Amber to go over to the Gordons, and then slipped out the door to walk to church.

Shella was the only one out of the two families that attended Sunday school that morning, which was a welcome reprieve from her demanding brother and friends. She loved Christopher, but she didn't like the new role he was trying to play in her life. Her dad was dead, and she didn't need another one. He need not start trying to run her life.

Steve, the young preacher, greeted her with his usual huge smile of welcome. He was glad to see her without Tyler commanding her attentions. He had always been a constant friend, and now, he had been elected as the teacher of this class. He was a good teacher and learned in the Word of God. Shella really enjoyed the whole Sunday school lesson.

Steve was sweet, where most guys were not. He reverenced women in the highest regard, especially when it came to Shella. She may not be the most graceful creature, but she was the epitome of what he desired in a wife, besides, there were few to no girls in this town comparable to her. All in all, Shella was the only person, male or female, that ever showed true kindness to him.

Midway through the song service, the preacher asked the trio to sing, which was slightly difficult for Shella and Christopher. When she returned to her seat Tyler had slipped into her pew, leaving Shella wedged too snugly between her brother and him for her liking. She was feeling smothered, especially when he put his arm behind her on the back of the pew. Her pride and irritation rose. He did not need to push himself on her so much. Christopher did not need to push him on her so much, neither did anyone else, for that matter.

To Shella's relief, Paula, a young lady that was crazy about Tyler, swiftly occupied his attention at the conclusion of the service. This gave Shella the opportunity to escape and walk the short distance home without having any propositions. Constant company was not what she wanted or needed. She would much rather have a little time to herself, so she quickly ran to her room to throw on an everyday frock to wear to the lake, where she was able to spend a few solitary moments, before Christopher and Amber arrived home.

It was only a little while, before Tyler went home to change into some jeans and showed up on Shella's doorstep. He barely had time to knock, before Christopher let him in, and called for Shella. He said nothing, but was glad that Shella had agreed to go with Tyler. Their mom and dad would approve of Tyler.

Tyler smiled as she came from the kitchen, "You ready to go Miss Evans?"

"I have the bread right here." She held a hand up, which held the bag. When she caught a glimpse out the window of Teddy striding across the yard, she added quickly, "Let's go."

As they passed him on the porch, Shella ignored his, "Hey Shella."

She was still angry at his insult to her, and his lame excuse for an apology infuriated her. She was not going to let him off the hook that easily. One does not kiss another and then act as if it were the most horrible thing in the world. It is the ultimate insult to one's character. She reiterated to herself that she hated him.

The warm sun rays peeped through any branches that spread far enough for it to steal through, sending beautiful misty rays to the pine carpeted earth. It was something out of a fairytale setting. It seemed as if time stood still, as the wind lay still, and the only sound that could be heard was the quacking of the ducks on the lake. It was a little piece of heaven that God, knowing her turmoil and grief, had reserved just for her to enjoy at this moment. Across the way she could see children running and playing around on the playground.

"Is this not beautiful?" she thought aloud.

"It sure is." Tyler put her hand in the crook of his arm as they strolled.

All the girls had liked it, when he did that, but Shella quickly removed it under the ruse that she was ready to feed the ducks. "Here you go." She handed him some bread. "They will chase you, if you let them see you have food for them."

They fed and played with the ducks for a while, and then sat on the pine carpet shaded by the trees laid out by God's own hand. Neither had much to say, because neither knew what to say.

One duck took a liking to Tyler and started following him everywhere he went pecking at his jeans' leg, until the duck became a nuisance to him. Tyler threatened and shooed, but the duck just kept coming back much against his aggravation.

He listened to Shella's laughter at the duck, or maybe it was he, she was laughing at. It was not the same laugh he remembered it to be. She was not that little tag-a-long kid she used to be who sent him love notes. Her laughter was older, more mature, not annoying as it used to be, when she laughed at him.

He wondered if she still felt the same about him. Would she still send him love notes? Was she still in love with him? He knew his mom and dad accepted Shella as a contestant for his affections. They had met a couple of the girls he went with, but they strongly opposed them. After that, he stopped bringing any girls home to Mom and Dad, but he knew they loved Shella.

Tyler was a good guy that tried to please everyone. He was sweet, full of life, and good hearted. He loved and enjoyed every person he met. He was a little arrogant, because his charm and looks could win the heart of almost any girl he chose; although, Shella was one girl he had always found hard to understand. She would write him love notes and then hit him when he responded to them.

He was a taller, more social, and more outgoing version of his brother. He had more refined good looks, whereas his brother had the rugged good looks. Tyler was kinder and more compassionate than his brother, but Tyler was also quicker to throw a punch than Teddy.

The only flaws Shella could find in Tyler was that he was not as mature as she thought he should be, and he seemed lost at where his place in life should be. He was daring enough to try anything once, and Shella knew he had gone out with other girls. She didn't quite trust him.

Shella didn't know that he was not always quite honest with his mother, though. He would tell his folks that he was working late or out with Teddy, when he really wasn't. He always justified his lies by convincing himself that it would hurt them and he wanted to remain in his parents' favor. In truth, he just could not say "no" to all the girls asking him out. Sometimes, he would have two dates in one night. Because his mother would never approve of a girl asking either of her sons out on a date or calling, he never let his folks know his social business.

The changing relationship from best friend to girlfriend would be a great challenge for Tyler. He was not sure how he was supposed to feel about Shella. She would make a good wife and mother. She was beautiful and talented, and she was a Christian, whereas he might not be as straight laced as she. Was that the choice he was suppose to make?

When the duck pecked through his pants' leg and the beak cut into his ankles, Tyler was ready to leave. He wasn't much of an outdoorsman, and he certainly was not going to stand for this kind of abuse, not from a dumb old duck.

"Okay, Shella, I am glad this is amusing to you, but I can't take it anymore! Are you ready to go?"

"No Tyler, you will break her heart. She is sweet on you," she teased.

"Ha ha ha! So funny. I might take her home for supper. She would make a good entrée," he scowled.

"Poor Sassy. You would really eat her? She loves you." Shella playfully pinched at his leg. "I could put her in a frilly dress, and you could take her out."

"You are just a comedian, aren't you?"

"Come on Tyler. We better leave, before she decides to follow you home like one of your regular dates, then how would you explain her?"

"Remind me that I am not speaking to you, Miss Priss. I came here to share an enjoyable picnic on a beautiful afternoon with one of my oldest and dearest friends, and all she can do is mock my pain. I tell you, if that is not just cruel, then I don't know what is." He folded his arms in mock anger.

They had a short evening service at church, and then the relatives invaded their home once more. It was good, in a way, because so much food would have been wasted, but Shella did not like the intrusion during her grieving. It did not seem to bother Christopher, but Shella was ready for everyone to go to their respective homes and leave her alone. It was always overwhelming for her to be in a room full of people.

Like the previous nights, the young woman disappeared a little after ten o'clock to climb the rope ladder, lay her head beneath the open window of the tree house, close her weary eyes to fall asleep, after she said her prayers. Once again, the tears lulled her to sleep, but silent tears did not comfort her in the least. It seemed that all she did anymore was cry.

Next door, Tyler was keeping young Paula, whom he invited home after church, in converse. Mr. and Mrs. Gordon had taken the pastor and his wife out to dinner, and on the home front, Christopher was doting on his bride-to-be, while trying to be cordial to the straggling family who refused to leave.

Teddy stayed as far away from Shella as he could. He had gotten the message loud and clear that she was angry with him for his indiscretion. He knew he could never take back that kiss, no matter how much he wanted to or how much he regretted it. He had broken a lifelong friendship with one foolish selfish act. Did she tell Tyler about that kiss, while she was with him today? Self-reproach consumed him for his betrayal to his brother.

He spent most of the hours after church at his hide-a-way on the outskirts of town, alone, so Shella wouldn't have to see him and be reminded of what he had done to her. However, when ten fifteen rolled around, he realized he needed to head home, because he had to be at work early in the morning. He drove slow to prolong questions from his folks. They would be curious as to why he had not been there for Christopher and Shella during their time of bereavement. Maybe they would be in the bed by the time he arrived.

They had their own idea of how he should be living his life, such as they felt that at his age, he should be dating and planning on marrying soon, but Teddy Gordon had no intentions of getting married. Nonetheless, they rejoiced whenever he reported that he was on a date, so many times he would let his folks believe he was on a date, but in actuality, he spent a lot of time on this private land.

He was in luck. His folks weren't at home… wait a minute, drat it all! That little over zealous girl was at his house with Tyler. It was good that his parents were gone, but he did not want to contend with some silly girl chasing after his brother.

Like many times over the recent years, he decided to take refuge in the tree house to escape his troubles. He enjoyed many hours in the playhouse as a child, and since his adulthood, he would climb into his faithful old hideout to think about his plans, uninterrupted. It had been a haven from interrogation from his mom for years, even if he did feel like Goliath. This tree house was made for children, and his head would bump into the roof, if he tried to stand up, so he always had to crawl in.

This time, when he pulled up on the rope ladder, the childhood safe haven was occupied. Her deep breaths announced clearly that she was sleeping soundly, so he planted himself quietly a short distance away, trying to catch a good look at the stars. The moonlight gleamed on her hair and face, illuminating a peaceful soft expression, a glory shining bright. She certainly was not that little kid anymore. He watched her sleep, trying to forget the fact that he had tarnished her perfection.

Teddy became lost in thought, while his eyes rested on Shella's pleasant face. He eased on his side with his head resting on his propped up hand, remembering how much fun he and Christopher had torturing her and Tyler when they were little. He didn't know how long he had sat there staring at perfection, before she bolted up with alacrity.

"Teddy, what are you doing here?"

Teddy's voice was calm, as if he was simply communicating to himself. "You are the only girl I know that would put a worm on a hook by herself or climb a tree *almost* as fast as I can. You are the only girl I know that would eat ketchup on your eggs with me on a dare. You may have grown up, but you are still the little Shella you have always been. You are charming, elegant and sensible on one hand. On the other, you are still the same uncoordinated tomboy I remember. I've been sitting here thinking what a fool I have been for messing up our friendship. I have missed having you around these last years." He looked down awkwardly, "You and Christopher have been my best friends my entire life. I don't want to lose my best friend, because of *my* forwardness. You were vulnerable and hurt, and I took advantage of you. I wish I could, but I can't take it back. I don't blame you for being angry with me for kissing you, and I'll do anything I can to make it right, if you will just forgive me. "

Shella sat listening the whole time he was speaking his heartfelt confession. It had pacified her to an extent. She responded earnestly, "Teddy, I am not mad at you for kissing me. I was not so vulnerable that I was incoherent. Since you didn't notice, I *did* kiss you back. It is not like I have loose lips and go around kissing just anybody."

"I know that," he averted his gaze shamefully.

She continued, "I am mad, because I do not appreciate you assuming that I am Tyler's girlfriend. I am not his girl, and if I *want* to kiss someone, I can. I do not have to get your brother's permission to do so." She tried to make him see that his kiss did not bother her one way or the other.

"Okay, I am really sorry I called you Tyler's girl."

"You should be. I want you, and everybody else, to stop it! I don't have to have Christopher's permission to kiss someone either. He can just get that through his thick skull right now. I do not belong to Tyler!"

she commanded.

"Shella, I hope you know I'd never hurt you for the world." Teddy put his hand on her foot, smacking it playfully. "Is everything okay between us, now?"

She rubbed his hair to muss it. "As long as you have it in your brain, that I do *not* belong to Tyler, we are okay."

"Okay. I got it," he agreed.

"Okay, but I know how hard it is for you, since you don't have a brain." She laughed at her joke and pushed the shoulder he was leaning on with her fist, causing him to fall over.

"Yeah? Well, at least I don't wear pajamas with pink elephants on them. You wore those when you were what, five maybe?" He was glad the mood was more jovial. He hated having Shella mad at him.

"I was twelve, thank you, and for your information, they are very comfortable." Another awkward silence ensued. Teddy was not sure if he should be having fun just yet. Her parents' death was still fresh. Shella reassured him, "I may still be able to wear my pajamas, but at least I didn't come home with some goofy hack job of a hair cut like you did in seventh grade?"

"Haircut? Oh! I remember. Don't be so quick to laugh, my dear. I have seen you at your worst, too," he threatened.

"Why in the world would you try to cut your own hair? That was pretty stupid."

"Do you promise not to tell?"

Shella laughed, "Tell what?"

"Promise me," he insisted with a mischievous grin.

"Okay, I promise," she conceded.

"I lied to Mom and Dad because I knew they would whip me hard, if I told them the truth."

"You have me curious, now."

"Bobby Jenkins, Roy Miller, and Toni Suttles bet me on a football game. They knew beforehand that our quarterback had mono. How was I supposed to know?"

Shella gasped, "You lost?"

"Sure did. They shaved me from head to toe. I was lucky Mom did not find my shaved legs. I would have been in trouble for sure. I was so miserable. I don't see how girls can stand shaving under their arms. It was quite painful."

Shella laughed heartily. She had missed talking to her old friend. She was glad they were back to normal again. "I wish I had known that back then. I would have laughed even harder at you. Your head was so white, it looked like a cue ball. I would never have let you live that down."

"I am glad you are always laughing at my expense. You want to hear funny? I remember the time you climbed up the oak tree at my cousin's house and got poison ivy all over your face, well it was all over you, not just your face."

"Ooh, I remember that. I was never so miserable in all my life. I itched all over."

"You looked like an Indian with his war paint on, with all that white stuff your mom put on you. You looked so funny."

"That wasn't funny. It hurt, and since we are talking about climbing trees, I beg to differ with you, Theodore. You have never beaten me in tree climbing. I have always been able to climb a tree faster than you."

"Whatever. You keep telling yourself that, and maybe you will start believing it. There is no little pip squeak ever going to beat me!"

"Sounds like a challenge. Are you challenging me? I think you want to race."

"Now?" He faked weariness. "I am too old to do the tree climbing thing anymore. You are not really serious, are you?" He tried to distract her challenge by nudging her playfully, but she was not to be distracted so easily.

She teased him mercilessly, "Chicken! Teddy is a chicken. Teddy is a chicken," she sang.

"Oh yeah? We will see who the chicken is Shella Esther Evans," he charged as he descended the ladder. "I will be back up in the tree house before you get half way up your tree."

Shella followed, "Whatever!"

"Want to make a bet?" he defied. His face came close to hers.

"No thanks. I don't care to shave my head. This is a clean race. I will make a deal with you, though. Loser buys the winner dinner. In other words, you buy me dinner."

"Oh, I see. That is how it is going to be, huh. You are on. Which tree is yours? I get that one."

After Shella picked the tree next to his, they scrambled to the top and then back down just as quickly as they did ten years ago. Their feet hit the ground almost simultaneously, as they both plopped to the ground with a thud.

"Shh," Shella urged, as Teddy groaned a little loudly. She deftly lit across the yard to the tree house, before someone caught them.

Teddy came up behind her, putting his arm around her shoulders. While putting all his weight on her, he gasped for breath, "You cheated!"

"How?"

"I don't know, but you did."

They barely had time to climb back up the rope ladder, before the kitchen door lighted across the yard, and Christopher appeared to see what the commotion was all about. They both crawled in the small space to fall on their backs in exhaustion. It was a few minutes before either caught their breaths enough to speak. They looked silently at each other, until Christopher went back in and then burst forth with laughter.

"I guess that is improper behavior for a girl that is grieving for her parents, huh?" she sobered.

"There is nothing wrong with relieving tension, Shella. You've done nothing wrong."

"You never see that I do anything as wrong."

"I do. You just rarely do things you shouldn't. You are a good kid, Shella." They sat in silence, while looking at the stars for a few minutes, and then Teddy realized the lateness of the hour. "I am glad we are good again. You love me?" Teddy fumbled, as he sat up.

"Of course. Just because I was mad at you, didn't mean I stopped loving you." She, too, sat upright and laid her head on his shoulder. "I am glad we are good, too. Since I am going to be around for awhile, it is good to have my best friend in my corner."

"You are going to be around for awhile? What about school? You didn't graduate without inviting me, did you?"

"No, I haven't graduated yet. It is just that Grandmother still needs someone to take care of her, and Mother is not here anymore. It is the only logical choice. Christopher will probably be going back to Maine, and there is no one else to do the job."

Teddy frowned, "So you are giving up school?"

"For the time being. I can finish later. I really need to be here right now. I am going to check out the hospital here to see if I can get a job in the therapy department, temporarily. I can always go back to school later."

"Are you not concerned that later may never come?"

Shella lifted her head proudly. "I suppose it could happen, but that is something I will deal with at the time. There are always local colleges."

"Shella, I will take care of your grandmother, so you can finish school," he offered.

Shella faced him with a warm smile. "Oh, that is so sweet. I know that you would, too, but for now, I need to be here for her. She needs a familiar face, and it is my place. I appreciate your offering, though. Who knows, I may take you up on that offer later on."

"Well, it is an open offer. Anytime you need me, I am yours. You know that, don't you, Shella? I would do anything I can for you."

"I *do* know that. That is why I love you. You are such a good friend." A thought suddenly came to Shella. "I do have something you can help me with, if you can arrange it."

"Name it. If I can, I will. What is it?"

"I need a ride back to my college one day this week in order to complete my finals. I spoke with the dean, and he is willing to work with me under the circumstances, but I have to be up there this week or next, or I will have to repeat the courses. He is really trying to help me out."

"I'll see what I can do? What day did you want to go?"

Shella watched the kind features of her friend. She pushed the lock of hair from his forehead that had fallen. "Any day that is good for you. I know you work, and if you can't, I certainly understand."

"I have some vacation time built up. I shouldn't have any trouble getting off."

"I know you might get bored sitting around all day, but I could introduce you to my sorority sisters. Who knows, maybe you will find one you like." Again, she nudged his arm with her fist.

Teddy smiled at her jest, but inside, smiling was the last thing he felt like. Like Shella, he didn't go around kissing, and he *did* notice that she kissed him back. That is why he lost his senses for so long during that moment. She had awakened his senses with her reciprocation, and in the last thirty-four hours, forty-two minutes, and seventeen seconds, new feelings for Christopher's kid sister had been aroused.

She was talking about liking other girls? He had no intentions of liking or kissing anyone else. He was content to have this attraction for Shella, because she was safe. Nothing could ever come of his temptation for her, because of Tyler, and Teddy liked having that security. He did not *want* to like anybody. He was not going to get roped into some marriage with any girl.

His tone was subdued, as he tried to change the subject, lest she read his thoughts. "You never told me why were you sleeping up here."

"I can't seem to fall asleep in the house. I just tossed and turned all night."

Checking his watch, "Well, it is almost midnight, so I better let you get some rest. Do you need anything, before I go? Do you need another blanket?"

"Thank you, but no. I just need some sleep." She planted a kiss on his cheek softly, where the stubble pricked her lips. "I love you, Teddy Gordon."

He spread a crooked smile for the touch of her lips pleased him. "I'll let you know what day I can take you up to school. Good night." He started down the ladder, but stopped and popped his head back up, "I love you too, Shella. I am glad we are good. I do not like it when you are mad at me."

She laughed at him again, "Goodnight." His head disappeared, but she called after him, "Teddy!"

His head surfaced again. "You never told me what you were doing up here in the first place."

"Oh that? I guess it is for the same reason you came up here. I always come up here to think and be alone. I just never expected to find anyone sleeping up here. I'm sorry I intruded."

"No, I am the one intruding. I'll not invade your safe haven again."

He threw the small pinecone that lay on the floor of the house at her, "You better. I have enjoyed spending my thinking time with you. I can think of no one I would rather spend it with. Good night, Shella. If you need anything, just throw that at my window, and I will be here in a jiffy."

Once again, he disappeared, but this time for good. Shella heard his back door click, as he silently closed it behind him. His bedroom light came on briefly, before she closed her eyes again. She smiled at the memory.

As it worked out, Teddy was able to free himself from work on

Thursday and Friday. Shella made arrangements with Christopher to take her place with grandmother, while she was to be gone. She did not tell him the purpose of her trip, lest he try and force her to go back with him. All week long, he tried to guess, but she kept him in suspense. If she could not even finish this task on her own, how could she finish the rest of her life?

Because, the company was pleasant, the two and a half hour drive passed quickly for Shella. In addition, she was not looking forward to her finals, so it made the ride pass too quickly. Teddy enjoyed the remembrances of days gone by, but his urge was to pull Shella across his truck's seat to be close to him. He wanted to smell her hair and feel the touch of her hand on his arm as she gestured animatedly.

Once there, she directed Teddy to the sorority house, where she resided. None of the other girls were home, so she started packing her belongings to take back home with her. It would be a while, if ever, before she could resume her classes, and there was no sense in keeping any of it here. She placed each of her personal belongings in boxes with great sadness in her heart and a lump in her throat. Teddy watched each sad feature with regret in his heart. She should not have to give everything up. It was not fair.

Her first test was scheduled at ten o'clock that morning, and it was only eight fifteen. She fingered her textbook, opening it at a page, where she must study for her exam. Pretty confident she knew the contents, she closed it again, putting it in a pile to give to someone else in need. Teddy was relaxed on the couch, almost to the point of falling asleep, when two of her sorority sisters returned after their classes. The other two were off campus somewhere.

"Celia, this Teddy. Celia is a junior this year. She is majoring in Speech Therapy," Shella introduced.

Celia shook his hand. "Nice to meet you, Teddy. Do you have a brother named Tyler?"

It was in Teddy's nature to blush as he did, when he answered, "Yeah."

"Shella tells us stories about you guys all the time."

"Well, if she told you she beat me at climbing trees, I will have to challenge her word," he directed toward Shella.

"You're not still on that, are you?" Shella laughed. "It is sad to see a pathetic loser, isn't it Celia?"

Pomalee, Shella's best friend and roommate twinkled with merriment, as she came from the kitchen. "Shella, you are going to have to race to take your test, if you do not get going."

"You are right, Pomalee. I have to go. Will you be all right here, Teddy? You can always take off to do something, if you would rather. We have a great library on campus, and…"

Pomalee cleared her throat, " Huh hem!"

"Oh Teddy, this is Pomalee."

"We will take good care of him for you Shella. Your brother is our brother," Pomalee promised.

Shella could hear Angel, the third sister, begin teasing Pomalee as she closed the door behind her. "Pomalee, don't you have class in an hour?"

The exam proved to be hard, but Shella was a worthy student. It was a forty-five minute test, and Shella finished it in forty-three.

Slowly, she trudged back to the house to find Celia, alone, trying to be sociable to the awkward Teddy.

"Did Pomalee wear you out?" Shella asked of him.

"She was fine."

"She is a good girl. Her folks are missionaries based out of Norfolk." She plunked down in the chair across from him. I have always been envious of her looks. She has the most beautiful black hair I have ever seen."

"She is pretty," he confirmed. "How did you do on your test?"

"I'm not sure. It was grueling. I hope I did good enough. Shall we go get some lunch?"

"Your wish is my command."

Shella lifted her voice for the friend who had gone into her room, "Angel, do you want to go to lunch with us?"

"Thanks Shella, but I have to cram for this major test."

As the two sat in the little café right outside the campus, Teddy announced between mouthfuls, "I think I will try out the library this afternoon."

"Was it really that bad?"

"No, Pomalee is going to meet me there and give me a quick tour of the campus after her class."

"That is wonderful!" Shella flipped open her next book, which she brought along to study. "My last final is not until seven-thirty, tonight. I can't ask you to wait around. It will be late driving, if we wait that late to leave. If you want to go back home, I can find another way home tomorrow."

"Nothing doing. I am off till Monday, so let me enjoy my mini vacation."

"Are you sure? I do not mean to put you out." Then a thought came to her. Maybe he wanted to stay to get better acquainted with Pomalee. Why did it bother her that he might have feelings for her best friend? "I really appreciate it, Teddy," she covered.

"No problem."

"I know for a fact Pomalee is free after four o'clock, if you want to ask her out." Whoa! Where did that jealousy come from? "We can put you up in our brother fraternity house for the night. I don't know about a change of clothes, though." Shella tried not to let the disappointment show in her voice.

"All that sounds fine," he responded in distraction. "I'll take you up on it," but Teddy's reasons for staying had nothing to do with what Shella was thinking his reasons were.

"Good."

୨ৡ

When Teddy met Pomalee for the tour, he invited her to supper that evening to please Shella. With that out of the way, Pomalee, finding out that he was staying the night, took him to the fraternity house and introduced him to all the brothers.

This is Ted, Luke, and Rusty," she introduced in the lobby. "Guys, this is a friend of Shella's. He needs a place to crash tonight."

"No he doesn't," Rusty's hearty voice boomed. "He is staying right here. Any friend of Shella's is a brother to us."

"How good of a friend to Shella are you?" one boy asked a little antagonistically.

"Luke!" Ted's fingers smacked the back of the boy's head lightly.

"What? I was just wondering what Chapman's going to think."

Teddy looked in puzzlement, until Pomalee explained, "Lawrence and Shella have been an item off and on for a couple of years," she turned to Luke, "but Teddy is taking *me* out tonight, Luke."

The boy threw his hand out to Teddy embarrassedly. "Sorry man. I didn't mean to be rude."

"No harm done." Teddy grinned. "Shella is like a sister to me. We have been next door neighbors all our lives."

Rusty joined in, "Pomalee, do you have your Physics notes?"

"Yes." She rifled through her book bag and promptly produced a notebook for him.

"Thanks." Rusty took the book and motioned to Teddy. "Come on

Teddy, I will show you where you'll be sleeping."

Pomalee readied to leave, "Okay, take care of him guys. Shella will not be happy, if you don't. I have to get to class. Teddy, I will see you around seven."

"Okay."

"Bye guys."

ೞ⋙⋘ೞ

In between exams, Shella managed to get everything packed and ready, except her nightclothes and an outfit to wear in the morning. One more test and she could cast her weary mind and body into her bed one last time. It had been an exasperating day. After this last one, she will have taken six finals in one day.

"Oh God, help me, I pray. Let me pass them all."

She arrived early at the classroom and studied the last twenty minutes before time to start. Her dear mom and dad, and the awful accident were completely pushed from her mind.

The test was difficult, for she was exhausted. She barely finished in time and feared she had missed too many to pass, but it was finally over.

"Whew!" she thought as she turned in her paper.

She slowly made her way back toward her house by means of the path, which had been worn down through the woods, when a voice startled her out of the dark, "You shouldn't be walking out in these woods this late by yourself."

Shella's heart jumped, "Lawrence! It doesn't appear that I am alone, does it?"

"But you didn't know I was with you," he argued.

"Maybe not, but God is always with me."

"True."

"What are you doing in this neck of the woods? Your last class ended hours ago," she questioned.

"The guys told me you were back at school, and I came to find you. They said you were going to be leaving for good. Are you really leaving?"

"I am afraid so. My grandmother needs me."

He touched her arm in a gesture of stalling her, "*I* need you."

"Lawrence, we have been over this before. We are not together anymore. We broke up, remember?"

"No, you broke up. I still love you."

"But I do not love you, Lawrence, not in love least ways. Sandy Bishop is better suited for you," she contested.

"Sandy? She is a nice girl, but Shella, she is not you."

"You are my friend, my very *good* friend, Lawrence. I don't want to ruin that."

The boy's temper was quick to flare. "Curse being your friend, Shella. I guess Teddy is just your friend as well?"

"As a matter of fact, Lawrence, Teddy is my best friend. We have been friends all my life, and I don't appreciate your tone of voice. Jealousy does not become you."

Understanding that he was not to be heard, Lawrence changed his strategy. "Can I have your address to write to you? I wanted to come to the funeral, but I didn't know where to find you."

Shella stopped long enough to take the pen and paper he was handing her, under the light of the porch, because by now, they were at the house. Lawrence took Shella's books and set them on the porch, after stuffing the paper and pen into his breast pocket.

"Come on Friend. Let's go to the swing set. I don't want to have to leave you yet."

He was referring to the wooden swing set belonging to the preschool behind the girl's sorority house. The owners didn't mind, because the students from the Christian college were respectful and kept everything neat. Twice a year, the sorority girls would come clean up the grounds and road in front of the preschool, and sometimes the girls would volunteer with the children.

As Lawrence and Shella rounded the corner of the house, they could see another couple on the far side of the playground perched on the barrels. Shella suggested, "Maybe we shouldn't intrude."

"They are way over there," her escort protested. "Please don't go yet. This may be my last chance to say goodbye. I don't want you to leave."

Shella sat on the swing seat as she had so many times before. She was going to miss being here. This life was comfortable, and no one likes change. She had a sinking feeling in her heart that she would never get to complete this life. She wanted to get her bachelor's in Physical Therapy and Music. She had come so far, only to stop a foot before the end of the race.

"I don't either, Lawrence, but I have no choice. I hope to finish school someday. Granted, it may not be at this college, but I do want to graduate."

"Don't talk like that Shella. Of course you will finish here. I have three more semesters, and you better be back here to graduate with me."

"Christopher is getting married and will probably move back to Maine. There is no one else to take care of Grandmother. It is my responsibility."

Lawrence, sitting in the swing next to her, pulled the chain of her swing toward him. "Take the semester off to find someone dependable to take care of her. Christopher could help pay someone."

"No, Lawrence, this is a family matter. I could never let a stranger take care of my grandmother."

"I told Teddy that was you, Shella," Pomalee announced, as the couple from the other side of the playground approached.

Shella shaded red. How much had they heard? She didn't want Teddy to get his feelings hurt after his offer to take care of her grandmother, or was it that she didn't want Teddy to assume that she had feelings for Lawrence, when she did not.

Lawrence objected their intrusion and remarked sarcastically, "Pomalee, your timing is always perfect."

Shella neutralized, as if she had not heard her escort, "Teddy, are the brothers treating you well?"

"They sure are," he responded trying to sound jovial, but he could not help responding to Lawrence's sarcasm. "They are making me feel like I am back in my old fraternity again. Chapman plays basketball too."

"I know." Shella turned to Lawrence, "Teddy played for the Wildcats in college."

The converse between the two men picked up as Lawrence responded, "Why did you go so far away?"

"I had an athletic scholarship from Arizona."

Lawrence frowned, "What is your last name?"

"Gordon."

"You know, I think I have heard of you. Coach makes us watch all the old games. I am pretty sure I heard your name mentioned several times. You graduated last year or the year before, didn't you?"

"Yeah, a couple years ago."

Shella interpolated, "Teddy, Lawrence had a scout meet with him about going pro, when he graduates."

"Are you going?" Teddy asked.

"I am seriously thinking about it. It is the opportunity of a lifetime, one that many just dream about."

Teddy finalized, "That is true."

Pomalee shined as she always did. "Well guys, I must head back. Some of us have finals tomorrow, that they must study for."

"It is getting late," Shella agreed, "and Teddy and I have a long drive in the morning."

In her apprehension she had twisted a piece of her clothing into the swing's chain somehow, and when she went to stand up, it jerked her back, causing her to fall on her backside. "Aaah!"

She burst forth in laughter, followed by Teddy and then Pomalee. Only Lawrence refrained from laughter, as he cautiously helped her to her feet. "Are you okay, Shella?"

She was laughing too hard to be embarrassed, "I am fine." She used his offer to help her rise, "Thank you. That is one thing you can never say about me, I am definitely not graceful."

"Do you need someone to carry you?" Teddy teased. "I mean, I understand how hard it is to walk with two left feet."

Lawrence gave a look of reproach to Teddy for laughing at the lady in her despair. He was being a cad. He waited for Shella to dust herself off, and then he carefully led her by the elbow to the porch.

At the door, Pomalee gave a friendly kiss to Teddy's cheek to say goodnight. "I really enjoyed meeting you Teddy Gordon. I had a lot of fun getting to know you."

He blushed soberly, "Same here."

Pomalee went inside, while Teddy descended the porch steps to wait on Lawrence to walk with him. Lawrence didn't like having an audience as he held Shella by the hand to detain her.

Lowering his voice so Teddy could not hear, "I am going to miss you Shella."

As he let her hand go, she walked to the railing and looking up at the blanket of stars above, responded, "I am going to miss it here, too." She felt his arms fold around her waist and nervously shifted.

"I hope to see you soon."

Shella was very uncomfortable, especially knowing that Teddy was watching from the shadows. Why was it that suddenly she should care what Teddy Gordon thought about her personal relationships? Why didn't she want Teddy to think she and Lawrence were involved?

"I can't tell you what you want to hear. I may never get back. This is goodbye, Lawrence. Goodbye."

He reached behind her shoulder and kissed her dimple. "Goodbye Shella."

He left immediately, without giving her a chance to give rebuke or rebuttal. She had been his fancy for the last three years. Yes, she kept breaking things off with him, but he always intended to marry her. Now, it just felt as if she were disappearing for good. Since they were not dating, he could say nothing about it.

ᔦ∽ᔨ

Shella shut the door while receiving mischievous grins from her sisters. Pomalee wrapped her arm around Shella's shoulders and kissed her cheek.

"What did he say?" Celia inquired giggling.

Shella blushed. "Just the normal. He wanted me to stay, but enough about me. What about you and Teddy, Pomalee?" She stood to climb the stairs for bed.

"Teddy is very nice. He is very polite and cute," Pomalee sighed as they climbed the stairs.

"Yes, he is. Why do I feel like you didn't like him?" Shella hoped her best friend could not see the truth.

Pomalee plunked down on the bed beside Shella. "I do like him, Shella. He is perfect, but he is already in love with someone. I don't stand a chance."

"He is? He never mentioned anything to me about having a

girlfriend. I am so embarrassed that I urged you two to go out."

"I'm not. I had a good time." Pomalee completed the conversation.

Shella lay in the dark wondering about her friend's words. Teddy had all the time in the world to tell her about a girlfriend, yet this was the first she had heard of it. It must be the real thing, or he would have brought her around. Sleep evaded her that night, as her heart was sad. Her pride was wounded.

છॐ

Shella settled into the new routine back at home disheartened that Teddy had surfaced these feelings in her with that kiss, and the whole time, he had a girlfriend. Her days consisted of taking care of her grandmother and Christopher. She couldn't convince her brother to go back and live a normal life in Maine. He insisted upon playing big brother to her and acting like her dad, which infuriated her haughtiness.

Tyler would encourage her constantly to go out with him on weekends, because of his parent's persuasion. He loved her, but as a sister. They had been through too much as kids for him to see her as a lover, but his parents had told him they wanted him to *marry* Shella, a couple weeks ago at the table.

"But Mom, what if she doesn't love me?" he argued.

His dad injected, "Then I suggest you sweep her off her feet. Face it son, she knows all your bad qualities as well as good. If she still loves you after all that, you better keep her."

"Dad, does it not matter that I don't love her as a wife? Come on Teddy, help me out here."

Patrick Gordon looked in annoyance at his eldest son as if to say, 'Keep out of it, Son.' Teddy shrugged his shoulders to Tyler to announce he was not getting in the middle of their conflict.

"That is what marriage is for Tyler. You will learn to love each other."

"Are we living in the first century?" He did not mean it, but his voice became sarcastic.

"Son, your tone is on dangerous ground. I suggest you keep it in check."

Tyler looked at his brother, suppressed his rising anger, and intentionally sweetened his voice. "Dad you can't seriously think I have to marry somebody, just because *you* want me to. Don't I have a right to marry for love? I am not saying I will never have those feelings, but I don't now."

"What your dad is trying to tell you is that we *do* know what is best for you. Shella is a good girl. She is smart, funny, and very pretty. She would serve as a wonderful wife and mother."

"Mother? Now you have us having kids too? Mom, I don't know if I want kids at all."

"Nonetheless, your mother is right, Tyler. You know how we feel, so there is no point in continuing this further."

Tyler lost his appetite quickly. "May I be excused, Mom?" he asked sulkily.

"Me too?" Teddy was getting out while the getting was good.

"Yes." She patted Tyler's hand, hoping he was not too angry with her.

Both young men took their dishes to the sink and promptly threw on a clean shirt and left to go their separate ways. Tyler had a lot of thinking to do, and some time away was exactly what he needed to clear his mind.

Tyler was not a rebellious son. He just couldn't force feelings that were not there. He tried to start a relationship with Shella over the next weeks, but Shella was really boring. She always wanted to be with her grandmother. She didn't go to the movies or anything, when she did take time off to go out with him. She wanted to go to the park or lake, and he just did not get any joy out of these things. It was hard to find things to do with her.

Another problem he faced was the other girls he had promised to take here or there. He couldn't restrict his dating to just one girl. None of his steadies would understand if he suddenly stopped having anything to do with them. He did not *want* to give them up. Shella was great, but he didn't want her solely.

He fell into the habit of using Teddy as a crutch, whenever he wanted to avoid a date with Shella. On the same token, Teddy wanted his parents to think he was involved with someone, so they wouldn't do the same thing to him that they did to his brother, so he gladly filled in for Tyler. The last thing he wanted was his mom picking out some girl for him to marry. In the end, the parents thought both sons were bidding their wishes, so everyone got what they wanted, down to Teddy getting to spend time in the refuge of Shella.

"Teddy, I am supposed to take Shella to some Bible meeting at church tonight, but Bob and Fred want me to go over to Milledgeville with them. Would you go to the Bible meeting with her for me?"

"Tyler, how do you plan to get the girl to marry you, if you do not go anywhere with her? Here lately, I have seen her more than you have."

"Please, Teddy? I know what I am doing. Shella will marry me when the time is right."

"Can she not go to this Bible thing alone?" Teddy wasn't too keen on going to this Bible meeting either.

"I guess she could, but *I* don't want her to. Steve Griswold will be there, and he has eyes for Shella, too. Please, will you do this for me, Teddy?"

"Okay, but you owe me big."

Shella was not stupid, so when Teddy showed up in a nice shirt and jeans, she knew she had been stood up. Her only question was why did Tyler keep insisting that they go out, if he really didn't want to? She looked at Teddy pitifully. What must his girlfriend think? What was going on with these two brothers? Why was it that they thought they had to keep her entertained?

"You got stuck with me again, huh? You are absolved from your brother's commitments, Teddy. I can go by myself." Embarrassment overcame her. She didn't mind going by herself, it was just that Tyler shouldn't ask her and then renege on it.

"Nothing doing," he reciprocated.

"I refused Tyler's request after the last three times he bailed on me, but he insisted he would come this time. I know you have a life of your own, and more than likely a girl of your own. You really don't have to baby-sit me and should not be bound by his promises." Her fishing expedition about his girlfriend did not bring the results she had hoped for. His expression hadn't changed, when she said that.

Taking her hand in his, he pulled her on the path to leave. He needed to get out of sight, before his folks came home and caught the ruse. "There is no other girl I would rather be out with tonight, than my best friend. Besides, Tyler's loss is my gain."

At the meeting, Shella noticed how uncomfortable Teddy seemed, shifting back and forth in his chair. She realized he had not really wanted to come with her, after all. Well, next time she would refuse his invite, as well as Tyler's. Once again, her pride was insulted. Of all the nerve! Tyler was arrogant and too self-assured, and so was Teddy. He should not have come, if he was going to be embarrassed to be with her. She *was* capable of going to church alone.

She refused his converse on the ride home. Teddy threw side-glances at his friend, who was determinedly staring out the window. He took her silence as anger, which filled him with self-doubt. He surmised that she really wanted to be out with his brother, when she ended up stuck with him. No wonder she was so angry. He was just going to tell Tyler he was not going to do this anymore. He loved the safety of spending time with her, but not at the cost of her finding out his true feelings. It was not worth straining their friendship.

"Shella, thanks for letting me go with you tonight. I really enjoyed it," he tried to appease, once they emerged from the car.

"Teddy, I am glad you went, but I will not do this anymore. There is no sense in you being miserable trying to keep me company, just because your brother can't keep his word. I am not a child. I know you are my friend, and I know Tyler is my friend. Neither of you should have to do things with me to console me about Mother and Dad dying."

"Tyler wants to be *more* than friends with you Shella. He is very interested in you," he sustained.

Shella laughed at his jest. "Okay, whatever. Goodnight Teddy."

As she walked away, he continued to hear her laughing. "I love you, Shella," he called after her.

"I love you too, Teddy."

The next time Tyler asked her to do something, she flatly refused, without even giving him the opportunity to use his charming art of persuasion. Tyler knew this wouldn't work for his mom. He had to forget about all these other girls and start dating Shella for real, so he showed up on her doorstep one evening to execute plan B. Tonight, he was not going to take 'no' for an answer.

Shella hadn't been home from the nursing home very long, "Let's go, Shella!" He took her arm.

She hesitated, "Where are we going?"

"It is a surprise."

"Tyler, I have to cook supper for Christopher. I can't go anywhere."

The older brother, who happened to come down the stairs at that time, buttoning his shirt, responded, "You don't have to cook for me Shella Esther. I am on my way to Maine for the weekend."

Trying to ignore Tyler, Shella joined in the change of topic. "So you are getting to go! That is wonderful. Give my love to Amber."

"Will do." He gave her a kiss and ran out the door, where Teddy was waiting in his car to take him to the airport.

"See, you have no excuse, Miss Shella Esther." Tyler was not about to let this chance go by.

He promptly took her hand and led her out the door and to his car. Shella's mind was on her brother, so she reluctantly allowed him to lead her away, where he drove to the state park on the outskirts of town. He knew she liked this kind of entertainment and he had to make things right with her, after canceling so much.

"Did you bring your fishing poles?" Shella asked as she saw the lake.

"Fishing poles? You mean to tell me you still like to fish. I thought when you didn't want to go the last time we came to the lake that you outgrew fishing."

"I could never outgrow fishing. It is very peaceful. You have all the time in the world to talk to God, while waiting for a bite. I went and got my license again."

"Well, would you settle for a boat ride?" he improvised, as he directed their steps in the direction of the boat rentals.

She laughed, "Sure. That sounds interesting. I would like to see you navigate a row boat these days."

Her laughter was refreshing to his ears. Most of the girls he was used to being with had silly giggles. It was only a few that had pleasant laughs. Paula, from church, had a pleasant laugh, then again, she had a pleasant everything. Shella was just Shella grown up.

She was like one of the guys, not a girl you would want to kiss. He did love her in a familial way. Could his mom and dad be right? Could he grow to love her like that after they were married, or vice versa? She was very nice to look at. He supposed that could be a starting place.

Tyler proved to be quite the oarsman. He took her to a little inlet at the far edge and pulled the oars in. He leaned back on his elbows, while watching Shella play in the water with her fingers, and then queried, "How serious are you with that guy at college that you are dating?"

Shella continued moving her fingertips through the water. "What guy?"

"I don't know. The one that Teddy said was your boyfriend."

"Lawrence? We don't date anymore."

"Oh, I am sorry about that," he responded, but his voice betrayed his true gladness.

"I'm not. We were better suited as friends than lovers. He is a good guy." She gave Tyler ample opportunity to respond, but when he did not, she added, "Tyler, I am not a broken child that you and Teddy have to keep occupied all the time. Stop feeling like you have to entertain me all the time. I am sure you would much rather be on a date right now, than making sure my evenings are not spent alone. I love you Tyler, but get a life."

It was Tyler's turn to laugh. "Shella, what do you think we are doing right now?"

"Sitting in a boat," she reported.

"On a date," Tyler corrected.

"No we aren't." She made a funny wrinkled face.

"Lo all these many times we have gone out together, we have been on dates," he insisted.

Shella rebutted, "No, we haven't."

"Yes, we have."

"No, we have not."

"Yes, we have," he maintained.

"That is just sick!" Shella retorted in an effort to end the argument.

"Oh? And why is that sick, might I ask?"

Shella wrinkled her face again. "Because, by your definition, I have been *dating* you and your brother, and that is just plain sick."

"You've not been dating Teddy." He was trying to understand her logic. "You are just two friends."

"So why is it dating, when you and I do things together as friends, but not when Teddy and I do things together?"

"It just is. You and my brother have no romantic intentions. You are *just* friends."

Shella flicked the water on her fingers to spray Tyler. "As are you and I. You and I have no romantic intentions, either. Tyler, if I thought this was more than that, I would never have agreed to it. Please tell me that I have not been encouraging you in this notion."

"Okay, fine. Have it your way, but technically, it is a date!" He realized that cutting his nose off to spite his face would only stunt any progress he had made, so he conceded to drop the topic for now and continue his pursuit in a different manner.

This time, she cupped as much water as her palm would hold and flung it at him. "Shut up!"

"You shut up!" He began rocking the boat from side to side, until she thought they were going to tip over.

"Stop it, Tyler! You are going to turn us over!"

In her attempt to get him to stop rocking the board, Shella ended up falling overboard, sending Tyler into hysterics. "That is pay back for the duck," he joked.

"Christopher," Shella was calling him in Maine late that same night. "I think this is absolutely ridiculous!"

She could hear the weariness in his voice. "What is ridiculous, Shella Esther?"

"Your life is in Maine. You have a job there, not to mention a lovely young fiancé. I don't see why you feel the need to come back here to live."

"Shella Esther, I am moving back to take care of you and Grandma for Mom and Dad."

"Christopher, I am thoroughly ashamed of you! I have been on my own at college for three and a half years now, without anybody *taking care* of me. Mom and Dad died, not me. I *am* an adult. I have the means and resolve to take care of myself, thank you very much. As for Grandmother, I can take care of her also. Stay in Maine and stop worrying. That is your home now."

Christopher had never been one to boss his sister around, but now he felt responsible since mom and dad were gone. He tried to appease, "I know you can take care of yourself and Grandma, but do you think Dad would want me to abandon my family?"

"Honey, it is not abandoning. I just don't see why your life has to be turned upside down because of me. I appreciate your feeling responsible for us, but you truly are not. If I were a minor, then you would have every responsibility toward me."

"And what about you, Shella Esther? Are you supposed to turn your life upside down? You say you can handle everything on your own, well what about college, or have you decided to forget all your dreams?"

"No, I have not. I can find a job here and finish school at the local community college, while I take care of Grandmother," the sister contended. "My scholarship will transfer."

"Shella Esther, can we talk about this when I get home?"

"That is the whole point. Why should you come back, if you don't have to?"

"I still have a lot of loose ends to tie up, even if I do come back to

Maine to stay, so can we please finish this then? Stop being selfish and stubborn."

The sheer exhaustion in his voice made her relent, "Yes, Brother. You sound tired. You need to get some rest and stop worrying about everything." She didn't like being called selfish, because it reminded her of the truth.

"Are you okay there by yourself? Teddy and Tyler are next door, if you get scared."

"Have you ever known me to be afraid to be alone?"

"No."

"Good night, I love you, Christopher. Be careful."

"I love you too, Sis. I will see you soon."

Shella lay her head down in the old tree house that night, with Christopher solely on her mind. She never intended him to be her keeper or give up his life to be a dad to her. She was an adult and could provide for herself.

Somewhere in her thoughts, the rain began to patter rhythmically on the roof, until she was singing Jesus Loves Me in her head to the beat of the pitter pat. The rain cooled the earth, so that it chilled Shella thoroughly.

ംഇ

"Teddy, let's go out tonight," Tyler suggested. "Shella, me, and you, and this girl I want you to meet."

Teddy scowled. He was not going to go on some blind date. He had no foolish intentions that Tyler had about girls. Teddy was perfectly happy without a 'girlfriend'. He didn't enjoy the practice of taking a blue million girls to the movies, until he found one he could tolerate. Besides, he didn't want to actually be there when his brother was out on a date with Shella. He couldn't watch the two of them smooch and cuddle. That kiss was still fresh on his lips and in his senses.

"Thanks, but no thanks, man," he replied glumly.

"C'mon Teddy, please. You know what Mom and Dad are making

me do. Won't you help me, please?"

Tyler truly wanted to please his mom and dad. He also wanted to try and woo Shella, but he knew it would not be that easy. That is why he wanted his friend and Teddy to go with them, just in case things went sour with Shella, he would have backup. "I have been helping you Tyler, or have you not noticed.

"I would do it for you," Tyler threw in for added guilt, knowing Teddy would respond to it.

"Where are you going?"

"I thought I would take us to that new restaurant that just opened up on Fifth Avenue."

"Tyler, they serve beer there. You know Shella won't go anywhere they serve beer."

"Oh, I didn't know they served alcohol. Where would you want to go?"

Teddy knew where Shella loved to go and suggested, "How about the old diner out on Hwy. 217? Christopher used to take her there and she loved it."

"Fine. Where do we go afterward? Shella will not go to the movies or clubs, and I don't want to go to another church meeting."

"Well, all I can suggest is that we go out to eat, and you take it from there," Teddy shrugged.

Tyler slapped his brother on the shoulder, "So that means you will go?"

"Whatever, but if you stick me with some gabby girl, we'll end the evening immediately after the meal."

Teddy changed his clothes, but nothing as fancy as his brother. Tyler always dressed to kill, but Teddy was most comfortable in jeans. Considering where they were going, fancy clothes seemed pointless.

He came back from getting ready to go, but Tyler had gone to pick up his blind date, so Teddy headed over to Shella's house to meet them. When there was no car in her drive, he plopped down on the porch swing wondering how he managed to get roped into this blind date. He did not want to do this. Tyler's demands were becoming more than he could deliver.

Shella still had not come home, when Tyler drove up a little while later. "She must still be at the nursing home," he guessed.

"I don't know." Teddy half shrugged.

Tyler eyed the young guest nervously. "Oh yeah! Teddy, this is Sandy. Sandy, my brother, Teddy."

"Hi," she squealed perkily.

"Hello," he returned, scooting over for the girl to have a seat.

They ensued in converse, mainly Tyler and Sandy. Teddy learned a long time ago that one could learn a lot about people by just listening, but he was doing little listening.

He sat in nostalgia, remembering a time when Christopher, his mom, and he were on this porch churning the ice cream crank. That was the best strawberry ice cream he had ever tasted. Of course, Tyler came home with a bloody nose, and Christopher's mom gave him extra, because she felt sorry for him.

Shortly, the two men saw their mom pull up, and directly Shella pulled in her own drive. She threw her hand in the air and smiled at Mrs. Gordon across the way. "Thanks!" she called.

৩৯৶

"We have been waiting for you," Tyler elevated his voice to meet the distance.

"You have? I have been with grandmother."

"C'mon, get your duds on and let's go get something to eat."

Shella smiled her sweet smile, upon seeing a guest. "Shame on you two for making your guest wait on the porch. Why didn't you go on in?"

Neither Tyler nor Teddy wanted to go inside anymore. It was not the same anymore, now that Mr. and Mrs. Evans were gone. It would be disrespectful or something. It was not their second home from childhood days, where Mrs. Evans always had some kind of delicious homemade snacks waiting for them. One couldn't just walk in without Shella or Christopher there.

Tyler met her at the foot of the steps and took her arm. He did not need someone to tell him his mother was watching from the kitchen windows, because he could feel her eyes on him, watching to see if he was going to do the right thing.

"We wanted to leave as soon as you got here," he directed her up the steps.

"Well, come on in the house. I will have to change clothes." She smiled at the young girl, "Hi. I am Shella."

"Sandy," the girl reciprocated the introduction.

Once inside, Shella quietly chided Tyler in the kitchen. "You should not assume things, Tyler."

"What should I not assume?" he grinned mischievously.

"I am tired, and frankly, I don't want to go anywhere with you. I would not want you to think we were on a date or something."

"C'mon Shell, please? You are not still mad at me about falling in the lake the other week, are you? Teddy has a date, and I will be the third wheel without you. Please, please, please? I will do anything, if you will go."

She sighed wearily, "Fine, but don't do this to me again. I want it understood that we are NOT on a date."

"Understood. Thanks." He stole a kiss to her cheek.

She began up the back stairs. "I need to change, I will be down in a few minutes."

৩০৫

Within the hour, the foursome was sitting at a booth down at McNally's Diner. Shella couldn't help remembering the first time she ever came here. Her dad brought her mom, Christopher, and her. It was a rare treat for the whole family to go out and eat in those days. Shella must have been seven or eight at the time, and she remembered how big her dad had seemed to her that day. She concealed her sadness with a precious smile and happy converse, trying to get to know this friend of Teddy's.

"I graduated two years ago and started working at the department store," she was explaining. "I'm going to start Tech school next year to become a beautician."

Tyler could read Teddy's expression. He thought this girl was a flake, and he was probably right. This would be a short night, so he sat back and placed his arm around Shella's shoulders, but she gracefully waited a few seconds before leaning up to the table, which resulted in a retreat of his arm. It was done so discreetly, that no one would realize the meaning of her actions, nobody but Tyler.

He looked at his date with much thought. Even though Shella was a pretty girl, his feelings for her were still strictly platonic, and no matter how much his folks or he wanted them to change, there was just no chemistry between them. He still could not see her as a datable girl. Again he wondered, could his dad be right? Could he have a life long relationship with someone that he did not long to kiss? Maybe that was it! He would kiss her. Maybe that would trigger some romantic feelings in him. "Nah," he thought. "That would be like kissing Christopher. Yuck!"

Nonetheless, considering his brother's warning look, which he took to heart, Tyler took Shella home, immediately following the meal, and decided to give the idea of kissing her a try. Teddy grudgingly took Sandy home, which gave Tyler the opportunity he needed. He knew that if he asked, she would tell him what lake to jump in, yet Shella was the kind of girl one asked before doing something like that.

ûœû

As he sat on her couch, he continued contemplating how to complete this task. "Shella, do you think you could ever love me?"

She laughed innocently, "I *do* love you, Tyler. You know that."

He nervously looked to the floor, "I mean, could you ever *fall* in love with me?"

"I suppose I could, if God put that kind of love in my heart." She watched his awkwardness in amusement. What was Tyler up to?

"You know, ever since we were kids, we have been betrothed, according to our parents. Everybody expects us to get married. Do you think they know something that we don't know?"

"I think they see us so much alike. We have always been like bread and butter. That is why they see us as a great match, but Tyler, you should never marry someone, unless you love them. Marriage is hard enough with two people that are in love, let alone with two people that are not. Are you in love with me?"

"Not exactly, but Dad seems to think we'll fall in love, after we are married."

"I will not disrespect your dad by disagreeing with him. He is older and knows more about life than I do. It is times like this that I wish my own dad were here to talk to, my friend."

Then the opportunity came. Shella reached over and treated him with a hug. Tyler saw this as his chance. He held her in an embrace, until he mustered the courage. He kissed her hair, which made Shella uncomfortable. She was aware that something was amiss by Tyler's sudden nervousness.

Next, he kissed her forehead. No, he was not feeling anything like love. With her face in his hands, he kissed her cheek, but Shella immediately stopped him from proceeding further.

She removed his hands and stood up. "It is getting late, and we have church in the morning. Goodnight, Tyler."

His embarrassment took him to the door in long strides. "Good night Shella. See you in the morning." He turned a red face and fled her presence.

ço∂

After enjoying the wonderful weekend with his sweet love, Christopher came back Sunday afternoon, bringing glad news with him. He towered over Shella, leaning his elbow on her shoulder, as he munched a carrot in her ear.

"Guess what?"

"What?" Shella answered half-heartedly.

"Amber and I decided to not waste anymore precious time. We are going to get married in two weeks."

"It is about time!"

"So, you are really okay with it?"

"I think it is wonderful Christopher!" she wiggled from beneath his sharp elbow. "I will be glad to finally have a sister." She clapped excitedly.

"I am glad you approve, sister dear. She likes you, too."

"Two weeks? That doesn't leave you much time to prepare."

Christopher bit off another chunk of carrot, "It is not a matter of preparation. Amber and her family are doing all the preparing," he noticed her discouraged expression, "but you can help, if you want."

Shella shrugged. This was just another way to say that Christopher had his own life and didn't need her, so why did he think he had to *take care* of her? "Christopher, answer me a question and be honest with me, please."

"I would not lie to you, Shella Esther."

"What made you decide to speed up the wedding? Are you getting married just because of me?" She searched his face for the truth.

Christopher's mouth fell open with crunched up carrots and all, "What on earth made you come up with that cockamamie idea?"

"You had no intentions of doing this right now, until Mom and Dad died. All of a sudden, you feel you have to go get married right now?"

"Truthfully, Shella Esther, Mom and Dad's death does play a role in this, but make no mistake, Amber and I were going to get married soon, anyway."

Shella's proud nature swelled, "Christopher don't do it for me. Don't get married for the wrong reason."

"You misunderstand. Maybe you were a small part of the reason, but not the only reason. I wish Mom and Dad had met Amber. I should have brought her home a long time ago, but I was embarrassed." He dropped his gaze and swallowed hard the last remnants of carrots in his mouth. "I was embarrassed about how Mom would react and insist everybody come down here for the wedding. Amber's family is different than ours."

"Different or better? Do you think they are better than us?" Her feelings were getting hurt.

"I was stupid in thinking that, before. I'm not proud of that fact. Now, I can never make it up to Mom and Dad. Maybe it's different now, because Amber has come to see who I am."

"Amber didn't seem to be the kind of person to think that way."

"She's not, but I never gave her the benefit of the doubt."

She put her arm around his broad shoulders. "I love you. I do not know what to say to you, except, Mom and Dad loved you, too. They would have adored Amber. It is a pity they never met her, but that's the past and cannot be undone. You have to forgive yourself. What's important is that you love her."

"I do love Amber. She is a wonderful woman and serves the Lord. Hey, she loves me, what more could I ask for?" He drew her into a full embrace. "Don't worry Shella Esther. I know what I am doing. Amber is the best thing in the world for me."

"Just don't do this on my account. That is all I have to say about the matter. Other than that, I am happy for you."

Christopher continued thoughtfully, pretending he didn't hear, "Teddy has always been my best friend. I want him to be my best man, but we were thinking about getting married in Maine. That *is* Amber's home, and I don't want to have to fly everyone in her family here. Do you think I could con Teddy into flying up for my wedding?"

"I am sure he would. Ask him."

"Of course, you will be there, but I can't think of anyone else that would want to be there, except maybe Tyler. See, it would definitely be better for us to go there, don't you think?"

"Absolutely. It is settled. I guess we are going to Maine. Have you a house, or are you still living in that apartment? Is that where you two will live?"

"No, Shella Esther, we are moving back home. I told you that we were going to take care of Grandma, so you can finish college. I have discussed this, in depth, with Amber, and she completely agrees with me."

"Christopher, I have told you that I don't need you to baby-sit me. I am perfectly capable of taking care of us, and I do plan on finishing school!"

"It is not negotiable Shella Esther. You are going to finish college, because you only have six months left. It is no big deal for us to come home for that short period of time. Can't you stop being stubborn for one minute, and listen to reason, please. We are not out to get you. We love you and are doing what is best for you. After you graduate, you can come home and be by yourself all you want."

The phone rang at that moment, which ended the conversation, but as Shella contemplated things, her stubborn nature refused to let her waiver in her opinion. Her pride couldn't let her see that he was right.

It was not much of a sacrifice for them to move home for a little while. Christopher could work here, just as easily as he could in Maine, but Shella felt the need to prove to her brother and Teddy, who thought she was a kid, that she could do it on her own.

She continued to spend every day with her Grandmother to spite her brother. She tried to visit in the evening hours, so that if she found a job, she wouldn't have to make much of a change in the schedule. In another method of action, she hired a health care giver to watch her in the morning hours.

Some days the grandmother faired well, but other days, Shella left the nursing home in tears. Many times, the grandmother would throw fits and become physically abusive with her, but Shella would wipe all signs of tears away, before Christopher came to pick her up. She was not about to let him see her troubles. Meanwhile, Shella put in an application at the local hospital's rehab unit, in hopes that she might find a job.

꽝

The weekend came in which Christopher and Amber were to be married. All the plans were perfected with the minutest detail. Christopher only had to be responsible for him and his best man, while Amber contended with all the rest of the plans. Shella respectfully declined the honor of participating in the wedding as the maid of honor or even a bride's maid, because she had only recently met Amber and did not feel it was right. Amber's friends should hold those positions.

On the groom's side, Tyler and Teddy flew up with Shella and Christopher. Teddy agreed to be best man, with a smile on his heart for fulfilling such an honorable responsibility for his friend. He didn't even mind putting on a suit for Christopher, too much.

As it turned out, the wedding was beautiful. Christopher and Teddy looked handsome, and the bride was unmatched in beauty as she paced down the aisle to meet her groom in her snow-white gown. Her bride's maids wore lavender gowns, as they carried deep purple irises with white baby's breath.

Christopher's eyes twinkled, as Amber came down the aisle. He had a smile of contented pride, as he unveiled his bride. Nonetheless, as with normal weddings, it was over in a matter of minutes. All the money and months of preparations ended in a short amount of time.

Tyler and Shella felt a little out of place, for they knew only Teddy and Christopher, besides barely knowing Amber. The bride's family and friends tried to be cordial to the outsiders, but they still didn't feel as if they fit in. Christopher's call was right. This group of people seemed to be in a higher social class than the Gordons and Evans. Shella noticed that Teddy fidgeted uncomfortably, too, but Christopher appeared to be right at home. As a matter of fact, Christopher looked like he belonged with this class of people. Living in Maine really had changed him. Seeing him in his element showed that he did not fit in at home anymore.

At the rehearsal dinner the night before, Shella noticed what a lovely young woman the maiden was, but could not help thinking that Teddy was too good for her, yet. The young couple seemed to connect immediately, with Teddy smiling a lot, which was rare for him. His shy passive nature prevented him from smiling a lot on a normal basis. Generally, his smiles were coupled with red blushing cheeks, but his unblushed cheeks made Shella wonder, if he really liked this girl.

Christopher had his eyes on the couple also, thinking proudly how he might have made a match for his best friend through his new bride; however, he didn't notice how Shella was studying the girl critically, as jealousy crept in. Could Teddy really fall for a girl like that?

The bride and groom wouldn't be leaving until the next morning for their honeymoon trip, and per prior arrangements Shella, Tyler, and Teddy were staying in Maine for one more night. It was more pleasant the second night without the pressures of a wedding hanging over them. It took some arguing to get Christopher to let Shella stay by herself at the hotel. In the end, this was one fight she conquered. Much to her chagrin, he arranged for her to have a room that joined his and Amber's on the other side.

The night held a double couple dinner with Tyler and Shella and Teddy and the maid of honor for a fun filled dinner. Tyler and Christopher were hoping that Teddy and Amanda would develop a special kind of friendship, which would continue for a long time to come.

Instead, Teddy surveyed his brother, as he doted over every need that Shella had, in envy. Tyler was a good, decent man, and Shella deserved a good decent man. His mom and dad were right, he and Shella were a good match, and he was a cad for having feelings for her that exceeded friendship.

This night, Tyler seemed like a different person to Shella. He was not preoccupied with trying to make her swoon over him, even though he was very attentive to her needs. He even went as far as completely ignoring one of the flirtatious bride's maids, which was highly out of character for Tyler Gordon, yet he was very reserved toward Shella.

"I could possibly learn to get along with *this* Tyler," Shella told herself, when he left her for the night without trying to get a goodbye kiss. "I like this Tyler a whole lot better."

As Shella and Teddy watched this transformation in Tyler, a growing up of sorts, a wicked seed was planted in Teddy, a seed that would soon grow and fester out of his control. It was born from guilt, cultivated with jealousy, and fertilized with idle time and evil temptations.

Christopher called to check on his baby sister, before he left the next morning. All the many months she had been away at college, she could count on one hand the times Christopher had called her, and now his calls were numerous. It infuriated her that he thought of her as a child, and it made her mad that even Teddy was treating her like a child. It seemed that the only person treating her like an adult was Tyler. Nobody treated *him* like a child, and Tyler was a couple months younger than she. It was discrimination!

Even after she arrived home, and Christopher was in the middle of his honeymoon, he called her daily. Even if she refused to answer the phone, he would call back way into the late hours and then chide her for being out so late. He was worse than Dad.

It seemed like a lot changed after the wedding. Tyler, for one, became more monogamous in his intentions. He seemed to have matured overnight. He became serious in pursuing her affections and attempting to love her like a husband loves a wife.

Shella picked up on these intentions, and in return, tried to acquiesce his attentions to a certain degree. It was just so hard for her to look at her best childhood friend through the eyes of a lover. She tried to convince herself that she was trying the best she could, but her heart truly lay elsewhere. She did not want to love Tyler, and it did not help that Christopher, Teddy, and his folks were all pushing it, especially Teddy.

The nicest change was Tyler's parents, who tried harder to be more available for them. The many years of having them side by side with their own boys made them like their own children. Aaron and Rebecca Evans had been much more than neighbors and friends to Georgia and Patrick.

The most dreaded change was in Teddy, though. He quickly went from joyously quiet and insecure brother, son, and good friend to a more unmannerly man. He was trying very hard to forget the growing fondness for his brother's girl. He started spending more and more time away from his mother's house, anything to keep him away from seeing Shella every day with Tyler. She had told him she did not like Tyler in that way, but she was spending a lot of time with him these days. Every time he turned around, Tyler was comforting her or coddling her.

The other big change was that the rehab at the hospital hired Shella. She wasn't able to handle clients alone without her degree, but her job would be to float between therapists as an aid. Technically, she was doing the work of a licensed therapist, but she just could not be recognized as one. This was a good means of occupying her time. Between this job and her grandmother, she had little time left over to socialize with Tyler or to think about how much she had enjoyed her first and only kiss.

When Christopher came home from his wedding trip, he was not happy with his sister's decision about not going back to school immediately, but Shella was in no hurry. He didn't understand why she didn't want to start in the middle of the semester, or rather just pick up in the middle. Another reason Shella did not want to go back just yet was because she knew how agitated grandmother got, and didn't want to inflict that upon her new sister-in-law. Christopher was displeased with Shella's hiring of a nurse for the grandmother and her taking a job. It looked to him as if she was not planning on ever going back to college.

The new set of Mr. and Mrs. Evans living in the old Mr. and Mrs. Evans' house was really awkward for Shella. Of course, they would never disrespect Christopher's mom and dad by staying in their room, but it still was strange. So many things had completely changed in such a short time, and Shella did not care too much for change. She missed her mom and dad terribly, and it seemed to her as if it did not faze Christopher at all.

In order to help her new family, Amber insisted on going with Shella daily to learn how to take care of the grandmother. Yes, it was per Christopher's request, but Amber was glad to do it. The old woman took to the new granddaughter-in-law quite well, which made Shella feel more comfortable about leaving her in Amber's capable hands, but the older woman still thought Shella was her mom as she was living in her childhood again.

As time passed by, Grandmother slowly went further into her own world. At one point, she even withdrew from Shella and Amber completely. She would chatter incessantly to no one in particular at intervals, but mostly, she simply sat staring out the window, silent and oblivious to anyone around her. Her eating habits were dwindling.

This gave Shella another reason to refrain from going back to college. She understood that her grandmother's time was limited, as she was heading into the seventh year of what people call, 'the seven year death'. Soon, grandmother would join with her daughter on the streets of gold.

Lawrence Chapman came to visit Shella one weekend to try again with her, but returned to college ready to move on without Shella Evans. He had tried and tried to make a relationship with Shella for years to no avail, but he agreed to settle for being just friends, for now.

Christopher, who had taken a leave of absence from his job in Maine, took a temporary job at the local accounting agency. They hired him to work for different corporations in the accounting departments in order to prepare them for the tax season.

Tyler grew more determined in his pursuit for Shella, when she became too busy for him. He may not have liked her being in demand all the time, but it did open the opportunity for him to slip out with a couple other girls that he was interested in without anyone knowing about it.

On the rare occasion that Shella had a few hours free, Tyler made sure he catered to her desires. There were a few times, that Tyler had to work and asked a reluctant Teddy to be his last minute replacement. He hated being alone with Shella. He hated the feelings she stirred in him. He hated Tyler, and he hated himself. His time with her was miserable.

"Teddy, why is it that you always have time for me? How come you do not have some lovely little lady occupying all your free time?" she asked of Teddy one day, as the two were taking a road trip to watch the sun set.

He laughed as he pulled into a field, "Lovely little lady, huh?" He shifted the point of converse back to her. "How come you don't just marry my dumb brother and make everyone happy?"

It was Shella's turn to laugh. "Marriage!" she cried. "I love your brother, but not like that. We are just *friends*, Teddy."

"Just friends?" he repeated, "Friends don't date each other exclusively. Friends don't…"

"Date? We are not dating. Tyler and I have an agreement. He knows I don't like him nor does he like me in that way."

Teddy barely heard her as he was crossing the front of the car to open her door. "Come on, Shella. I have seen the gleam in your eye, when you look at him."

"That 'gleam' in my eye, as you call it, is really tears, because I am in your presence. You see, I am in agonizing pain, whenever you are around." She used her trademark tossing of her hair across her shoulder proudly. "Furthermore, I do *not* want to be the topic of your stupid conversations anymore."

"I love you, Shella," he tried to appease, taking her hand.

"No you don't, you horrid meanie!"

He had been leading her along a little footpath through a thick of woods, but now, they came to a clearing. He took her hand and fell to one knee mockingly, "My name is Tyler. Marry me Shella, oh marry me and be mine forever."

She shoved him away, until he fell over. She gasped, "Teddy! This is beautiful!"

ༀ

Standing before them lay a panoramic beauty unfolded as if God knew she was coming and prepared her a banquet of awe. Perfectly placed on a luscious green hill was the beginning of a two-story house. Two huge bay windows looked over the dell below.

"I think so," Teddy agreed.

"Are we trespassing?"

"No, I know the owner." He opened the door and waited for Shella to step through.

"We cannot just walk in," she protested.

Teddy smiled mischievously, "Why can't I walk into my own

house?"

"Oh Teddy! You are kidding!" She touched her fingers lightly to the intricate workmanship of the banister. Her eyes were big with awe.

He elated in the joy of her face, "No, I am serious."

She was half way up the steps by now, "How? Why?"

He began the explanation, "I can't live with Mom and Dad forever you know? A friend of mine had this piece of land, didn't want it, so he sold it to me a little over a year ago, and I started building this shack. I really should have moved out by now, but Mom has a hard time thinking of Tyler and me leaving the nest, besides, Dad is not able to work like he used to. He needs us to help." He chuckled, shaking his head. "I am twenty-three years old, and I still live with my mommy."

"They love having you both there."

"Be that as it may, it was time to begin plans to get out on my own, so here we are." Teddy followed her into one of the rooms upstairs.

"And you have built all this by yourself?"

"Not completely. I have had quite a bit of help from my friends."

Shella wrapped her fingers around his muscles of his upper arm, "Can I help too? I don't know how much I can do, but I am willing to help any way I can."

"I would be honored." Teddy removed her hand, keeping it in his, as he led her down the back stairs. "I do not have any electricity yet, and it is getting dark in here. I want to show you the best part of this house." He sat her on the window seat beneath the left bay window, "Look." He pointed out the window.

Shella held her breath, because she was witnessing the most incredible sunset she had ever seen. The window facilitated the perfect spot to view God's glory. His awesome greatness reflected and shone on Shella's young face. Words would have tainted the moment, so both sat in silence, until the last ray disappeared.

"Thank you for sharing that with me." Shella moved toward him, but quickly jerked her hand, as she received a splinter from the unfinished seat. "Ouch!"

"What is the matter?"

"I think I got a splinter in my hand."

"We can go outside. There is a little more light out there." He took her hand and carefully led her outside. "Let me see."

After a few minutes of probing and picking, the little culprit found its way to the surface. "Thank you. That little sucker hurt."

Teddy relinquished Shella's hand reluctantly. "Does it feel any better?"

"Yes, thank you, Dr. Gordon." She gave his cheek a lingering kiss. "I still can't believe you own all this."

He smiled shyly, "All seven acres."

"Well, it is absolutely gorgeous." She looked out over the few lingering blossoms of wildflowers, which blended with the green of the grass that blanketed the pastures with a beautiful quilt.

"I think so," he could not explain his contentment that anyone else should care if he thought it was beautiful or not.

"Oh Teddy! Would it not be lovely to have a balcony off this front bedroom, where you could sit and watch the sun rise every morning?"

"Yes, it would be lovely. I wanted to build a wrap around porch, also."

She had forgotten about the wounded handed in her glee. "It will be so wonderful. Over there, you can plow a garden, and are you going to get some horses for the barn?"

"I might. Will you come ride with me, if I do?"

"Of course, and you could build a ring in the pasture on the other side of the barn. You are going to clear a driveway through here, are you not?"

"Yes, yes, yes to everything," he laughed, holding his hands in surrender, and then he put his arms around her waist in a hug. "I love being able to share my secret with you. I have wanted to tell someone for so long."

"And I love you for sharing it with me. It will be our little secret. I will tell no one. She turned around in his arms to face the last fading remnants of the day. "God is awesome! He gave us these incredible colors in the sunset. Imagine the cascade of hues we have never seen here, but we shall see in Heaven."

Teddy's only reply for a few minutes was a grunting of, "Mmm."

Over the next several weeks, Shella watched Amber embrace her grandmother as her own. On one hand, Shella was glad for the improvement in her grandmother's health, but on the other hand, she had a tinge of jealousy. It was, to her, simply another person leaving her life, because Grandmother no longer needed her. Mom and Dad left her without even saying goodbye, and Christopher and Grandmother preferred Amber. There was always Mr. and Mrs. Gordon, and of course Tyler, but the one Gordon she wanted had little to do with her lately.

The days turned into weeks, and the weeks quickly turned into months, until three months passed by, and it was time for enrollment for the next semester of college, and Shella could find no reason not to return and finish her last two semesters in order to graduate at the end of the spring with Pomalee and the rest of her class. Feeling lonely and sad, she made the choice to quit her job and return to school. What was left here to hold her? She needed to get away from Teddy and everything that made her want him to kiss her again.

Grandmother was fairly frail these days, but that was okay, too, because Amber was very loving toward her. Shella watched the new sister treat the older woman with extra care. Amber seemed to have a touch with Grandmother, which even Shella didn't have. Grandmother saw too much of her own demon past in Shella for her to be of much use. There was really nothing that Shella could do for her that Amber could not. Besides, was that not the whole reason Christopher gave up everything in Maine to come home again?

Needless to say, Christopher was glad of her choice. She would finally finish what Mom and Dad had started all those years ago. Both of the Evans children would be college graduates. There may come a time, when he and Amber could return home, and Shella being on her own two feet with a college education would enable them to do that sooner.

Though he would never tell her, Teddy wanted her gone, because the farther away she was from him, the less tempted he would be to have feelings for her. That kiss that they shared opened up a can of worms.

Teddy was ashamed of his growing guilt, as his fondness for Shella grew increasingly. He knew he could never have her. No matter how much she denied it, she belonged to Tyler. He couldn't just drop out of her life, as long as Tyler kept asking him to keep her occupied, so that no other guys would entice her. He would never know how hard this favor was destroying his brother.

As for Tyler, he was crushed that Shella was leaving. He couldn't stop her from getting close to Lawrence, if she was that far away and alone with him. He wanted her to stay, until he could establish a permanent connection. "If we got married," he proposed in one last effort to keep her from leaving, "you wouldn't have to work at all."

"Tyler, you are so funny!" she laughed.

"I am not trying to be funny, Shella. I am serious."

She looked at him across the table at a restaurant. "Tyler, you know you don't feel that way about me. What brought on this married thing? I don't understand why you have to say things like that. I thought we had been over this before."

"You know I'd marry you, Shella. You would be a great wife and mother. My folks love you. They would love to have you in the family."

"Well, I think you would be a great dad and husband too, Tyler, just not to me. We can't marry just because we are good spousal and parental prospects. You say you *would* marry me, but you do not *want* to marry me, or anybody, for that matter."

"I do want to marry you."

"Can I get you some coffee?" The young waitress winked at Tyler with a big smile.

He turned without paying the girl any attention, "No thanks."

"Let's go out to the lake and watch the sunset," Shella suggested in order to change the topic. "We can talk there."

"Sunset? The sun sets every day. Why do we need to watch the sun go down? Besides, I need to go back to the house. We could do it later, couldn't we?"

Shella would agree to anything at this point in time, as long as it kept the subject of marriage under wraps. She said little on the way home, disappointed that her attempts to dissuade Tyler all evening had been in vain. She conceded to let him wallow in his self pity. She would not placate this marriage talk. As a matter of fact, she was getting pretty tired of all this talk of dating and marriage with Tyler. She wished he would just drop it and never mention it again. She decided right there and then to never go anywhere with him again, if he ever mentioned the word date or marry again. It was absurd, and she was going to clear any notions Tyler Gordon had in his stupid head about him and her.

"Are your folks out for the evening?" Shella asked as they pulled up in front of the Gordon driveway, where the house ahead was dark.

"Yep," he grunted.

Thi was one of the few times Tyler offered to walk Shella across her yard to her front door. She was glad, because her own house was dark and foreboding. Christopher and Amber must have gone out, even though the old family car was still in the drive. That was weird. She wondered what was wrong.

She could not help feeling sad every time she entered the empty house. Opening the door slowly, dreading that feeling of loneliness she would face inside without her mom and dad, she opened the door and reached for the light, and then squealed with a jump of alacrity.

ぺん

"Surprise!" a crowd of guests, led by Amber, shouted.

Tyler grinned at her knowingly, "Are you surprised?"

"Tyler, of course I am! Very much so. You are a dog for not forewarning me, Tyler Gordon. I almost had a heart attack!"

Amber fell on her neck. "Sister dear, I am going to miss you so."

"What have you and my awful brother been up to?" Shella blushed modestly.

At the mention of Christopher, Amber threw a loving smile to her husband. "We could not let you leave without a farewell bash."

"You know you shouldn't have."

Christopher threw his arm over her shoulder which weighted her down, while stuffing something in his mouth. "You're right. We shouldn't have, but my wife needed an excuse to throw her first party," he rambled with his mouth full.

"Shella, I don't know what Tyler's going to do while you are gone," Mrs. Gordon interrupted.

The young girl smiled graciously. "It is very nice of you to come, Mrs. Gordon."

"Well, Darlin'," the Gordon patriarch patted her cheek, "you and Christopher are like our family. Where else would we be, when you are about to leave us for so long?"

That conversation, as many others that night, was interrupted, and the evening was filled with lots of mingling, hugging, and farewells. The young preacher was there, along with the young Paula. Tyler was discreet in his attempts to keep the two of them occupied and away from Shella, until the party ended late that evening. Tyler lingered after everyone had gone home.

"Can we go out on the porch for a while." He asked her after all had gone. "I want to ask you something."

"Let me get my sweater first," she complied reluctantly. She dreaded what she knew he was going to say.

Tyler helped her put her sweater on and held the door open. He began nervously, as they sat on the swing, "I know Christopher is supposed to drive you up tomorrow, but if you don't mind, I would like to take you."

"That is an awful long drive, especially for you to have to drive home by yourself," she excused.

"My boss man has already agreed to let me off tomorrow. I really would like to, if you would let me."

"If it means that much to you, then you may take me, if Christopher doesn't mind. We had better ask him. There is a condition, though. The first mention of marriage or dating, I will get out and walk."

Tyler kissed her cheek affectionately before rising. "I love you, Friend."

"I love you too, my friend. Do we understand each other?"

"We do."

∽∾

The journey was much more pleasant that Shella had expected. Tyler surprised her. As an odd turn of events, he was more childish than Shella had seen him be in a long time, which brought back many memories. It was as if they were ten years younger again, with Tyler reminding her of some slightly embarrassing moments, like the time Shella threw up on him, when he spun her too fast on the tire swing. The pleasant reminiscence made the time pass so much faster.

As they drove up the maple-lined lane to the college, Shella's heart began to race. Her old alma mater was a welcome sight. There stood the Lyndon dorms. She could see the dome top of the campus church. There was the gym with the indoor pool. Excitement ran up her spine, at the thought of coming back to graduate.

She directed Tyler to her old sorority house. This time, she was going to have to forego her beloved sisterhood house in lieu of a dorm, because when she moved out, someone else had moved in, yet she wanted to see all her lovely sisters first. She didn't really mind that she had to stay in the dorm, except for missing the girls terribly. It was only fair.

ॐ

At the house, Tyler held the door open for her, and upon entrance, Shella smiled at the usual hustle of the annual preparations of rush week for all the sororities and fraternities.

Pomalee was in the process of putting up a banner with Angel, not noticing the newcomers' entrance. Celia and some other girls that Shella did not know were scurrying hither and yon accomplishing other tasks. The memories of rush week brought a smile to Shella's lips. She was still a part of this, but it would not be the same.

"Am I intruding?" Her eyes laughed merrily.

Pomalee squealed, "Shella! What are you doing here? You're early." She hopped from the ladder and ran over to place a big hug around Shella's neck.

"Pomalee, this is my other brother, Tyler. This is Teddy's younger brother. He offered to drive me up so I wouldn't have to wait for Christopher to get off work." She turned to Tyler, aware that everyone had stopped what he or she was doing and was gathering around. Shella continued, "Tyler, this is my best girlfriend, Pomalee."

Tyler grinned at the raven beauty, "Hi."

"Do you guys need help preparing for rush week? Tyler and I will be glad to pitch in." Shella looked at her friend for approval.

"Rush week? Oh, we have got it under control. You are just early, and threw us off," Pomalee repeated.

"Yes, I explained that already." She frowned oddly at the strange behavior.

Pomalee threw a guilty glance at the others and turned to re-climb the ladder without a word. She lifted up the banner for Shella to see, because it was halfway up and hung over in the middle. It read: 'Welcome Home Shella'.

Shella looked at Pomalee, "I don't understand."

Pomalee was at her side again, but it was Angel that spoke gleefully,

"Surprise!"

All the others chimed in, "Surprise!"

Then, Angel explained, "You were not supposed to be here, until we got it finished.

"Celia finished and is graduating in the spring with us, hopefully. Her moving out is opening up your old room."

"But I lost all seniority to this house, when I left. One of the younger recruits should have first rights."

A young girl Shella knew as one of the new girls from last fall touched her arm gently. "You and Pomalee are a legend to this sorority. No one would dare take your place."

"Thank you, Belinda, but I wouldn't want to impose." She realized at this point that they had left Tyler nervously shifting from one foot to the other near the door.

"We voted on it, and it is settled Shella." Pomalee followed her gaze and approached Tyler. "Tyler, please forgive us for being so rude. Come on in. We have not completed preparations for the party, or I would offer you something to eat and drink."

He willingly allowed her to pull him by his arm further into the room. He grinned at Pomalee again. "I am fine, thank you."

"Shella, are your suitcases in that car in front of the house," Angel queried.

"I will get them," Tyler announced while striding to the door, glad to be breathing fresh air that was void of all those girlie screams.

Pomalee leaned over to Shella's ear, "Two gorgeous guys in one family. You sure know how to pick them. Is he taken?"

"He is all yours, Dear." The two were huddled and whispering, just like they were back in high school. "He has been out there for a few minutes," Shella suggested. "Why not go see if he needs help?"

Pomalee kissed her cheek. "I love you."

"I love you, too."

Shella helped the other girls prepare for her party. It was a good thirty minutes, before anyone saw Pomalee or Tyler again, but Shella knew that her dear friend would talk anybody's ears off that would listen.

In fact, Tyler was quite taken by this lovely young lady. She was fresh and exciting, young and full of life. Her lips looked soft and happy. Her hands were dainty, as they animated her words. She was so excited, making everyone around her full with her joy.

He chided himself for having these thoughts for someone other than Shella. He was not going to get anywhere with her, if he had such thoughts of other girls. If everyone, especially his folks thought he and Shella should be together, then he should heed their wisdom over his desires and forget such beauties as this.

Tyler was a ladies' man and couldn't help always flirting with them all.

Teddy Gordon's jealousy, guilt and restlessness had been mounting. Whenever he was around Shella, his palms would sweat and he would become tense. The few occasions he replaced Tyler at youth meetings at church, or simply sitting at her house to ensure she did not go out with Steve, put a strain on his emotional well-being.

He didn't understand that the emotional turmoil really did not have that much to do with Shella Evans at all. In fact, it was the conviction of an almighty God knocking at his heart's door, wanting to be let in, but Satan had him blinded, as he does so many people, into thinking that he was saved when he was seven. He and Christopher went up the same year to be baptized, so he allowed Satan to lull him into a false sense of salvation. The fact that he did not believe all the stiff beliefs of his parents didn't mean anything, except that they were old fashioned. He went to church, most of the time. Conviction from God was the last thing on his mind. The apprehension he felt each time he was at church could not be because he wasn't saved.

After graduating college as an engineer, he had secured a job with the local paper factory. He loved being an engineer, and he was good at it. He had his land and was building his house. He had an incredible relationship with his folks, so why should he have these feelings of doubt and insecurity. He had everything he could ever want, except the girl next door.

He ventured to talk to Steve about it in a round about way, but Teddy was a proud man and would not speak to anyone about his own personal business. He coyly questioned the young preacher without revealing anything specific, but no there was no feasible explanation for the void in his life.

Christopher had married leaving Teddy without his old confidante, but he really couldn't talk to Christopher about Shella. That wouldn't work, because Christopher wanted her with Tyler. Even if Shella hadn't gone away to college, he could not talk to her, because she was the problem.

He was having feelings for her and emotions that no other girl had ever stirred in him. Why did it have to be Shella? Why did she have to be the one to initiate these feelings? They had always been friends, and both comfortable being around each other. There was no weirdness between them at all. Now, he thrilled whenever she touched his arm or gave his cheek a kiss. It was as if he were in the presence of glory. That was definitely not the desires of friends.

Not only was he betraying Tyler, he was also betraying Shella, because she had no such feelings in return. He had given her the opportunity to reveal any hope for him, but she had made him painfully aware of that fact, in her rejection of his kiss. She loved him only as a friend. In the beginning, he had appreciated the safety of loving her, because of the fact that she couldn't return his feelings, but oh the agony showed only blindness to that refuge now.

Boy, would Mom and Dad not love to hear how shameful he was, lusting after his brother's future wife. They chose Shella for *Tyler*, and he found it very hard to face any of them, hence his downfall began. It began innocent enough, but it began, nonetheless.

He worked on his house religiously, working each evening, after he finished up at work. He spent so much time away from home, so he would not have to face his family.

First, he finished the outside. Then, he put on the deck he wanted, before building a beautiful balcony off the master bedroom per Shella's request. He was not even aware how much he was trying to please her.

He built it as if he were seeing through her eyes. Would she think was beautiful?

He couldn't forget the glory on her face, as the rays of the sunset shone on her, sitting on that window seat.

By the end of October, he had a brainstorm and began to build a tree house, identical to the one that their dads built between their homes. Shella slept in it before she left for college. He had watched her climb up the rope ladder quite often, wishing for a moment alone in her good graces. The tree house was something he knew she would love. Next, he began on the barn.

He had done it all, before he could stop himself, but when the work was all finished, Teddy's hands became idle, and we all know that idle hands are tools for the devil. This was no different. He could not stand to go home every night and look at his mother's face, knowing her heart would break, if she only knew. If he hung around enough, they might see his feelings for Shella in his actions, and that could never happen. He even distanced himself from Tyler, almost to the point they rarely spoke. Teddy tried really hard to be anywhere Tyler was not.

It started out as just friends relieving the tensions of a hard day at work at the local club, but when he recognized some of his parents' friends, Teddy figured he would be safer finding another pub in the next town over, than to risk being recognized by one of them. His friends did all the drinking, at least at first. He would just sit around shooting the bull with his friends, while watching them drink. He did have enough respect for his parents to not drink.

That was how it began, anyway. He would pay the fee at the door and just sit around accepting the flirting of little barhops. This put his arrival time at home very late, if he came home at all, or sometimes, it would be very early the following morning. It was not long, though, that the boredom of watching everyone else being lulled into that faux happiness and inflicted bravery became more than tempting. The girls were little to satisfy his taste, because he set his standards by *her*, so he turned to the demon that could make him forget her, make him numb for all the misery he was feeling, and make him brave enough to face another day. He tried desperately to fill that void in his life with multiple women, to no avail. The drinking seemed to be the only amnesty he could find.

He did not drink enough to get smashed to where he stumbled home;

nonetheless, it only took one swallow for his mother to smell it on him. She had noticed for a few weeks now, that her firstborn had come home smelling like cigarette smoke, but now he was coming home smelling like alcohol.

ৎৡৡ

Georgia Gordon was devoted to serving the Lord. She had raised her children as such, but she knew not to question her son about this. He would only argue and deny it, so she went to the only One she could confide in and trust to help him. She fell on her knees in prayer.

Why could Teddy not be more like Tyler? Tyler never gave her a moment's worry, but Teddy, she worried about him. He never dated, he never really had friends, except Christopher, and he was always withdrawn. Now, he is drinking and staying out all hours of the night. What was going on with that boy?

Christopher was a good boy. Maybe she could get him to talk to Teddy. No, Christopher had a new bride. She would be embarrassed to talk to Christopher about it. She could talk to her husband, but he would fuss at Teddy, and Georgia knew that rebellion would increase with rebuke. He was at that age, where no one could tell him what was best for him, because he knew it all. She had seen too many young men break their momma's hearts, because of rebellion. No, fussing was not the answer.

Shella had been a part of the family, and was in love with the Lord also, which made her a credible ally. She was a prayer warrior, that Georgia knew she could count on, and Shella was faithful to call every weekend from college, and in return, she would check on Shella's grandmother and report back to the granddaughter about her condition.

That was who she could turn to. When Shella made her call one week, Georgia tested her theory. "Hello dear," she responded to Shella's greeting. "Your grandmother had two good days this week."

"Only two?" Shella knew her surrogate mother would highlight any good report to avoid any bad news. "Is she treating Amber good?"

"She doesn't treat anyone at all, Shella Esther. Most days, she just lays there without doing or saying anything."

"Truthfully, Mrs. Gordon, does she have much longer?"

The older woman hesitated, "No, Sweetheart, I don't believe she does. I do not mean to be so blunt…"

Shella interpolated, "Oh no! You are not being blunt. I asked you for the truth, and you are telling me the truth. Thank you."

"They have been having trouble getting her to eat enough." Georgia explained.

Shella knew the signs, "I know she is ready to go. I asked her on one of her last good days, before I left, if she was ready to meet the Lord. She assured me she was. Thank you for keeping an eye on her for me. Does Christopher seem happy?"

"Oh yes, Dear. That Amber is good for him. You can tell they are crazy about each other. They seem very happy."

Shella politely asked, as she always did, "How is all your family? Is everyone well?"

"Mostly. Tyler is getting a promotion. He will be supervisor." She explained, thinking Shella and Tyler were more than what they were.

"That is wonderful. Tell him I am proud of him," she appeased.

"You know I will, Shella Esther. He adores you, you know."

"How are you doing, Mrs. Gordon?" Shella heard some anticipation in her voice. "Are you doing well?"

"I suppose I am well enough."

"And Mr. Gordon? Is he well?"

"Why yes, he is."

"Is Teddy okay?"

Her hesitation gave it all away. "I am a little concerned about Teddy."

Shella chose her words carefully. "Is he hurt?"

"Not yet, but I am afraid he is heading in that direction."

"Is there anything I can do to help?" Shella offered. She did not want to pry, and she did not want the blessed little mother to have to explain her child's faults.

The mother smiled. She knew she was confiding in the right person.

"Just pray, if you will, Dear. I believe he has been frequenting some dubious places and keeping questionable company." She hesitated before adding, "Shella, he has taken up drinking."

Right then, Shella bowed her head and prayed with the mother. "Dear Jesus, please be with my friend, Teddy. You know his heart, as we do not. Please touch him in a mighty way. Direct his paths and keep him safe from the devil's snares, please. Touch his little mother, also. Please give her peace. We thank You for the victory You have already claimed over this matter. We pray Your will be done. In Jesus name, Amen."

This meant more to Georgia Gordon than Shella would ever know.

Each morning, afternoon, and evening, before she would climb into bed, Shella prayed for her dear friend. She was dedicated to continue to advocate to the Father for Teddy, because she, too, knew God was the only One that could help him now. Oh how she longed to be there with him. Maybe she could help him if she were there. She wanted to be in his arms, but he had made it clear that he didn't want her there. She was glad she was gone.

Was that why he was drinking? Pomalee said he was already in love

with someone. Maybe his girlfriend had broken his heart, and that is
why he had taken up drinking.

Teddy had seemed so happy, when she left, building on his glorious
home. He seemed to be on top of the world. Shella would never think
ill of him for the world. It was almost like a mother's love for her child
that excuses any behavior, only it was God's love in her. She could
only assume what had happened to him since she had gone.

છે

In spite of the ordeal with Teddy, Shella was glad when, a couple
days later, Pomalee announced that her parents were going to be in the
Philippines for the next eighteen months. As a missionary, Pomalee had
spent many years in the Philippines, and it was normal for her to be
alone in college, while they were gone.

Shella was elated. She could have a new sister. She invited her best
girlfriend to go home and stay with her. It would be a sweet reprieve
from the loneliness she faced at home without her parents.
Thanksgiving was almost upon them, and Christopher would want to
have some stupid big dinner, and Pomalee would help the situation.

Much to her delight, Pomalee and her parents accepted. It was set. Much to their delight, Amber, Christopher, even Georgia were glad to approve of Shella's idea. They would all make Pomalee a member of the family.

Per his request, on one of the phone calls to the Gordon home, Tyler drove up to bring the girls home for the Thanksgiving holidays. Shella was pleasantly surprised to find his mother had wanted to ride up with him. Her presence would make the journey appear proper as apposed to two young girls riding alone with one man.

Shella sat in the back seat with Mrs. Gordon, as they carried on an enjoyable conversation. The always cheerful Pomalee kept a smile on Tyler's lips for the most of the ride.

The Gordon parents naturally invited the Evans clan to feast at their house for Thanksgiving. Christopher politely declined for him and his new wife. He understood her being homesickness and agreed to take her back to Maine to celebrate with her family. They left Wednesday night.

Shella smiled and laughed on the outside, but inside her heart was breaking. This was the first holiday she was to celebrate without her beloved mom and dad. She wondered how Christopher could be so gay about it all.

As for the invitation, Shella and Pomalee happily accepted. This was not an unusual request, for over the years, until the kids had become grown; the two families had been together at holidays on many occasions. Even after Teddy and Christopher went to college, Shella remembered both families getting together at one house or the other for most holidays. It had been several years, since they had all been together, though.

Shella and Pomalee cooked and prepared what they were going to bring the night before. They had so much fun in doing so, although it took more than half the night to clean the mess they made, with flour here and there, butter on the floor from where they dropped it, and breadcrumbs scattered all over.

Shella made her mom's recipe for pumpkin pie with a longing in her heart to see her mom, just one more time, as she peppered the cinnamon into it. Tears threatened more than once, but she maintained control over them.

ço~e

That afternoon, her thoughts of loneliness were relieved when they were welcomed at the neighbor's house.

Patrick and Tyler were watching a football game on the television. Tyler stopped watching long enough to answer the girls' knock, greet them briefly, and then return to his chair, leaving them to carry all their goodies to the kitchen by themselves. Patrick was chiding the television screen audibly as he disliked the call of the referee. Shella smiled because all was as it should be.

Pomalee and Shella carried the food baskets into the kitchen, where, although wearing a smile, Shella could see a disturbance in Georgia's features. The young girl knew the matriarch long enough to identify sadness, however it might be disguised. Shella kissed her cheek and gave her a quick hug.

"I will take your fellows something to drink," she announced cheerily, while getting three glasses from the cupboard, trying to lighten the woman's spirits. She couldn't talk to her with Pomalee in the room.

"Oh, they will appreciate that," the woman continued mashing the potatoes.

Shella heard Pomalee as she pushed through the kitchen door, "What can I do, Mrs. Gordon?"

Patrick barely noticed his hand taking hold of the glass, but Tyler broke his concentration to flash a bright smile of appreciation. His eyes twinkled merrily.

"I thought Teddy was in here," Shella claimed, holding up the third glass.

Tyler shook his head. "Haven't seen him." He threw a side-glance toward the kitchen and lowered his voice. "He has not been around all day long. I don't think he even came home last night."

So, that explained Mrs. Gordon's veiled worry. Shella entered the kitchen with deliberate enthusiasm. She had an idea that she knew where to find Teddy. "I forgot something, Mrs. Gordon. I will be back before dinner is ready. Do you need anything else?"

Georgia answered distractedly, "No, Honey."

Pomalee, whose apron was covered with flour, offered, "You need me to go with you?"

Shella laughed, "I think I can handle it, thanks." She kissed the Gordon matriarch's cheek goodbye.

At her house, she gathered the keys to her dad's car and maneuvered the huge beast to a more rural part of town, where Teddy had surprised her one night a while ago. Though she had been there on several other occasions, she almost could not remember the way to Teddy's land, but as she went, she recognized landmarks, and then she saw his car parked in the same place.

The onset of winter made everything so dead and bare. The woods Teddy had initially led her through were thin, since the thickness of leaves was gone. As she broached the edge of the trees, she could see how much work had been accomplished on the house. It was beautiful. He had the balcony on the second floor, with a tri-level deck below with intricate railings that covered two sides of the house. Oh Teddy was a wonderful creator! He had also placed shutters on the windows over the brick walls.

She could hear muffled hammering, which she assumed came from inside the house. The young woman had no qualms about pushing the door open and entering in. The cushion she made for the window seat was perfected on the bench where she had placed it, the day she made it. Her homemade curtains obscured the incredible panorama outside. The electricity had been turned on, because she could see a light shining from upstairs.

She topped the steps, "Teddy?" All sounds stopped abruptly. "Teddy?" she repeated, as she ventured into the master bedroom. "There you are. Didn't you hear me calling you? Did you lose track of time?"

"What are you doing here, Shella?" he snapped, keeping his back to her.

Shella was taken aback. He had *never* spoken to her so harshly. She tried again in a pleasant voice, "I thought you might have forgotten what day it is. Your mom has Thanksgiving dinner almost ready."

"Well, I won't be there." He offered no explanation.

His sharp words cut like a knife into her heart, forcing tears to threaten her. She was truly uncomfortable for the first time, being around Teddy. She tried to select her words carefully, as she softly began, "Teddy, are you mad at me? Have I done something?"

"Who are you to care whether I go home for dinner or not? Tyler's there, go be with him and leave me alone."

Shella stood her ground, fighting hard to keep the tears from coming. "You are breaking your mother's heart Teddy, and I am your friend that loves you."

Her words fazed him only a little. It did bother him to hurt his mother, but how dare Shella come here after him? He should never have shown her this place. "Go home Shella. You shouldn't be here."

Shella turned her head, so he would not see her cry, as she began to leave. As she reached the door, she halted her steps. Without turning around, in a quivering voice, Shella relayed her last comment to him. "Teddy, one day you will not have your mom to spend Thanksgiving with."

Teddy had been angry and full of self-pity for so long. Those words were the proverbial straw that broke the camel's back. He had deliberately avoided Shella ever since she had come in on Monday, because he was afraid he would not be able to control his feelings around her. He was consumed with selfishness, pride and guilt, but Shella was not fighting fair.

His thoughts of only himself were manifested as selfishness now, by the fact that this was her first Thanksgiving without her parents, yet her thoughts were on everyone else but herself. Who was comforting her unbearable loneliness? Suddenly, he wanted to envelope her in his arms to do just that.

His voice grew tender as he followed after her to the head of the stairs. "You are right, Shella. I'm sorry." When she began to descend the stairs, he quickly added, "I am not mad at you, Shella. I just can't go sit at my mother's table and act like everything is wonderful."

"Everything is wonderful, when we are all together. Why can't you go home…to please your family?"

He turned away in shame, "My family will not be pleased with me. I can't face my brother and mother with what I have done."

After turning around, she was within inches of his face. She could smell a horrid odor. She knew what the stench was, because she had see the bottle over near the window. "What do you mean 'with what you have done'? There is nothing you can do so bad that your mother wouldn't want you at her table."

"You just don't know what I have done, or you would understand."

She searched his eyes in which he tried to hide from her. "Teddy, your mother loves you, just like you love her. Are you saying that if you found out she made a mistake you would stop loving her?"

"You don't understand. She knows I have been drinking."

"Teddy, I have made more than my share of mistakes. Does that mean you don't love me anymore, or that you cannot stand to be around me?"

"No, but…"

She barely gave him time to answer. "There are no 'buts', Teddy. It hurts your mother, when you don't come home."

"I think it hurts her more, when she knows I have been drinking.

She has not said anything, but she looks at me as if she knows."

"At least she knows you are safe, when you are at home, even if you have been drinking. If she doesn't know where you are, then she worries whether you are dead or alive."

"Mom doesn't worry about *me*, Shella. I am not Tyler. She does not care if I drink myself into oblivion, as long as no one knows about it. I am an embarrassment to the family."

"Theodore Patrick Gordon, you know better than that. I cannot believe you actually said that."

"It's true, and you know it. It has always been Tyler. Tyler is the good-looking one. Tyler can do no wrong. He has always had everything just given to him, and now you…" he quickly caught his words, before she could catch their meaning. He came close to cutting Tyler to the quick. He wanted to tell Shella how much he hated his mom and dad for giving her to Tyler. Tyler may be his brother, but he hated him for taking Shella.

"Teddy, you know, deep in your heart that is not true. Remember when Tyler had to have that heart surgery, when he was a few months old? He needed the extra attention, whereas you were healthy and didn't. Your folks love you equally, just in different ways."

"Whatever."

Shella proceeded down the stairs, "As for good looking, you are better looking than Tyler. You are also strong, tenderhearted, and honest, but if you want to throw yourself a pity party, you go right ahead, but you are having it alone. I'll not join you." She had never been so angry with Teddy before. He should be grateful to have his mom living and well. He should appreciate her life. He should not be allowed to torment his beloved parents that way.

Having longer legs, he quickly caught up with her, hands shoved in his pockets, and a scowl adorning his otherwise gorgeous face. They walked in silence through the woods to where their vehicles were parked. Teddy pushed passed her to open her door.

In one last attempt, Shella faced him, "You have changed, Teddy. I don't know what has gotten into you, but I really miss my old Teddy. I love him. When he finds his way back, let me know."

"I'll drive. I know how much you hate driving this big car."

Shella smiled to herself. He was coming! Yet, she would not allow her voice to portray her joy of success. "I would appreciate that." It had completely faded from her mind that he had been drinking.

At first, the ride was somber, but Teddy was not happy that Shella was upset with him. He couldn't stand the thought of her not liking him, as she did now, so he tried to lighten the solemn expression from her face.

"So you think I am strong?" he began. She nodded. "And you think I am honest?" Again, she nodded. "And I beat you in our tree climbing race?"

As he knew she would, Shella broke her silence, "I don't think so. You know I beat you fair and square, you cheater!"

"I don't remember it that way," he insisted.

"You have problems, then. You are not only a cheater and a liar, but you are also pompous, pigheaded, and a lousy rememberer," she accused, almost back to her old spirit.

"But I am good looking?" he prompted.

"And add conceited to that. There is nothing worse than someone being gorgeous and bragging about it."

Her words made Teddy glad. Yes, he was guilty of trying to get her to say them, as he had briefly forgotten she was supposed to fall in love with his brother. He wanted her to love *him*, but in his attempt to get her over being mad at him, he thought of nothing of his jealousy of Tyler.

"Do you still love me?" he queried.

"I am not going to stop loving you, no matter what you do."

He felt bad about getting angry with her for coming out to find him. "I am glad to hear that, but Shella Esther, I don't know if that Teddy still exists."

Shella emerged the passenger seat of the car with her eyes fixed on Teddy. "This whole conversation is just between the two of us, Teddy. Please don't say anything to anyone."

He appreciated her saying this. She had a way of taking the shame off him with her words. He knew Shella would not judge what he shared with her today. "Oh God, I love her," he thought, "and curse

Mom and Dad and Tyler. The love he held in his heart for Shella equaled his hatred toward his brother.

The young woman ran to her house to grab something, at the last moment, to make her excuse for leaving valid. This enabled Teddy to go home on his own, without them knowing Shella chased him down.

❧

Shella waited till dark, when everyone was comfortably engrossed in a movie at the Gordon house, before she offered to take Teddy back to his car. None of the gang in the house would miss Shella or Teddy for the short amount of time it would take her to drive him back out there. Tyler happily entertained Pomalee, while his dad dozed in his recliner. Georgia, happy to the gill that her sons were home and safe, turned in early, because she was genuinely tired.

The jovial part of the day was over. There had not been two minutes for Teddy to ponder on anything in the past during the festive meal or even cleanup, but now that his mind had time to idle, he felt awkward around Shella.

He hadn't meant to, but he had told her too much before. Had she seen through his façade? Did she know he loved her? All he knew for certain was that the forgetfulness that comes along with being drunk was his desire right now; hence, he was anxious.

He was fidgety and nervous during the ride, wishing he had something strong to drink. It had been, what seemed to him, forever, since he had a drink. He was in the presence of an angel, and suddenly was feeling inadequate and vulnerable now that his intoxicated bravery had worn off. His uneasiness increased, when Shella presented him with a personal question.

"Teddy, are you saved?"

Of course he was saved. Yes, he had a desire to have a beer in his hand at that moment, but that did not stop him from being saved. So how come he couldn't answer her without hesitation, without questioning himself? How come he could not say, "yes" to her question? Was it her piercing honest eyes? Was it her goodness?

"You know Shella, any other time, I would say yes, but right now, I just don't know," he answered after some time had elapsed. "I think I am."

He pulled up and parked beside his own car. Shella touched his arm with her fingers. She closed her eyes and did not say anything audible for a moment, and then turned to search his eyes. "I will be praying for you. You were once the best of my friends. I miss you so much. I love you Teddy, and I will be praying for you."

Before her very eyes, Teddy turned into a little boy, laying his head on Shella's arm. She thought she even saw tears in his eyes. Like a child in pain, he accepted her strokes on his hair and comfort from her arms. He had forgotten his strangeness around her. She put his heart at ease to the point he enveloped her friendship. She was the only one he felt he could talk to. She had proven her friendship and loyalty to him. True to his belief in her character, Shella remained comforting him with a gentle stroke, until he rose up. It was as if her hand were an extension from God, sent to comfort him.

"I miss you too, Shella. Things are happening to me that I cannot control. I don't know how to stop this spinning wheel, and I don't know how to get off. It scares me."

"*You* can't control it, Teddy. Without our Heavenly Father, we can only yield to the temptations of the flesh. Only when you *want* Him to, will God intervene. Only He has power to direct your actions and deliver you from all temptation."

He did not know how to respond to that. He believed it was true, but he felt that God had deserted him, because Teddy had dove head first into the flesh. Everything seemed to be going wrong. Where was God, when he needed Him to stop him from falling in love with his brother's girl? Where was God, when he needed Him to stop him from drinking? Where was God's mercy, when he took a perfect angel, like Shella, and killed her parents?

Her soft kisses fell on his hair, like a sister comforting a brother. He closed his eyes and relinquished his anger under her touch. His love for her kept crossing his mind. That was the reminder he needed that he was an infidel, screeching his joy to a halt, he jumped up ashamed, once again, for his feelings for Shella.

That was the last time he saw Shella, before she went back to school. He made a point to be gone for the remainder of the weekend. After she left, he had nothing to make him feel guilty about his actions. Teddy knew that if he dabbled in the things of the world long enough, he would soon join in the world, but none of it seemed that bad. He was not really doing anything that was going to send him to hell, as long as he did not love Shella.

Teddy had been under the preaching of the Word all of his life, so he knew. Yet Teddy associated with the world in order to drown out his sins. He needed to forget that last few moments he spent with Shella at Thanksgiving. He needed to forget he was Teddy Gordon all together, until he was not hurting anyone. What harm could be done by his occasional frolicking with alcohol?

He was glad she was gone. Once again, he would be able to push Shella to his subconscious with the help of alcohol. He would occupy his time with other girls. He had managed to do that when she left for college before, but the minute she walked in his house on Thanksgiving, he was slammed with the responsibilities of his actions. He was glad she was no longer there to be a reminder of what is right and good.

The worst part of his downward spiral was that he could never tell anyone how he felt. His parents, Tyler, even Christopher were all pulling for a Shella-Tyler union; therefore, he was forced to bury it, which made it fester and boil inside, until he just wanted to die.

Little did he know that the secret he could not reveal to anyone was that he questioned the love of God in his heart, and that was the true reason for his misery, because God kept working on him, trying to draw him to the cross. It basically had nothing to do with Shella at all.

Every Sunday morning, he attended church with his family, although the words fell on an empty heart and deaf ears. He would push away the Holy Spirit that tried to draw him nigh. He was living a lie in every aspect, and was not willing to give up the pleasures in sin, which made him more miserable.

ೞೲ

On the home front, his mother became his advocate to the Father, pleading for her wayward son to find salvation, full and free. Tyler grew angry with his brother, because he was being cruel to their mom, but Tyler's anger included mostly ignoring Teddy. Patrick was not oblivious to what his son was doing, he just knew the boy would have to sow his wild oats and later reap the wages of sin. When the time was right, he felt confident Teddy would answer the Savior's knock, because he claimed his whole family, according to the Word.

Shella prayed vigilantly for her dear friend to find the right path. He had scared her quite seriously, when he announced he did not know if he was saved or not. She was concerned about his drinking and whatever else he might be getting into. She realized that only God could intervene and take this desire away from him. Although she prayed diligently, she refrained from calling or writing him. She felt as if God had His forbiddance on her contacting him. If that was the case, she realized God was working on His own and did not need her help.

Meanwhile, Shella became considerably involved with her school. She delved into her studies to be worthy of her straight A status. Finals would be upon them soon, and then she would have only one more semester, before she graduated. Still, she made time for prayer. She didn't mind the distractions school offered to get her mind off of that kiss. If she would allow it, that kiss would hinder her prayer life for Teddy.

Every year, at Christmas, the music department put on respective concerts. Much practicing and preparation ensued for the events. Shella was both in the choir and in the band, as she played the violin, which made her a dual participant. She, Pomalee, and two other stringed instrumentalists were grouping together for the recital to play a medley of carols, which highlighted each instrument.

Another constant distraction for Shella was Lawrence. As usual, he favored her company. She had completely assured him that they would remain only friends, and if he kept expecting more than that, she would take that away, too. It was only then that she complied to attend this event and that event in his company.

Lawrence didn't need much encouragement. The fact that Shella came back to school so soon was enough to get his hopes up high, and when she agreed to go with him to the Thanksgiving festival, he assured himself that he could win her heart. He was incorrigible.

Just when all seemed to be going steady, Shella received the call that her grandmother had gone. Shella could hear great sadness in Amber's voice, as she broke the news. Once again, she felt she had to be strong for everyone else. There was no time for her own grief.

Getting permission to go home was easy, because she only had two more days, and she had planned on going home for her birthday for the weekend. It would not affect her classes much, so she could leave that evening. Lawrence arranged to miss classes, so that he could drive her home, because Christopher was busy with the arrangements for the funeral.

Shella was not glad that Lawrence was the one to drive her home, because she knew the assumptions he would make. However, beggars could not be choosers. Besides, there was not much of a selection. Against her wishes, Christopher had asked Tyler to come get her, but he had to work. Of course, she was glad she was not stuck with him.

Lawrence chose to be there for Shella and prepared to stay for the whole weekend. Naturally, Georgia and Patrick offered him to stay in Teddy's room, since the wayward son rarely came home. Momma Gordon knew how this young man felt about Shella Esther. She wanted to keep her eye on him.

The throng of consolers was not as large as when their parents died, but all of their mothering family was there, again. Shella and Christopher were required to stand at the end of the casket of their loved one and accept hugs, kisses, and handshakes, along with an aunt and uncle, and their children.

Tyler took what he thought was his rightful place behind Shella, even though Lawrence had pretty much put a claim on her. The two sparred through sharp stares all evening, but Shella paid neither one much attention. Of course, Tyler's mother aided her son's efforts by occupying Lawrence with conversation as much as possible.

Teddy slipped out of his house, as soon as he saw that no good Lawrence drive up with Shella and headed straight to his haven of escape. He had no intentions of accommodating her being with that scumbag. He certainly was not going to hang around, while Shella rubbed his nose in that punk kid. Shella could say what she wanted, but something was going on between her and Lawrence. Even Tyler could see that.

The wicked imaginations were running wild, so when he arrived at the tavern, and found Shelley, Teddy thought about how sweet it would be to rub her in Shella's nose. Besides, his mom and dad had strongly requested he show his respects, and he did not want to disappoint them anymore, so he told himself. Yes, this would be sweet revenge.

He showed up fifteen minutes before it was to end, with his date wearing a leather mini skirt, six-inch heels, and a backless top. Her pretty black curls appeared as if they had not been washed or combed in days. She was very young, with a persistent cough and a strong voice.

Teddy occasionally felt *her* eyes fall on him. He knew she was watching him. Well, he hoped she was watching him and suffering as miserably as he was. He let his date, hang on him like an ornament in hopes it would make Shella jealous. He plastered a foolish grin on his lips, so that she would think he was happily doting over the girl, as she whispered in his ear.

Shella was not the one watching, though. Christopher had caught a glimpse of him with that hussy girl and critically watched the disgusting display of affection. At one point, he started to go to Teddy and expedite the visit, but was not able to get away. He became protective and wanted to shield his wife and sister from that kind of behavior.

He didn't know what was wrong with Teddy. He had not come around much since he and Amber came back from getting married, and he came around a lot less than that after Shella went back school. As a matter of fact, they had hardly seen Teddy across the way even. He came to church, but would not participate, and as soon as the service was over, he was gone. To think that his, once, best friend had been up to these shenanigans. He would never imagined Teddy with girls like that.

When he approached, Christopher stepped in front of Amber to hide her. He could tell that Teddy and the girl were pretty drunk. He went to ease Teddy past Shella, but she had already seen them, and her reaction pleasantly surprised Christopher.

As the two came near, Shella had to hold her breath. Both had put on too much cologne, but that only veiled the foul odor of alcohol. The overkill odor of mint expounded the nauseating combination. Teddy shook Christopher's hand, then Amber's, but hardly looked at Shella as he walked on by.

"I will show her I have no feelings for her," he thought.

Shella smiled pleasantly at Teddy's date and took the girl in her arms without second thought. This is a friend of Teddy's, and she must show herself friendly. She discreetly held her breath, so the loud perfume would not choke her. Was this the one he told Pomalee he was in love with?

"Thank you for coming," she put forth graciously. "You are so kind."

The gum in the girl's mouth retaliated loudly, following a horrible cough, as the girl quickly pulled away. She was not so free with her hugs, not with girls, anyway. Who is this that should hug her neck and not even know her?

Then the young worldly girl turned to Teddy, with no regard to the volume of her voice, "Dead people give me the creeps. Let's get outta here, Teddy Bear."

Teddy and Christopher exchanged an embarrassed glance, for the girl's voice carried. Tyler stepped up and mumbled something to Teddy and directed him to the exit. Teddy was glad to have a good excuse to leave without coming in contact with Shella.

Even half blitzed, he could not stop his love for her or his desire to comfort her again. Her fresh innocence, as she stood there so vulnerable, made him jealous that his brother had the right to stand behind her in support.

This made him more determined than ever to lose himself and the torment of his soul in the bottom of a bottle.

He held on to one flaw that he could find in Shella and tried to make her into a horrible monster to ease his own hideousness. Shella claimed to not be involved with Lawrence or Tyler; however, they were both right here as a lover would be. Teddy clung to that as a fact that she was a liar and two-timer, trying to convince his own mind that he could never love her because of that flaw.

He would try anything to expel her sweet innocence from his thoughts, but beneath it all, he knew she was neither liar nor cheater and could never be anything less than perfect. She was most certainly too good for all the horrible things he had done lately. She could never love a drunken fool.

$\wp\!\!\sim\!\!\wp$

Teddy left the funeral home with a vengeance in his heart. How dare Tyler escort him out like some heathen? Just because he was with Shella did not mean Tyler was better than he. How dare he treat him that way? He was the older brother. He was a man. What did Tyler know? He was just a boy trying to show off in front of Shella. And how dare Shella be so uppity? Who did she think she was?

He took Shelley back to the hole where they tried to drown out the memories of dead people. The girl drank to forget the dead body in the coffin, and the boy drank to forget the friend that he once had, but now was dead to him.

Teddy forgot the beer and went straight to the hard stuff. He ordered a bottle of hard liquor, which he consumed by himself, save a half a glass that Shelley drank, and then ordered another. Shelley didn't drink the hard stuff, because she was only eighteen and did not want to be thrown out.

His drunken buddies surrounded him with the encouragement to drink on. Any time someone wanted to make a fool of themselves and drink a lot like that, they would always stand behind them and cheer! This was the first time Teddy had been the one they cheered.

The head cheerleader was a brute named Stanley. Stanley was a two-time loser who couldn't hold a job for more than a couple of months. He was just as lucky in his love life as he was in his career. He was once married to a beautiful girl that left him the first time he hit her, and any girl unwise enough to look in his direction, generally regretted it within a minimal amount of time afterward. He preyed on the new blood that came in the bar, especially young ones like Shelley.

There were always plenty of young ignorant girls willing to give him a chance.

His friends were only his friends, because they feared him. He was big and would get physical in his drunkenness, and it was just easier to go along with him than to anger him. Teddy was not one to follow anyone much, but it was just easier to stay out of his way and ignore him, but tonight, Teddy's intoxicated boldness made *him* Stanley's target of entertainment. Teddy did not care. He was just happy that someone was buying him a bottle to help him forget what's her name.

After his second bottle, Teddy Gordon became more talkative than he had ever been in his life. Being one that never said much, he ran his mouth about idiocy he didn't even know a thing about. Another first for him was when he became too fresh with Shelley. Naturally, she had tried and tried to win this handsome man's affections for the last few weeks, but the most she could get out of him was a quick kiss one night before he threw up. Tonight, she was happy that he was paying that much attention to her, but she was uncomfortable with the audience that Teddy was trying to impress. He had let her really kiss him at that creep show, but she had the feeling that was for someone else's benefit also.

Stanley came to her rescue and insulted Teddy, making everyone laugh. Stanley may be a drunk, but he was one of the few who actually grew smarter with alcohol in his system, being that he was pretty stupid to begin with. He laughed heartily and pulled Shelley behind him in a method of protection and handed Teddy another glass full of the liquid demon.

"Momma's boy, let's go have some fun," he slapped Teddy on the back. He always called Teddy a momma's boy, because Teddy never delved too deep into this drinking. He had decency and a few morals, which Stanley associated with being tied too tight to momma's apron strings.

"Wherer ya wanna go? I thought we's havin fun here."

"Yeah, you're having fun, but the rest of us want to have fun too. It's not fair that you are having all the fun."

"We could go back to your place, Teddy Bear," Shelley offered.

Stanley put his arm around her shoulder and pulled her face close to his. "Don't worry about Momma's Boy, Sweet One. You'll be with me. I know how to treat a real lady. You shouldn't be around somebody like Momma's Boy, here. You need a real man."

The girl fluttered her eyes while donning a smile, because Stanley thought of her as a lady. "Can we get out of here?" she asked of him, touching his arm in flirtation.

"In a while, Sweet One. Me and Momma's Boy, here, are going to have some fun first."

There were three other men and two other girls cheering Stanley on. They were laughing at Teddy's drunken stupidity. He laughed uncontrollably, "G'ahead with im, Shell-lla. Me n the boys are gonna have some fun."

"What are we going to do?" asked one of the other men.

"We could go over to the Great Escape," offered another.

But Stanley already had plans of his own. Something about Teddy rubbed him the wrong way and he had never been too fond of him. He had the ultimate humiliation in store for him, besides taking his girl away. "No. I gotta better idea. C'mon, let's go." He motioned.

He and the other guys had to help Teddy stand and walk, because his legs were like wet noodles. "C'mon Shel-la," he stammered.

Shelley became more furious, "I'm not Shella!" Of course, this sent the rest of the gang into laughter again.

Teddy stumbled back to her. Throwing one arm around her, he got close to her face, trying to kiss her, "I'm sor-ry. I know yere…" he trailed off, forgetting what he was saying.

Stanley ordered the girls to stay put, until they returned, and herded the others out of the bar loudly. John, one of the men, asked, "Hey Stanley, where'r we going?"

"Trust me. We're gonna have a good laugh. Momma's Boy, you're going to become a man tonight."

He drove them all stuffed in his little old beat up car about a mile down the road to a place that had signs hanging up advertising body piercing and tattoos. In the abyss of his drunken oblivion, Teddy agreed to and allowed Stanley to inject the green ink filled needles into his shoulder. Being that Stanley could not spell very well, his 'Momma's Boy' turned into 'Momas boy', marking the eldest Gordon boy for the entirety of his life with a hideous tattoo. He would not be held responsible, because Teddy agreed to it.

As he woke up the next morning in a place he knew not, he had not the slightest idea of what he had done the night before. His shoulder was sore, but he never would have imagined he would have scarred his body this way. It would have been a shame to him had he known his actions, so he went around for weeks without knowing his indiscretions. Every time he was around his 'friends', they laughed mockingly at him, but none revealed what they had done, because he never mentioned it. They just assumed they were laughing with him.

That was the result of the night Teddy drank so much he became oblivious to anything having to do with Shella. He couldn't even remember Shella Esther Evans existed. He threw his life away in a moment of carelessness. He would rather die than ever face his feelings for that girl again.

Shella returned to her classes with a heavy heart. She wanted to cry, again. She had left the funeral home that night, her birthday, with the image of Teddy's lips freely kissing that girl etched in her burning eyes.

Had he always been so carefree with his kisses? That meant that *the* kiss meant absolutely nothing to him. She had just been available for a passing moment in which Teddy Gordon would not remember the next day. It really had meant nothing to him.

She had opened up all these feelings for him, that he never even pretended to reciprocate. He told her from the beginning. She was so stupid!

She cried herself to sleep. While everyone thought she was grieving for her loved ones, really her heart was ripped, minced, and broken. She talked about this with no one, not even Pomalee. She was embarrassed. If she told Pomalee about that kiss in the nursing home, she would think how much of a fool Shella was.

Teddy was about to break his momma's heart as well as hers. That girl he brought to the visitation was the kind of girl he preferred? This was his true love?

He did not love *her*. She couldn't hold on to that kiss as a token of unspoken affection. It was just as Teddy had said it was. It was an act of pity, because he felt sorry for her. The vision of that girl's lips on his smile tainted the memory of the kiss *they* shared. Now it was ugly and revolting, yet she found herself reliving that moment over and over in her mind.

＄◦◅

Each day, she grew closer to the end of the semester by taking exam after exam, with everything having happened in this last year, she was mentally strained. Only one more semester, after this one, and she would graduate and be finished with school forever. Oh how wonderful that thought was to her!

They were not back at school very long, after the funeral, before it was time to go home on break a second time.

Christmas time was always exciting, and with Pomalee and Shella preparing for the break by taking their final exams, they grew more joyful in the spirit of the Holy day.

However, Shella's weekly calls to Mrs. Gordon drew her down, somewhat, as she could hear the worry in the mother's voice, knowing what all Teddy was in to, and now he was rejecting everyone that loved him.

Once again, Lawrence came to the rescue in driving the girls home, before going on to his own home. This was wonderful for the girls, because Christopher had to work. Lawrence was all too glad to accommodate, especially after Shella turned down his invite to the fraternity's Christmas formal.

Lawrence finally collected enough sense to stop pressing her so hard, and for that, she was grateful, but it was Pomalee's constant cheerfulness that brightened the trip a little.

The journey home went too quickly, for Shella dreaded going home. Mom and Dad were not there. She would never hear the joy in her mom's voice, as she called them to Christmas dinner again. She would never get to watch her dad's eyes sparkle, whenever he opened the tie he received every year, and still remained surprised. She would never receive that precious kiss from them both, as she lay her head on her pillow.

Christopher and Amber were gone, when they arrived home, which made the house feel so much emptier. Something was different about the dark foreboding loneliness, though. She could not put a finger on it, but something was definitely unusual.

She and Pomalee took their belongings to their rooms, while Lawrence waited in the living room, hoping to get an invitation for a date. He became nostalgic as Shella descended the stairs. At last year's formal, she wore a deep purple gown and he had thought he had never seen anyone so elegant as she descended the stairs of the sorority house. It was déjà vu, except the dress. He had the same anticipation pounding in his chest, especially when Shella reached the last three steps that turned at an angle, because her foot caught on something, she slid the rest of the way down.

Lawrence was quick to jump to her aid, as Pomalee came running from the top of the stairs. "Shella, are you okay?"

Lawrence helped her to her feet, while she laughed at the sight she imagined she was. "Oh yes. Just call me grace."

Both friends gave her the once over to ensure she had not any visible cuts or marks, before continuing on. "Shella, you need to be more careful," he chided.

Her gracious laugh adorned her lips, "Lawrence, would you like to stay for supper? I do not know what we have in the freezer, but I would be glad to throw something together."

"How about I take you two lovely ladies out for supper?" he suggested.

"You don't have to do that, Lawrence. It would be no problem for me to check."

Pomalee came from the kitchen with a glass of water for Shella, "Okay, what are we cooking?"

Lawrence offered, "Nothing. I would be very honored if you girls would let me treat you to supper, before I have to head home." He took Shella's hand, "Please, Shella?"

She conceded, "I guess you do have to be leaving soon. We do appreciate the offer, but save your money, I know exactly where we can go."

She threw her coat around her shoulders and led them out the door and across the yard. As soon as she opened the door, she could smell the rich aromas in which she had expected to permeate the Gordon house.

"Hello girls," Georgia greeted happily, though her smile faded, somewhat, at seeing Lawrence. "I saw you come in, and have been expecting you. Did you have a safe trip?"

"Yes ma'am. Christopher was not home, so we thought we would crash supper over here."

Georgia completed her hug on the girl's neck. "You cannot crash. I have already set extra places."

"What can we do to help?" Shella and Pomalee laughed, because they asked in unison.

Shella noticed that Mrs. Gordon looked pale and strained. She seemed uneasy and sort of jumpy. From their conversations on the phone, Shella realized that things were not any better with Teddy. Why was he being so rebellious? She would have expected this kind of behavior from Tyler, maybe, but not Teddy. Teddy was truly sweet and kind, and it was not in his nature to be so rotten. His mom told her that he rarely comes home anymore. Shella knew he was probably staying out at his house, but that did nothing for the little mother, who did not know there was a beautiful home and that he was probably safe there. Teddy should be turned over his dad's knee and whipped.

Georgia seemed a little grayer this trip home than Shella remembered her being last time. She had dark circles forming under her eyes, obviously from not getting enough sleep and from hours upon hours of worry. Her happiness was veiled behind a weak smile and furrowed brow, as she pressed on vigilantly.

When Pomalee had taken a platter of pork chops into the dining room with Lawrence, Shella asked cheerfully, trying to lighten the burden, knowing that Georgia would want her to ask about him. "Where is Tyler?"

That was enough to get that faint smile out of her. "He should be here any minute. He got off work about fifteen minutes ago." She drew close to Shella. "He is a good boy, Shella, and he is really fond of you." Just then, they heard a car in the drive, so the little mother quickly changed the mood and converse. "You and Christopher and everyone *will* be having dinner with us next Tuesday, won't you? I expect you to bring your famous potato salad. You can bring whatever you like, but you will share it with us, won't you?"

"I cannot answer for Christopher and Amber, but as far as Pomalee and I are concerned, my potato salad is your potato salad.

The older woman saw the sadness in Shella's eyes. This first holiday season without her folks was becoming increasingly hard to bear. Their absence suddenly overwhelmed her to the point she could not breathe, and she still had over a week to prepare for Christmas "I miss them so much, God." She cried out in silence.

Pomalee burst through the door with laughter on her lips, "Tyler's looking for you Shella, but he had to wash up first. He is not happy that we are having carrots, and he said it was all your fault."

Shella laughed. Whereas carrots were her favorite, Tyler always slipped his onto her plate, when his mom was not looking, because he hated them. Georgia always fixed them, whenever Shella was over just to make the girl happy, which Tyler resented fully.

He bounded in about that time, expecting his mother to fuss at him for running in the kitchen. Accepting reprimand was not on his mind just now, because his blessed mother was deathly white. The color had evaporated completely from her face. He watched as slowly, her legs gave way beneath her. By the time she hit the floor, he had reached her side and was weeping over her crumpled heap.

"Mom, can you hear me?"

Pomalee ran to the living room, to summon Mr. Gordon, while Shella turned off the stove and oven and called 911.

The poor woman's eyes were fixed with a terrified look of wildness in them. She lay motionless, without the ability to respond to Tyler's calling her name. Before the husband made it into the kitchen, her eyes closed, and her body became limp.

Within minutes after that, the paramedics were surrounding her with skillful reactions. They all could hear the voice on the radio transmitter speaking to the emergency room, as he reported, "…apparent heart attack."

Shella did not realize that Mr. Gordon was holding on tight to her, and had she not been supporting him, he, too, would have fallen. His life had been knocked out of him. She was more than a wife to him. She was a part of his own body that was being ripped from him.

Tyler almost cursed in asking where his brother was, and he meant for him to be there for his mother. Tyler paid no attention to Shella,

Lawrence, or anybody, except his mom. His dad rode in the ambulance, and he drove Pomalee to the hospital in his truck.

Lawrence and Shella stayed behind. Lawrence pled apologies, as he reluctantly needed to head home. He offered to take Shella to the hospital, first, but Shella had another goal in mind. She quickly loaded into the old family car and set out to find Teddy. Hopefully, he would be where she found him the last time.

ﻌﻌ

She prayed for Mrs. Gordon, "Lord, let her be okay, if it is Your will. Please heal this broken family, I pray." She continued, as she drove in the direction of his house. "What is that boy thinking?" She was unaware that she was pressing on her gas pedal so hard in her haste, until amid her thoughts and tears, she heard a brief shrill of a siren. Looking in her rearview mirror, she, now, saw the blue flashing lights.

Once she was pulled over, she wiped any signs of tears from her face, which enabled her to see a navy blue uniform approaching. She quickly fumbled for her license in her purse, trying hard not to let the tears flow again.

"Shella, is that you?" the officer asked, bending down to face her.

"Dan! Yes, it is me. What is the matter?" she responded to her brother's old high school friend.

"What is your hurry? You were going a little fast."

"Oh, I am so sorry. I was trying to find Teddy Gordon. His mom had a heart attack, and they took her to the hospital."

"Teddy? Why are you heading in this direction?"

Shella didn't want to reveal her friend's secret, but this was an emergency. She answered regretfully, "He has a house out on Hwy 25. I was just going to see if he was there."

"Well you go on, and I will check at the Dew Drop to see if he is there. He hangs out sometimes over there. Now, you be careful in this rain, and slow down. I will meet you at Jaryd's Grocery in about thirty minutes. If I do not see you then, I will assume you found him."

"Thank you so much, Dan. I will definitely slow down for sure."

Shella had not noticed the rain, until Dan mentioned it, so she carefully maneuvered the big old car back on route again. This time, she did pay closer attention to her speed, and she became more conscientious of her driving.

"Please let us find him in time, God." she cried out hopefully.

When she reached the place where Teddy always parked at his house, her hopes were dashed. His car was not there. For reassurance, she ran through the rain to his house to see if he was there, but amid the beautiful creation that lay before her, no Teddy was found. On nimble feet, ignoring the splatter of raindrops on her head, she returned to her car.

The blanket of wetness chilled her, which made the heater feel wonderful. Tears threatened again in her disappointment, because his absence here meant he was off drinking somewhere. "You are going to accomplish nothing being a big baby, Shella Esther Evans," she chided herself audibly. "Stop blubbering."

Dan was already waiting for her at the local grocer, but his expression revealed he had not found him either, before he was able to say a word. She pulled her car beside his, so that neither would have to get out in the rain.

"He was not there?" Dan asked through the two opened windows.

"No sign of him. I take it you found the same results?"

Dan conveyed grimly, "Talked to some of the fellas, and they said he mainly goes out to the Camel's Back, over in Sandersville. I would go for you, but I am on duty."

"I appreciate it anyway. You have been a big help. I will ride out and see if I can find it. Meanwhile, if you find him, will you tell him to get to the hospital?"

Dan had strong reservations about Shella going to such a place as this. He questioned in concern, "Sure will. You don't know where that bar is, do you?"

She tried to smile, "No, but I can find it. I have to."

"Do you know where Dandelion Road meets up with Hwy 217?"

"Is that before or after the carpet place?" she queried.

"After. About three miles past it on the right."

"Okay. I think I may have seen it before. I can find it. Thank you again, Dan."

He concluded, "No problem, Shella. I wish I weren't on duty. You shouldn't be in a place like that."

"Thanks," Shella retreated as she rolled up the window and then added to herself, "Neither should Teddy."

In her heart, she prayed for the little mother of her dear friends. Too much loss and death had taken place lately, and Teddy would resent not being with his mom, should something horrible transpire. The trip to the next town took several minutes in which she prayed, yet again, that she would find him.

Her heart sank the closer to the carpet store she got. She thought she had talked some sense into him at Thanksgiving, but his mother had talked like things had only gotten worse. Maybe he would not be at this bar. Maybe he was somewhere safe and Godly. Maybe things had changed, for the good, in his life. The streetlights danced on the raindrops on her windshield, as she searched the signs.

She was saddened and relieved, when she found his car in the parking lot. She did not want to hesitate in getting him to his mother, but she did hesitate momentarily to see if the rain would slack up. Truthfully, she did not want to go in there.

Opening the door, she held her breath in anticipation of what was to come. She meekly approached the counter, where a huddle of people was on each end. Single individuals were scattered across the distance between the two. She knew she was out of her element. Only a couple of the strays bothered to turn their heads to acknowledge her entrance. Everyone else was full of drunken jolly.

"What can I do for you, Little Lady?" asked the man behind the bar. "You have to be twenty-one to drink"

"I am looking for someone…" She had not finished her question, when a man beside her interrupted rudely.

"Well Baby, you've found someone."

Shella ignored the oaf to speak directly to the man behind the bar.

"Have you seen Teddy Gordon?"

The bartender motioned with a nod in the direction of the corner of the place, where tables and booths held parties of people. Shella briefly caught a glimpse of her friend with a young girl draped across him, but the boorish lout, once again, stepped in front of her to block her vision.

"That old square? What do you need him for, when you have me?" He touched her cheek to push back some of her wet hair.

Shella stared directly into his eyes to stand her ground. She was not to be bullied. "Please do not touch me."

"Ooh, a little fireball, heh!" He deliberately obstructed her view, as she tried to get Teddy's attention. "I like that in a girl, and you *are* a little girl, aren't you?"

"Stanley, do not patronize the customers." The bartender warned, but turned to serve someone at the end of the counter and paid her no more attention.

"I ain't patronizing her." Again, he dared to touch her delicate skin. "Me and her have a date, don't we, Little Lady?" He put his arm around her shoulder in an attempt to draw her toward him. "Come on Princess.

You look lonely. Old Stanley will take care of that for you."

He leaned his face dangerously close to Shella's in a bold attempt to kiss her. She reacted with a sharp hand across his face, which only enraged the bully. He grabbed her shoulders roughly to the point it hurt her terribly. She seemed to have lost all her strength.

"Looks like Stanley found him a new girl tonight," giggled Rita. "Look at her Teddy, acting all high and mighty. It kills me to see girls like that come in here. They act all 'don't touch me', and yet they're in a bar. What do they expect?" she rambled on. "Ouch! She slapped him. You know Stanley won't stand for that. Serves her right, the little snob."

Teddy took a drink from his mug, with a glance in the direction Rita was pointing, carelessly looking for some entertainment, but he quickly slammed the mug back onto the table in shock. He must be drunk! At first, he thought his eyes were playing tricks, because Shella would never be seen in a place like this. That was the whole reason *he* was here. It did not matter if it was a dream. His natural instinct to help any damsel in distress overtook him. Whoever she was, she had slapped Stanley, and he knew Stanley would never let that happen without retribution, especially since he was plastered.

Teddy rose, flinging the girl on his lap carelessly to the seat beside him. Someone had to intervene. He was by Stanley's side in only a few strides.

Meanwhile, Stanley touched his cheek in disbelief. "You little vixen!" with his large hand, it was nothing to knock her to the floor with one slap. "Next time you come in here, thinking you're better than every…"

His words were halted by Teddy's fist hammering his mouth. While the two men scrambled, Shella had a chance to escape. She did not know or care what the distraction was, but she gladly fled out into the pouring rain once again, having forgotten the whole purpose of being in that awful place. "Oh God help me, please," her brain cried out.

She did not hear as Teddy called after her, "Shella! Shella!" His legs were longer, so he caught up with her pace quickly. "Shella!" he called again.

The first natural instinct would be to run to Teddy's arms and let him be her protector, as when they were kids, but she could not do that anymore. He had lost that right, when he destroyed the old lovable Teddy.

Instead, she turned to him in devastation, with tears flowing freely, as he grasped her arm and repeated, "Shella, are you okay?"

She recoiled from his grip with a gasp. "Don't touch me!" Her emotions were still reeling from the touch of that horrid man inside. She did not fully understand who the person in front of her was or that he had no intentions of hurting her.

She was a pitiful picture indeed. Shella was literally soaked to the bone. Her hair was clinging to her face, and against her will, her teeth were chattering slightly. Her eyes were tired and puffy from the amount of crying she had done. Teddy could see a hand print still on her cheek. He wanted to engulf her in his comfort.

Instead, he let her crisp response cut through his compassion. For all these months, he had tried so hard to turn her against him, so that he could hate her, so he could be free from her hold on his heart. Now that she actually was angry with him, he did not like it at all. He suppressed his continual urge to pull her to his breast and apologize until their old friendship renewed. He loved her, and he could not bear to have her hate him. Her rejection stung, making him angry.

"You shouldn't be here, Shella," he retaliated furiously.

"You shouldn't be here either, Teddy," she turned to complete the short distance to her car, so she could run from this awful place.

Teddy quickly paced in front of her to match the fire blazing in her eyes. "Why *are* you here, Shella?" He could not imagine why she had come to this place. Was she trying to embarrass him? Was this payback for her grandmother's funeral?

"I came to find *you*. Your mother was taken to the hospital." His widened eyes and sobering concern for his mother came too late for Shella. She finished, "They think she had a heart attack." Then, she dodged him to leave.

"When?" he demanded, grabbing her arm, as if it were her fault.

She wiggled from his clutches, "A couple hours ago."

"Is she…okay?" he pleaded.

The raindrops that fell relentlessly were drowning Shella's tears. "I don't know. I haven't been to the hospital to find out. I knew you would want to be there. She looked bad."

"Come on, we will take my truck. I will send for yours later."

"I'll take it now." Teddy took her arm again and practically dragged her with him to his truck. He opened the passenger door, but Shella refused to get in. "You are drunk, Teddy. I am not riding with you. Let me drive."

He was a man. He could handle a little drinking. How dare she treat him like a child? "I am fine. I haven't drunk much. Get in."

The fire in the girl matched him defiantly, "No!"

He flung her arm from him. "Fine. Suit yourself."

He slammed the door shut, strode to the other side, and sulkily slammed his own door. If she was going to act like that, he would be content to leave her in this God forsaken place to fend for herself. His engine revved under the weight of his foot, while Shella ran back to her own car to leave. She knew she wouldn't catch up with his speeding, but to her surprise, she exited the parking lot before him.

The young girl who adorned Teddy inside came running out to catch him, since he left so quickly and curiously. She was angry that he had deserted her and would not be put off so easily. She stepped out from between two parked cars, flailing her arms wildly and running out in front of his truck, until he had to screech it to a halt.

"Teddy! Teddy!" she yelled.

Rolling down his window in frustration, he growled, "What do you want Rita?"

"Where are you going?"

"I gotta go," was all he offered.

"But Honey Bear, you didn't even say goodbye." Her whining hit his last nerve.

"Bye Rita." He spun his tires in his haste to leave and sped in the direction of the hospital, leaving the girl standing in angry awe that he had left her that way.

Who was that hoighty toighty girl that came in? Whoever she was, she was the reason Teddy took off that way. She returned to her den of evil, pouting and plotting her next trick to get Teddy back.

Further down the tree-lined road, Shella encountered a puddle of water standing on the road, which caused the old Evans' car to sputter to a stop. "Doggone," Shella said aloud to no one, as she tried to restart the car. "I have flooded her."

Carefully, she opened the door to look under the hood. Shella knew nothing about cars but had seen Christopher do this before, so she jiggled here and banged there and decided to give her another try, with hopes that this would work. As she rounded the driver's side, headlights blinded her eyes. She had difficulty seeing the handle in the bright lights.

"That must be Teddy," she thought, but her anger at him hoped he would not stop. She did not want him to try and insist on giving her a ride.

The impairment of the alcohol effected Teddy's sight. Through the rain, he blinked to make sure he did see something in the road ahead. With the speed he was traveling and the misjudgment in distance of how far the object was in front of him, slamming his brakes did little for the severity of the impact. He jerked the wheel in the opposite direction, so that in over steering, his truck went airborne off the embankment and into a tree below, leaving him dazed and confused and momentarily unconscious.

∾∾

Teddy lay stunned and still. Where was he? What happened? What was the last thing he could remember? Braking…skidding…losing control…Shella!

He scrambled from the seatbelt, but could not open the door. His chest hurt, but he ignored the pain in order to release his torso from behind the steering wheel, which seemed to trap him. It was a painful fight, but he finally freed himself, falling hard onto the ground. His head was busting and pouring blood. Breathing was hard and hurt excruciatingly.

Again, he ignored the pain for the thought of one he feared was lying dead on the road. He didn't think he was that close, but he distinctly remembered his truck actually contacting an object. Maybe, it was just her car. Maybe she was clear. "Oh God," he cried out to the

One who would not hear him, because Teddy did not belong to Him, "What have I done?"

He must have been out of it for a while, because when he topped the small hill he had flown over, he saw blue flashing lights. He ran toward the sight of a figure kneeling over a heap in the road.

"Teddy? Teddy Gordon? Is that you?" The officer recognized him, even with the blood smeared all over his head and face.

"Shella!" was all Teddy could say, as he fell to his knees beside her, "I am so sorry."

He didn't know why he expected her to look better than she did a few minutes ago, as she stood before him in the parking lot, but she did. Only now, she was lying on the ground in a fragile pitiful heap. A bruise had formed on her head and on her hand. That was the only part of her body that was visible. He would die, if God would take him right now, as apposed to having hurt Shella.

Her eyes were opened prior to Teddy's arrival. In response to Dan's question, she answered, "I don't need an ambulance. Thank you for the offer, but I am not hurt too bad." She tried to sit up with his help, wincing in pain.

"Wait Shella. Let me get EMS on the radio."

"No. Please?" She tried harder to sit up this time, until, with his help, she was propped up against Dan's arms and rejecting Teddy's help.

Again, he apologized, "Shella, I am so sorry."

Dan looked from Teddy to Shella. "What happened? Did you hydroplane?" He asked of Teddy."

Shella continued, so Teddy would not have to answer. "Dan, could you please take me to the hospital? I think my leg is broken." He started to say something, but she injected, "I don't want an ambulance." She hoped this would offset the pressure from Teddy. She wanted to protect him, because she could not help still loving him. No matter what things he had done, and God would probably whip her for it, but she still loved him.

Her anger subsided, as she looked into his haunted face. He was being punished pretty badly already. His cheeks were hollow and pale. He had lost so much weight that his clothes were sagging on him. The most pitiful feature of all was the hollowness of his eyes. He was hurting so terribly, but why? Why could he not tell her what was wrong? They used to share so much. What has changed?

Teddy reached down to lift her to the car, again Shella rejected his offer. As he did this, he moved close enough to the officer that Dan could smell the strong odor of stale alcohol. "Teddy had not hydroplaned at all! He had been drinking!" he concluded mentally.

"I'll get her, Teddy," he ordered, while gently lifting her to his backseat. He shut the door so she would not hear, and then turned to Teddy, "Ted, we go way back, and I hate this more than anything, but I am going to have to ask you to accompany me down at the station house, after you get checked out at the hospital.

Teddy couldn't look at Shella, neither could he argue. He obediently followed Dan. Together, they pushed Shella's car to a safe point, so that no one else would wreck because of it.

"Is Christopher at your house, Shella?" Dan asked, once they were on the road. "He would kill me, if I didn't call him about his kid sister getting hurt."

She replied weakly, "He might be home by now."

Dan mistook the tears he saw in his rearview mirror as tears of pain. In fact, they were tears of a broken heart for having lost such a wonderful friend. He slowed long enough to radio dispatch to contact Christopher to meet them at the hospital and to send a wrecker to pick up the vehicles. Christopher was his old buddy too. He dreaded telling him what happened to his sister, especially after losing his parents such a short time ago. He would be livid with Teddy to think he might have lost his sister in the same manner as his folks.

He drove the squad car to the emergency docks, where the ambulances entered. Immediately, three medics greeted them with a stretcher. As they rolled her away, she grabbed Dan's arm, preventing him from leaving.

৩৯৩

He leaned over her, "It's okay, Shella. I am going to make sure Teddy gets what he deserves for this. It is just a shame. I really don't look forward to telling your brother."

"Please don' tell him, Dan. Please, just keep this between the three of us. I know you have to do something according to the law, but I don't want to press charges. Teddy needs to be with his mother. The realization of what he has done will hit him full, when the alcohol wears off. He'll punish himself enough. Please Dan? His mom is upstairs, maybe dying, and she needs him."

"Don't worry, Shella. I'll take care of it."

"I mean it, Dan, promise me."

"Take care of her," he called needlessly after the medics, as they rolled her between two doors.

‿◞◟‿

Dan returned to the car, where Teddy was waiting in sheer fright for his order. "We'll go in the front way." Teddy had made him mad. As an officer, he had seen too many deaths due to drunk drivers. He hated them.

Teddy said nothing. His mother was upstairs, possibly dying, Shella was somewhere being treated for injuries and both situations were his fault. He had worried his poor mother, until she was sick to death.

When he saw Stanley hit Shella, he thought it was the worst thing for a man to hit a woman, but he took his vehicle and hit her with it. How much worse was that? He could have killed her! Through it all, he still longed for the forgetfulness of drinking. He wanted another beer, right now.

He had a long wait before they called him back into a curtained room to be checked out, not that he cared one way or another about his own health. He flatly refused to go to the emergency room for himself, but Dan insisted. Teddy didn't care if he died right now. He was a coward and did not want to face the consequences of his actions.

Dan filled out a pink paper, while they were waiting. "Here Teddy. I need you to sign this, if you can. Against my better judgment, Shella made me promise not to charge you for hitting her, so I won't be charging you for that, but I am required to charge you for driving while impaired. You are really lucky I don't take your license. By all rights, I should. I know your mom is upstairs, so if you will sign this ticket, you can go straight up to see your mom, when you are done down here."

Teddy scowled from the bed he was sitting on, as he signed the paper and was glad to be rid of Dan. He eyed around to see if anyone was around, and then he slipped off the bed. He did not need or want a doctor. Carefully, he replaced his clothes, threw the gown on the chair, and double-checked one last time to ensure a free escape, before walking out of the room.

Halfway to safety, he heard a familiar voice, "Teddy! You are here with Shella?" Christopher asked, and then Teddy had to turn around. "Oh my word! You look terrible. Is Shella okay? I got a call from the police station." He grabbed Teddy's hand in the normal welcome gesture of a handshake, but Teddy's hand was limp in his. "Are you okay?"

"Mr. Evans? Your sister is over this way," the nurse that had given him and Amber directions earlier, informed. Turning a critical eye toward Teddy, she added, "You are supposed to stay in the room, Mr. Gordon. The doctor will be in shortly."

Teddy looked at the floor shamefacedly, because the nurse's cool tone embarrassed him. He could feel Christopher's inquisitive eyes on him, and promptly retraced his steps to his curtained room to sit alone, sober and lost. How had he let things get so far out of his control? He woke up this morning on top of the world, but now, things could not get worse. He had done this all by himself. He had done this to his mother. He had done this to Shella, the one girl in the entire world that he loved more than his own life. He wanted an escape.

露

"Mr. Gordon, I am Dr. Guilde. I see you have been in an accident.
What seems to be giving you trouble? It looks like you need a few
stitches above your eye."

Teddy flinched under the touch of the latex gloves, "I am fine. How
is Shella?"

The doctor pulled out his stethoscope and listened to, first, Teddy's
chest, and then his back. The doctor distracted the topic. He was not
allowed to talk about other patients. "Are you aware that whoever put
your tattoo on spelled 'momma' wrong?"

"Mmm," was his diverted reply.

The doctor stitched his cut over his eye with the nurse's help. It was
obvious that the nurse did not like him. Her manner was abrupt, but
Teddy knew he deserved every bit of pain she inflicted on him.

As soon as they left him alone to order the x-rays and tests, Teddy jumped up as quickly as he could, considering his soreness. He turned and twisted, but could only see a spot on her shoulder. He could not turn but so far without too much pain. "It must be further down," he thought. When did he get a tattoo? He did not remember getting a tattoo.

"Think, you fool!" he yelled at himself in his mind. He started to use his trademark fingers through his hair in agitation and accidentally touched his wound, causing more pain. "You have a tattoo! Thank God Mom didn't see it. She really would have freaked," he continued chiding.

Teddy lifted the top to the little table beside the bed, revealing a small mirror. It was attached, so he pulled the whole table with him. After a little maneuvering, he was able to use it with the other mirror to catch a glimpse of green ink under his shoulder blade. It was a brief glimpse, because the nurse came in and he had to stop.

He sulked through the tests and x-rays, trying to understand what was going on. It was when he was laying flat on the cold hard table, waiting for the pictures to be taken, that he had a recollection of what might have happened.

There was one particular night, when he had gotten so very drunk that he did not know where he was or what he had done. It was Shella's birthday, the night of her grandmother's visitation.

He had been so humiliated and so angry, that he had been antagonistic to the guys, until they started picking on him. He remembered they had teased him in front of Shelley to the point that she had left the bar with Stanley that night. He did not remember much else that night, but what he did remember was that the next morning his shoulder was sore. Was that what happened? Had he run off to a parlor and marred his body?

Once again, he wanted to die, rather that face the consequences of his actions. A tattoo? He could never get rid of that. His momma would have to bury his cold dead body with it forever etched in it. He did not even know what it was a picture of. Again, he cried out to an almighty God that did not hear him, "Oh God, what have I done?"

The doctor took blood samples and wrapped his chest where the steering wheel had broken some ribs. The stitches were in place, where his head had busted the driver's side window, and now the doctor was ready to release him.

He was torn in which he should do first. He wanted, or needed, to
be with his mother, but he could not very well leave without knowing
about Shella. That would be like hit and run. He needed absolution
from her. He needed to be found in her good graces, and then he would
never make her lay eyes on him again.

He figured Christopher probably already knew he was responsible
for Shella's condition, and Teddy did not want to face that, so like the
coward he believed he was, he went to be with his mom.

He found out from the front desk nurse that his mom was over in the
EKG lab, in another wing of the hospital. When he got there, he found
Tyler, Pomalee, and his dad in the waiting room. His dad was haggard
and weary.

Tyler was obviously upset with him and said nothing to him except,
"It is about time. Where have you been?"

Pomalee tried to keep peace between all, while Teddy's dad lovingly
explained to him what was going on with his mother. The father knew
the son was going through some turmoil, although he did not know the

details, but as a father should, he loved his son and forgave him for all. One day, the prodigal would return.

"What happened to your head, Teddy?" Pomalee asked quietly, after a while, when Tyler and his dad were out in the hall talking. "You have so much blood on your shirt."

He stammered incoherently, "I…I…"

"What's wrong, Teddy?"

"I was in a wreck," he bluntly responded.

"Oh my goodness!"

"I need…oh…Shella…"

She interpolated in concern, "Speaking of Shella, did she ever catch up with you? I figured she would be here by now. The only place I could think she would be was finding you, but you are here."

"Shella… is in the… emergency room."

Pomalee gasped, "Oh goodness! Was she in the car with you? Has someone called Christopher?"

"He is downst…" the wound on his head was hindering his coherency. "Oh God in Heaven," he cried softly, to the point that Pomalee could not hear all his words, "Let her be okay." He closed his eyes to retain the tears that wanted to eject. "I love her."

Pomalee put her hand on his knee, "Teddy, look at me. What is wrong?" she required seriously.

He rambled, "I need to see Momma, and Christopher and Amber were with her. Could you go…"

"Of course."

"Will you tell her I am sorry?"

Pomalee frowned at not knowing what was going on. "I'll be back." She rose to leave, "Will you explain to your dad and brother?"

He nodded. How could he explain to anybody?

He wandered over to the window, after Pomalee left. He was in deep thought, just staring out, pondering the revelation of new events, when Tyler and his dad came back in a little while later. Tyler gave him a hateful look. He wasn't stupid. Teddy reeked and probably had not bathed in a day or two. How could he come here like this?

"Teddy, we thought we saw the doctor coming." Patrick came over to where he was standing. "I am sure you have a good explanation for all the blood on your shirt, and I want to know why, but I need you to clean up before you see Mother. She is worried enough as it is."

"Here, Teddy. You can put my sweater on." Tyler slipped his sweater over his head and gave it to his brother.

As Teddy pulled it over his head, Tyler noticed the place on his head where the stitches were, when the sweater pulled the hair back that shaded it. He started to make some well deserved remark, but the doctor had entered the room and was talking.

∽∾

"Tests show she has suffered cardiac arrhythmia. We are going to keep her a couple more days for observation. After that, we will probably be treating her with medications. Initial diagnosis shows it does not appear to be too serious."

"Will she need surgery?" inquired the beloved husband.

"No, arrhythmia is a variation in the normal rate of the heartbeat. Abnormal heartbeats occur when the heart has an irregular heart rhythm, beats too fast or too slow. The electrical system the heart creates signals that trigger the heart to pump. This controls the heart rhythm. Arrhythmia results from a problem in that electrical system of the heart, possibly caused by thyroid malfunction, too much caffeine, stress, or even alcohol. I believe it is minor. It can be fatal to some people, but Mrs. Gordon seems to be one of the lucky ones. Some require a pacemaker, but again, your wife is not to that point. She needs to make an appointment with a heart specialist and keep regular appointments. I will put her on medication before she leaves, but she will need to follow up."

"Thank you doctor." The patriarch called as he left. When the doctor turned around, Patrick reached out to shake his hand.

"They are putting a cot in her room, if you want to stay with her," he concluded.

"Thank you. Can we see her?"

The doctor stated before he walked out, "In a bit. They will be transferring her to a room in a few minutes. The nurse at the desk at the end of this hall can tell you what room number, after they move your wife."

Teddy mumbled something about being back later and followed the doctor out. He needed to see if Shella was badly hurt. The guilt was about to eat him alive. It seemed he had a knack for hurting the ones he loved.

Pomalee met him in the long corridor coming back from the other wing of the hospital. "It took me a while, but I finally found Christopher."

"Did you see Shella?" Teddy refused to look her in the eye.

"She is in surgery, Teddy. Christopher said she has a broken hip. I think he said something about having to put pins in or something like that."

"Is that all?"

"I think there may have been some minor stuff, but her hip was the only major injury. Have you heard anything about your mom?"

"Yeah. They came in just a minute ago. They are going to keep her a couple extra days," he half explained. "Are you going to see Christopher?"

"I will walk back with you," she offered, "I was just coming to let you know what was going on."

Teddy frowned guiltily, "Since I can't see Shella now, I will go back to Momma. She may be in a room, already." He did not want to have to wait with Christopher and answer the obvious questions burning in his friend's mind. He did not want to have to tell his once best friend that he almost killed his lovely little sister, who had done nothing but show kindness to him.

"Okay, then I will go back with you."

He didn't offer much converse on the way. It was Pomalee that asked the nurse at the desk for the room number, but considering all Teddy had been through, she thought nothing of his silence. She also asked the nurse for a toothbrush and toothpaste. Suggesting coyly to Teddy that he needed to freshen up before seeing his mother was not easy, but Pomalee managed to accomplish it without offending him.

"Teddy!" Georgia cried weakly, when they came in. "You are here." She smiled peacefully at his presence.

"Yes, Momma. I am sorry I wasn't here sooner." He reached into her open arms to grant her the hug she awaited.

Of course the little mother could smell the stale remnants of smoke and alcohol on him, no matter how well he cleaned up. "Teddy, what happened to your head?" She touched the wound.

Teddy pulled back quickly in embarrassment. "Oh, that is nothing for you to worry about, Momma. How are *you* feeling?"

"Better, now that my family is here, well, most all my family. Where did Shella get to? I figured Christopher and Amber would be up here, too."

"They are downstairs," Pomalee offered.

Tyler implemented, "Why? Didn't you tell them Mom was up here?"

Pomalee looked at Teddy to see if he was going to explain, but by his downward stare at the floor, she knew hew was not, so she began, "Shella was in an accident. Christopher and Amber are down with her."

"An accident?" Tyler and his mom exclaimed in unison, as Tyler threw a frown at Teddy. Was it coincidence that his girl was in an accident and Teddy looked like he had been in one?

"Where is she? I want to see if she is okay," he asked of Pomalee. Something was not right about this news.

Pomalee took Tyler's arm, "Come on. I'll show you."

The days went by until Georgia went home, but Shella was still recuperating from her surgery. The doctor had put in two pins on her right hip and one on the left. Her left wrist sprained, as she tried to catch herself in the fall, but a sprain would heal fairly quick. Minor abrasions adorned her entire body, and bruises were strongly visible, but all in all, she would recover. The wounds that hurt the most were the breaks in her heart. She had lost a truly beloved friend.

Of course, she had forgiven him, but he had not come to see her at all, since the accident, so she was left to assume that he had chosen to return to the dung heap of his drunken stupor. That meant he had forgotten all that had transpired. "Take this love from me, God, please. I love him, yet. Make him Yours, Lord," she prayed every day.

There was not much of a smile for her these days, because she harbored a dark secret alone. She would not and could not tell anyone about Teddy, so she opted to bear that burden solo. In return, she became greatly sad.

Upon hearing about her condition, Lawrence came down to visit the first weekend. Like Tyler, he suspected something was not right about the story, and resented Teddy. For both men, Shella's secrecy about the wreck made them angry at her protection over Teddy. Somehow, he had wronged her, and they wanted to know how.

Tyler and Pomalee were faithful to alternate visitations between the two invalids. Shella found out that the night of the accident, Christopher and Amber had been making arrangements to move back to Maine. Now that Grandmother was gone and Shella was gone, they could get on with their plans. Naturally, all plans would be put on hold, at least till Shella was healthy again and back at school. That was the reason the house was so foreboding that last night. They had packed all their belongings to leave.

Teddy stayed away completely. His self-reproach of the events that unfolded was more than he could face. Although she had not, Teddy was afraid that Shella had told everyone what he had done to her. His remorse was consuming his sanity, and he swore to never touch a drop of alcohol again. The only problem with that oath was that he had no means of escape from the torment he had created for himself. He saw no way of putting a stop to all the pain he had caused so many people, except in the bottom of a bottle.

Things just kept getting worse for Teddy Gordon. He was slipping into a reality that was manic. He methodically went to his job, came home, served his mother's needs, and tried to avoid his brother. Tyler didn't help the situation much with his quick words and looks of disgust that made the older brother want to die. That would end everyone's misery for good.

He sat in the tree house one morning, about a week later, with a pistol in his hand, fingering it thoughtfully. Mom had every reason to hate him. He bore her much shame and worry with his drinking and philandering. His dad hated him. Tyler hated him for much less, and

Christopher, well Teddy could feel the hatred in Christopher's eyes, but the one he could not bear to have hate him was Shella, and she had more reason than any. He could never face her again. The reproach of his actions was more than he could bear. He was already living in silent discourse with his family. He was only there to please his mother, anyway.

He rolled the chamber over and over, trying to think of a good reason not to use it. Yes, Mother would be hurt but she would soon get over it. She had Tyler to comfort her, so did Shella. Of course Shella would not mourn his death. She probably wished he was dead already. It always came back to Shella: beautiful, vivacious, courageous Shella.

He placed the pistol in his mouth two times, but could not get the courage up to pull the trigger. It must be that coward in him coming out again. He thought about that soft kiss and the taste of her tears that day so long ago. He remembered her reacting motions. She had kissed him so delicately, as if she had never done this before. His closed eyes relived that precious moment, but immediately flew open at the remembrance of her recoil. The last time he touched her, she had such disdain in her retreat. If he loved her, this would be the best thing for her.

Once more, he lifted the gun to his mouth. His finger was on the trigger, as he was actually geared to do it this time, when he caught a movement out of the corner of his eye caused him to lower it to investigate the motion. He certainly did not want a witness.

It was his dad at the woodpile, staring off in the sky, musing. Teddy watched as his dad stood there for several minutes. Occasionally, he would run his fingers over his hair, as Teddy had seen so many times before, whenever he was anxious.

Finally, his dad picked up the axe and heaved it into a log. Even by the sunless sky, Teddy could see the features of his dad's face. Teddy couldn't see how much he favored that man. He had the same hairline, the same nose, and the same mouth. He was shorter than his dad, but he had the same build. Even though neither used it very often, anymore, they both had the same smile.

This morning, Patrick Gordon bore saddened features. Teddy noticed how worn his dad looked. How long had he been dragging down? Was this the result of his wayward actions, as well? When did his dad turn so old?

Teddy descended the rope ladder, started over to his dad, and gently maneuvered the axe from his dad's calloused hands. "Let me do it, Daddy."

The younger man split enough wood for at least two days without stopping. His dad watched on in silence. He acted as if he had something to say, but didn't know how. At one point, Teddy thought he saw tears in the old man's eyes, so he stopped chopping and sat on a log beside his dad.

After a longer silence, Patrick quietly inquired, "Teddy have I done something wrong?" He searched the boy's eyes, in which Teddy kept hidden.

"Why do you ask that, Dad?"

"You don't talk to me anymore, not even in passing. You rarely come home and have been distant from the whole family. It is obvious that you have a burden."

Teddy shook his head, "No sir. You have done nothing."

"Then what is it, Son?"

"Would you go somewhere with me, Dad? I will carry this in, and stoke the fire first."

"The fire is fine, but let me tell your Momma we are leaving," the father agreed without question. Teddy noted that if he lived long enough to have kids, he wanted to be just like his dad. He would drop everything in a moment's notice to listen to his children. That was a precious quality.

Patrick waited for his son to explain why he wanted him to go somewhere else with him, but Teddy drove in silence, until he reached a spot off the road a little way down on Hwy 25. The dad curiously watched the son, as he led him through the woods to a house, yet he still did not understand. It was all too silent.

Pushing through the door, Teddy, jammed his pockets and began to explain, "This is my house. I have been building on it a little at a time. There is only a little more left before it is complete. I have spent many days and nights here fixing her up."

His dad stared in awe. "This is yours?"

"Yeah. A guy I know sold me this land a couple years ago. I know I cannot live off you and Mom forever, so I made plans to get out of your hair."

"Why didn't you tell us? This beats what I have been assuming you have been up to."

Teddy opened the door for him. "The time never seemed right. Maybe I was just being a coward. I am good at that. It is just, I love you and Mom, and I didn't want you to be hurt.

"You did not tell Tyler?"

"The only person I have told, except the people helping me build it and you, is Shella."

The gentleness in the way he spoke her name did not escape Patrick's notice. He was suspect of Teddy's feelings for her, but kept that to himself. Since Teddy had pointed it out, he could see a feminine touch in the curtains and rugs, as well as other things. Things were coming together, now. That is how come Shella always knew where to find him, when no one else could.

"Don't mistake what I am saying. The truth is worse than what you were assuming, Dad." Teddy strode to the refrigerator, opened it, pulled out the remainder portion of a six-pack of beer, and opened each one to pour down the sink. "This is the other reason I have been missing." He held up a can, "You don't have to worry, though. I will never drink again. That is a promise."

"I am sorry you ever started, but I sure am glad to hear you are not going to drink anymore."

After the grand tour of the house, his dad complimented, "You have done a beautiful job on the house, Son. I am just amazed."

His words were the first encouragement Teddy had received in a long time, but his shamefulness only let him reply, "Shella made the curtains. She said she would not allow me to put something ugly in the house." He sort of laughed to himself. Then, she shouldn't want him in there. His thoughts of trying to leave this world came back in full, now. Why did he not just pull the trigger, when he had the chance?

"Shella is a good girl. I hate to see her going through so much. We are blessed to have her in our lives," his dad admitted.

He mainly said this to get confirmation of his suspicions. Teddy lowered his gaze to the floor. His dad made him feel some better, but how could he feel anything but contempt for what he did to his brother's betrothed? It was not enough that he smashed her in his drunkenness, he also was recklessly out of control in love with her.

With his head held in utmost shame, he confessed bitterly, "Shella didn't have an accident, Dad. It was all my fault."

"I know. She told us how you lost control of the truck in the pouring rain. Is that what has been bothering you lately? Son, the roads can get bad in the rain. You can't blame yourself."

Teddy raised his voice in anger at Shella. He didn't understand why. Why didn't she just tell everyone the whole truth? "I was drunk, Dad. She came over to the Camel's Back to tell me about Mom being taken to the hospital. She literally came in to find me. We argued, and I was so mad at myself that I refused to let her drive me. I don't know what she was doing out of her car, but I tried to swerve and miss her, only I did not miss her, and now she almost died, because of me!"

There! He had it out. He immediately felt a load lift from having told someone. He expected his dad to be horrified at his confession and look at him in shame, but that was the farthest thing from the old man's mind.

"Now I understand what has been eating at you. Why didn't you come to me sooner?" He put his hand on his son's shoulder.

"I figured Shella had already told everybody. I didn't want to face your disappointment in me, again. I had disappointed you by not being at home in the first place."

"Teddy, I am only disappointed that you had to be afraid of me. I may get disappointed or even mad, but Son, I still love you. No matter what you do, your mom and I will always love you."

Teddy laughed apprehensively, "That is the same thing Shella told me."

"She is a smart girl, who has been through the wringer this past year. You would do good to listen to her."

He mused, "Maybe."

The old man prayed for the right words to convey to his son. "I am concerned, Theodore. Is God's conviction not on your soul? *His* disappointment is all that should matter."

Teddy laughed nervously, "That is funny. Shella asked me that, too. I guess it *always* comes back to that, doesn't it?"

"Yes, and what was your answer to her question?"

"I don't know, Dad. I do not feel anything, except angry. I knew drinking is wrong, but I didn't care. It was a means of forgetting everything that was going wrong."

"What was so wrong, Ted, that you had to get drunk to forget it?"

Teddy came close to saying it, but caught himself just in the knick of time. "Just things, Dad. You wouldn't understand. It is like I am so alone. It does not matter how many people are around me, I still feel so alone."

"Do you not hear God's voice?"

"I don't hear anything. I don't feel anything. I just don't care about anything. I am a void."

"*My sheep hear my voice*," his dad quoted, "If you do not hear His voice, then you are not His."

"I am scared, Dad. I do not want to go to hell, but I have done so many things. I have destroyed my relationship with you and Mom, Tyler, Christopher, and Shella. He would not want me."

"I cannot answer for the others, but your mother and I love you, Teddy. Your mom and I would move mountains to protect you and Tyler, both. How much greater is God's love, who sent His *only* begotten Son to die that *we*, being full of sin, might be free. He says to come as you are. You don't have to straighten your life up first. Simply come as you are. He came to save us *out* of our sins."

"I just don't know. What about Shella? Can she ever forgive me for trying to kill her?"

"Teddy, your relationship with Christ is just that. Your family and friends have nothing to do with your personal relationship to Him. It is strictly between you and Him. It does not matter what anybody else thinks or says."

"But Dad, I got saved when I was little. I am just supposed to announce, all of a sudden, that I got saved again? Who would believe me?"

"Why do you care what anyone thinks? You can't be saved a second time. Is it possible that you just got religion, not salvation, the first time; therefore, you are getting saved the first time, not again?"

"Could be, I suppose."

"So why do you hold on to this sinful life? Why not give it to Christ? He said, *"Come unto Me, all ye that labor and are heavy laden, and I will give you rest. Take My yoke upon you, and learn of Me; for I am meek and lowly in heart: and ye shall find rest unto your souls. For My yoke is easy, and My burden is light.* You don't have to bear this alone. If you are willing, He will carry it all for you. Don't you want all your sins and worries taken away?"

Teddy thought about his dad's words for a minute. "I do, but they are many. I have done some really bad things. There are a lot of other things you don't know about."

"But God knows about it all. Why not confess it all to Him and let Him wash you white as snow?"

"Will you help me, Dad?"

"Let's pray."

Kneeling on the floor of his beautiful new living room, Teddy Gordon fell upon the grace and mercy of almighty God for the sake of his soul's salvation. He cried out aloud for forgiveness, naming each sin individually, until he came to Shella, and then, he mumbled quietly in prayer.

⁓∽⁓

He helped his dad to his feet. "Let's go tell Mom. I bet that will fix her heart right up!"

"You are right. Let's go." As the two proceeded back to the car, one thing was still bothering the father. "You need to go see Shella Esther first, Son."

Immediately, a familiar sickness overcame him. "Dad, I am the last person Shella Evans wants to see. I am sure she hates me, and I can't say that I blame her."

"You are wrong, Son. Shella belongs to our Lord. She cannot hate you. Has she not proven that over and over again? She went into a bar to bring you home. What, in the world, would motivate a good Christian girl like her to enter into a den of iniquity like that, except love? You *have* to go to her. You haven't seen her one time, since you put her in the hospital. She has kept all your secrets. What better friend could you ask for? You owe it to her."

"Dad, I really don't want to do this."

His dad threw it straight at him. "Will you let her think she is dead to you?"

Boy, he knew how to tighten the screws! "I'll do it, but I can't imagine facing her. If Christopher is there, I will wait for a better time."

Nervousness flooded him, yet he was amazed how different this apprehension was from yesterday. He felt as if he had an Advocate with him to mediate on his behalf. It was not a sinking sick pit in his stomach like the void and hopelessness of before.

The whole ride took too little time, before he was standing in the waiting room.

"Shella girl?" Patrick tapped on her door, but she didn't respond immediately.

"Mr. Gordon!" she answered, after the nurse had her seated in the wheelchair. "It is good to see you. Are you alone?"

He hugged her neck and placed a kiss on her head. "You must be feeling better. You are out of the bed."

"Yes, they are wanting me to stand at least twice a day. I think they are going to begin therapy at the beginning of the week. I guess I get to practice what I will be preaching," she laughed half heartedly at her joke.

He pulled the chair from the other side of the bed and placed it in front of her. He sat down and took her hands in his. "You have been through a lot, little one."

"So have you and Mrs. Gordon. Is she well?"

"She sure is. She will be perfect, when her favorite daughter gets to come home. You know she wants to visit you, but I won't allow it."

"You are right. She needs her rest." He leaned over and kissed her cheek. "You need to rest, as well. You looked worn."

"You're just like your mother. Bless your heart. You are going through quite a storm, Shella Esther. You have a physical stumbling block to face now. You have lost your folks, and you feel as if you have lost a good friend in Teddy."

"I did lose my friend. The Teddy I grew up with no longer exists. I don't understand. I assume he is going through trials I know nothing about. I am sure he is full of losses as well."

"Teddy will be okay, now. I believe his storm is over."

"Oh, I am so glad to hear that." She shifted in her chair with a happy smile on her face. That was certainly good news.

The gentleman ran his rough hand through his wavy hair. "On the other hand, you still have a way to get through this one of yours."

"I don't know how well I will manage this one. It is quite painful at times."

"Just keep your eye on the Lighthouse to guide you through. The winds may crash around you and the waves may seem to suppress you, but do not pay attention to the storm. Shella Esther, as long as you focus on the Lighthouse, you will overcome. He will guide you through."

Shella smiled her graciousness. "Truly spoken, like my own Daddy. Thank you. It *is* easy to get discouraged. I admit, I have questioned God lately. It seems like everything that has happened lately are punishments for something I have done. If it had just been Mom and Dad, it would not seem anything out of the ordinary, but the storm just keeps going on. How much longer will it last?" She held her gaze away, lest he see through to her heart. "I have had some feelings that I am obviously not supposed to have, but I don't know how to stop them from remaining in my heart. I have prayed for God to deliver me from it, but He punishes me more."

"Shella Esther, it is not a punishment, when we go through the valleys. Sometimes it is a growing pain. You have to go through the storms to get to the rainbows. God is a just God. You would know if you were being punished, because God lets us know exactly why. Do you believe these feelings you have are the reason God is punishing you?"

"Not necessarily. I have harbored ill feelings in my heart because of it sometimes, but I try hard not to act upon them. If it isn't a punishment, then why does it just keep coming?" Shella's smile was sad.

"I can't answer that." Like a father to a daughter, he enveloped what little he could of her shoulders and held her in comfort. "The Lord knows what is best. It will all come about according to His will. Sometimes the mountains that we have to climb are high and the burdens seem too heavy to carry up it, but He will carry it for you, if you let Him."

"I know you are right." She used his shoulder as a pillow to cry on. "I am sorry for blubbering all over you." She laughed nervously, wiping away the tears. Patrick returned to his seat, and Shella continued, "I don't know what has gotten into me lately. I seem to bawl at everything."

"You are entitled with everything you have been through. You know you are like my own little girl, don't you? There is nothing I would not do for you."

"I know that. You have always been special to me also."

He experienced a little difficulty looking into her eyes, while he confessed, "Teddy told me what really happened the day of the accident."

Shella lowered her head and blushed, "I told you what really happened."

"Yes, you did, but you protected my son on the whole. He told me he had been drinking and driving. That is why he basically lost control of his truck. The rain only impaired his recovery skills."

She quickly responded to his defense, "He didn't mean to hit me. I know Teddy would never intentionally put me in danger, Mr. Gordon."

"And your protection of him is very precious. He does love you, more than even I had imagined, and you obviously care for him."

"I don't know about that, Mr. Gordon. I made him angry. He hasn't been to see me. He probably hates me, and for good reason."

"He is angry with himself. You made him face the wrong he was doing. Nobody wants to have their sins revealed." He leaned forward to kiss her head. "Would you like to go for a walk? I'll push."

"That would be nice." Shella smiled, "I didn't mean to do anything to hurt Teddy. I…I simply wanted to get him for his mother's sake."

"But, where did you have to go to find him?"

"I'll never do that again, that is for sure." She shuddered at the memory.

Patrick walked in a determined manner. "You should never have to do anything like that again. I don't believe you have to worry about Teddy ever drinking again."

"That would be fantastic!" Shella exclaimed, as he pushed her into a room with lots of windows, which displayed a fountain amidst a dead garden.

Teddy rose from his chair slowly. He had explained to his dad that if she had not wanted to see him, he was not going to force himself on her; therefore, he would remain here, until his dad discovered her feelings about it. The answer to his doubt came in the form of a smile across her perfect lips.

Unable to speak, Teddy humbly fell to his knees in front of her. He laid his head on her lap to hide the tears, which he could not stop. "I am so sorry. I am so sorry. I am so sorry," he repeated.

Neither noticed the dad slip quietly out, or the smile of satisfaction on his rugged old face as he left. He left the two alone to break down the wall that had come between them. He was glad his son had this girl as an anchor.

Teddy looked different to Shella. His hair was neatly cut, his clothes were ironed and appropriate, and even his countenance seemed to glow. She took her fingers lightly and brushed his temple. Her hospital gown became wet beneath his face. Shella's heart broke for him.

She lifted his face with a gentle hand. His nose was red and stuffed up, where he had been weeping. "What is it, my friend, that hurts you so?" Her tears flowed as well.

Teddy took at least a minute to clear his voice and sinuses, "How can you ask that? I have hurt you, Shella."

"I will heal, Teddy. It'll be okay."

"It is not okay that I almost killed you."

"My dear friend," she cupped his thin tanned jaws in her hands, forcing him to look at her. "What is it that I can do to make it better for you?"

His red puffy eyes pleaded, "Can you forgive me, please."

"Already taken care of," she leaned over and softly kissed the corner of his mouth and extended into an embrace. "I love you, Teddy."

"Not as much as I love you," he mumbled in her ear.

For over an hour, he lay in her touch, re-establishing a bond that had been broken, but through Christ, was now made whole. The tears had dried up, leaving only her grace in their wake. She would never know exactly how much he loved her.

"I am starving. Would you take me to lunch?" Shella broke the paradisiacal bliss. She knew she had to get back to her room in hopes that the doctor would come in for his rounds.

"I would be honored. Where would you like to eat?"

"I have a tray waiting for me, but let's go by the cafeteria and get you something, too. I do not want to eat alone."

Teddy was not in the mood to eat, but he would acquiesce her request, because he loved her with a new love in his heart. Standing to leave, Teddy noticed Shella had that glow on her face again, the look of glory she wore the night they watched the sunset together.

Once they had gone to the cafeteria and were back in the room, Shella began to twist and move to the edge of her chair in order to climb back into bed. Teddy immediately came to her rescue to assist, thinking nothing of his own hurting ribs. He was responsible for her, so he felt he deserved to hurt. He hid the wincing from her view as he reached down to lift her over to the bed.

"I am glad you are here, Teddy," she told him in almost a whisper.

He paused in mid action, looking deep into her soul through her eyes. He felt drawn to her pureness. He was so close to her lips that he could feel her soft breath. He drew close with the intention of kissing her for the second time.

"…not here this time, we will wait." Pomalee's voice intruded. She pushed the door open, "She is here!"

Teddy blushed deeply and turned his head, as he helped Shella the rest of the way into bed. He had almost kissed Shella, again, and this time, Tyler had almost caught him. He had been stupid.

"Shella! We have been looking all over for you," Tyler kissed her head, plunking down on the bed beside her.

"Teddy and I have been out walking," Shella responded. "We stopped to get something to eat."

Pomalee hugged her neck and kissed her cheek. "We came by a little while ago, but you weren't here. Tyler thought you might have gone home."

Tyler to Teddy, coolly, "I am surprised to see you here." He was still suspect of Shella's 'accident'. He felt there was more to it than Shella was telling, and he thought Teddy was more involved than either were letting on.

Although Pomalee went back to school a little late, Shella stayed home for a while, since she was bound to a wheelchair. She was unable to go back to school before Christmas break. Christopher and Teddy built a ramp on the back stairs, so that she could get out a little bit. She had no way upstairs, so she slept on the couch and bathed in the downstairs bath.

Her days were filled with boredom, even after Pomalee brought her class work to her. She hated being stuck inside all the time. Her outings to church meant more to her than ever before.

Twice, Tyler took her to a function his job presented, one of which was a New Year party. Shella was all too glad to get out of the house, so she agreed to accompany him.

It was the trips she and Teddy took out to his house, that she enjoyed most. He took her for a ride at least twice each of the three weekends she remained home, which generally ended up there.

She spent weeks in a wheelchair. Through therapy, she was able to walk with a walker, at first, and then a cane, but her doctor did not release her from the chair, until after she had gone back to school and had come home again.

Her progress was unusually fast, but then, Shella was a determined girl. She was not going to let something like a few pins keep her down long.

For a belated Christmas gift Teddy bought Shella a heart locket with a picture of her mom on one side and a picture of her dad on the other. She kissed his cheek in deep gratitude, which he savored for a long time after.

Her gift to him was a swing for his porch, but she had it delivered to his house, so his mom and dad wouldn't know about it. He accepted it under the condition that she would be the first to sit on it with him.

The late Christmas was celebrated at Shella's house, due to her inability to get in the neighbor's house. She hated not being able to help in her own home, but she was stuck in the chair. Both families made Pomalee feel like one of the family. There were gifts under the tree from everybody for her. One rule that Georgia Gordon had was that no one would ever feel like a stranger in her home.

Shella's first Christmas without her mom and dad was a little more than sad, because Christopher and Amber left the weekend before to go back to Maine.

Even though Shella smiled a lot, her heart was broken. The death of her mom, dad, and grandmother played heavily on her heart, although the entire Gordon family did all they could to take her mind off her sadness. The only consolation was that Teddy was back.

When Shella was well enough to go back to school, she became more self-reliant. Christopher was finally going to let her spread her wings and be responsible.

One way of taking matters into her own hands was that she and Pomalee drove the old family car back to college. Of course, Pomalee did most of the driving, but neither would be dependant on having to have someone else tote them somewhere.

Pomalee used the car for work travel, which was about the only time either used it at school, but the trips home were the greatest reward.

She and Pomalee made a couple of weekend trips home that last semester, in which Shella noticed that Teddy was staying close to home. He even came over with Tyler and spent some time with her and Pomalee.

A change had definitely come over him. It looked like Teddy had the real thing. The change in the old friend was part of her healing process. Teddy's salvation brought back the boy she had loved for so long. His ceasing to live for the devil anymore was all the medicine Shella needed.

He was fairing pretty well about keeping his feelings for Shella at bay. Even when his mother made Tyler call on her, or she pushed Tyler toward her, he did not let his jealousy get to him, like he did before. One asset was that, now, he had an Advocate, who could answer any need he should have to help with these feelings.

Through reading God's Word, he realized that, if he prayed God's will be done, *all* things would come together according to Christ's will. He also found that should Shella not be God's will, He would take her from his heart. God would fix things with Tyler, his mom, and his dad. It was as easy as letting Jesus take his yoke and burden completely from him, like his dad had said. He was not praying too hard about Shella, though. He wanted it to be God's will that she love him.

His heart quickened, at the sound of her voice on the other end of the phone, when she called. Coming to the realization either she called home or his mom called her *every* Friday, he began making sure he was home and available, just so he could talk to her briefly and hear her laugh. However he may feel about Shella, she showed no similar feelings in return. She remained the same old faithful friend of years gone by before the kiss, but he chose to secretly love her anyway.

When she came home, Teddy tried to be doting to her, because when all was said and done, he *was* responsible for her condition. He would accept her gracious smiles and bottle them tight as the Bible said God bottles our tears. He would occasionally release one to warm his soul, when she had been gone so long.

These trips home did little with Shella as far as Tyler was concerned, though. He had boldly made his claim on her, which Shella resented and flatly reported was *not* going to happen, so Tyler was left to resolve it by himself. It was challenging that someone would dare resist his charm, especially the little girl next door that had always been in love with him. His pride was crushed, and he would be a monkey's uncle, before Shella Evans rejected him. He was glad that his brother was back to normal.

At school, Shella and Pomalee stayed at the sorority house, although Pomalee had finished her school. She would have to wait till June for the graduation ceremony, so Shella asked her to remain with her, even if it meant they would have to rent an apartment separate from the campus.

Pomalee pushed her in therapy, too, in between the two jobs she held. She was so grateful to Shella for giving her a home, since her parents were on the mission field. In return, she worked with Shella's walking every day. She was determined to get her better faster. Pomalee was an only child, so she enjoyed having Shella as a sister and the boys as brothers.

Lawrence realized he was out of the picture with Shella and began a relationship with someone else. Shella was much relieved, when she saw him with a really nice freshman girl, however awkward Lawrence felt around her. That was one less inconvenience she would have to deal with. It was as if God were leading her out of the storm. It was time for her to get some relief.

⁑

In mid February, Shella's presence was requested at home. Tyler insinuated that his mother really needed her there, or she would not even have contemplated going. Even though, it was an extra long weekend break, there were about eighteen people staying on campus due to a music recital on Friday. She had not planned on going home that weekend, because Pomalee had to work, but per Tyler's insistence, Pomalee requested time off and they agreed to go.

The snow started peppering down on Thursday and then stopped. Friday was gray and gloomy, but the snow did not start back until the early morning hours of Saturday. The roads were rarely impassable in this snow prone area, because the snow plows were good about getting them cleared.

"Tyler, we are getting ready to leave," she was telling him over the phone prior to leaving.

"Okay." He was more interested in the score of the ballgame on the television, so he did not pay much attention to Shella.

She continued, "We should get there a little after three. Tell your mom not to cook. I'll do it, when we get there."

"Sure." He replaced the receiver without taking his eyes from the TV.

Shella hung up the phone, turning to Pomalee, "This is so much fun!"

Pomalee giggled, grabbing Shella's arm. "I know. I am so excited. I love the snow!"

"Oh! I have to run these by the library, real quick. I almost forgot." She held up some books.

"C'mon, we will run them over now," Pomalee suggested.

The two left the house laughing and chattering nonstop. Shella trudged through the snow with some difficulty. Pomalee was kicking it up gleefully. She would help Shella down, so they could make snow angels, and then help her back to her feet. They were like two girls at a party.

On the return trip, they were sidetracked, when they took time to stop and build a snowman. It took quite some time, since there was only a couple inches of snow. There was a lot of dirt mixed in with the big circles of snow, and the end result was a pathetic excuse for a snowman. They didn't care. They were having a blast.

"He will be covered up by the time we get back," shouted Pomalee with a red nose.

"It does seem to be coming down heavier now." Shella checked her watch, "Oh my goodness! It is two o'clock. Mrs. Gordon is expecting us within the next hour and a half. We better get on the ball."

"You are right. We better call before we leave to let them know we will be later."

However, when they called, there was no answer. It was still thirty minutes before they were ready to go, because they put the chains on the tires before leaving. Shella was moving a lot slower now, because the cold weather was really causing her some pain.

"Are we ready?" Pomalee asked, popping the gearshift into drive.

"Thank you, again, for driving, Pomalee. Every once in a while, I get this pain in my hips, and I do not want it to affect my driving.

"No problem. We really should have left earlier. The snow seems to be coming down so fast now."

"Wait a minute, Pomalee, we need to pray, before we go any further."

"How could we forget that?"

They stopped the car long enough to pray, and then they proceeded, slipping occasionally on the snow. Pomalee recovered well each time. She had not driven much in the snow before, but she was a cautious driver. She even suggested once that maybe they should not go, but Shella had given her word, because Mrs. Gordon needed her.

৵৶

Going up Toxaway Mountain was a little slippery, but they made it up without incident. However, coming back down was difficult. The whiteout made visibility impossible. A mountain guarded the edge of the road on the driver's side, but on the passenger's side, a deep ravine fell from the mountain on top. It grew less deep as the grade descended, and because the guardrails were covered in white, the parameters of the road were not observable.

Twice, the car slid into the guardrail, scraping the side of the vehicle with sparks flying from the friction. Pomalee recovered the best that anybody could under the circumstances. They both questioned going on, but they could not very well turn back now. They would have to retrace that awful mountain they just passed over. When they reached the town at the foot of the mountain, they would call and let the Gordons know they were not going to make it.

The third incident occurred about three quarters of the way down the decline. There were several feet of gap between two guardrails on one side. After the car skid about a hundred feet against the rail, it plunged through the gap and down the hill, until it plowed into a tree. The motor automatically cut out, leaving a somber silence, save the howling of the wind and steam escaping the engine. Neither stirred for several minutes.

Shella regained consciousness first. "Pomalee!" she cried, "Pomalee! Are you okay?"

The scene before her was brutal. The car had folded like an accordion in the front. As she looked over at Pomalee, the steering wheel seemed to have her pinned. There was blood on her forehead.

Shella's door would not open, so she was forced to crawl through the broken windshield. She paid no heed to her own painful hips in anticipation for the well being of her friend. Pomalee was moaning by the time Shella reached the driver's side, yet she was not fully concious.

Pomalee's door had flown open upon impact, but the opening to pull her through was very small. From this angle and close view, it looked worse than Shella had originally thought. After the initial investigation, she realized she could not get Pomalee out so easily.

"I am getting you out, Pomalee, as quickly as I can. Hold on. I love you. Can you hear me?"

"My legs hurt, Shella. I cannot feel my left foot."

Shella tried her best, but could not budge the wheel. The emergency brake was crushing her ankle. She was pinned beyond Shella's ability to help. She had to go for help. It was not much further to Cashiers.

Shella ran to the trunk, opened it, and brought all the clothes and picnic blanket up to the front. The whole while, she was sending up tearful pleas to her Father. She quickly wrapped all the clothes around Pomalee snugly, before putting the blanket around her. She was not able to do much with the legs, but did the best she could.

"I am going for help, Pomalee. You hold on. These clothes should keep you warm enough while I am gone. I promise, I will come back. You stay put. Do not try to get out." Shella kissed her cheek softly. "I love you. Bye."

Pomalee waited till Shella was gone from her hearing, before she let the tears go. She did not want to tell Shella how very badly she was hurting. She knew Shella was doing the right thing, but she did not want to be left alone. She was scared.

Shella pulled her coat collar up around her ears and trudged against the wind, which bit her hard through her toboggan. She had thrown her pink elephant pajama bottoms on, in order to have some protection on her legs. Her panty hose did nothing for the cold.

She knew the town of Cashiers was right down the road a mile or so, so she made sure she was going downhill. She had lost the road, because now she was in an area scarcely populated with trees. It seemed the more she tried to get back to the road, the further into the woods she went, but she was still going downhill, and that was all that mattered. Occasionally, she would break a tip off a reachable limb, to mark where she had been. This would make it easier to find her way back.

Although it seemed like hours, Shella hit level ground about an hour later. In town, she passed a diner and a little plaza with only two stores still in business. It had a pay phone, but it was not operating, so she was forced to go further into town. It was not too much longer, before she found a deserted service station that had a pay phone, which Shella used to call help for Pomalee.

She felt a rush of relief that help was on its way to her friend. Suddenly, she felt light headed from the rush but shook it off and proceeded to retrace her steps. This process was not easy, because the wind and continual falling snow had already mostly covered her tracks. Her hips were excruciatingly tormenting her, but she could not let that stop her. She had promised Pomalee she would come back.

"Oh God, help me I pray," she cried out against the wind.

The snow seemed lighter. It was not falling as fast, yet she could yell as loud as she wanted, and no one would hear her in this storm.

The wind still whistled through the tree limbs. Was that God's whisper of comfort to her? He takes care of the flowers of the field, yet they toil not, so how much more did He love her? Would He not also take care of her?

As she began to climb upgrade, finding the broken branches that marked her way and her steps grew increasing difficult. Her feet were numb from the cold. It was all she could do to lift one and then the other.

She did not realize that her body was ravaged with fever. Her eyes burned, while the sounds of the vicious winds tormented her mockingly, calling out her name. She stumbled several times catching her body with a numb hand.

"It is time to go Home," she thought. "I cannot make it. I will die a liar. I didn't get back to Pomalee."

With that, she fell to her knees, having given up completely, as a black veil fell upon her. She was enveloped in a cold darkness, waiting to see the Light coming for her.

⧜

Georgia and Patrick Gordon had gone on an excursion for a couple of weeks, leaving Teddy and Tyler to fend for themselves. Of course, their version of fending for themselves was fast food or foregoing meals all together. They were two bachelors and very bad at it. The house would remain upside down, until the day before their parents were due home.

Tyler set in motion a plan to help his mother. He was going to bite the bullet and ask Shella to marry him, thinking that this news would help his mother more than anything, so when he asked her to come down for her break, he was ecstatic when she agreed. Yes, he may have stretched the truth a little, but it was for his mom's benefit, not his.

He took her call in stride, proud that she was on her way to *him*, so he returned to his spot on the couch with a plop and threw the pillow at Teddy, who was engrossed in the game as well. Teddy was barely aware that the phone had rung at all.

"What did you do that for?" He threw it back at Tyler's head, the second a commercial came on.

"You are too involved with that stupid game."

Teddy scoffed, "Like you were not before the phone rang?"

Tyler rose from the couch and pounced on Teddy in playful wrestling. "That is different," he grunted in between punches. "You have to know when to quit being so serious and stop being a jug head."

"Oh shut up." He returned the punches. "Was that mom?"

"It…" punch, "was…" punch, "Shella." He got him in a particular hold, "Give? Do you give?"

"No way!" Teddy wrangled around, until he had the upper hand. "What did she want? That was a quick call. Do you give?" He would not let the disappointment show that he had not been the one to hear her voice.

"No!" Another attack of punches ensued, before he answered. "She just called to tell me that they are on their way."

"On their way where?"

"Here." He gained the upper hand, because Teddy stopped all

wrestling and sobered.

"Boy, when is the last time you looked out the windows?" He motioned with his hand toward the window.

"I don't know, why?"

"Cause there is a quarter inch of snow on the ground, here. Shella is in higher elevations, so she probably has more, and you are going to let her drive in that mess?"

Tyler looked guiltily out the window. "I didn't know. I'll call her back and tell her not come." Yet, when he called, there was no answer. "They are gone already."

Tyler watched curiously, while his big brother rose and left the room, only to return a few minutes later, donning his coat. Teddy grabbed his truck keys and made for the door.

"Where are you going?" Tyler queried.

"I am going after them. God willing, I will find them safe. If you were a decent friend, you would go with me to drive their car, so I can drive mine back."

"Hold on. I am coming, but we are taking my truck. It is four wheel drive, and your truck is a piece of junk, now that you have crashed it." He punched the off button on the TV, grabbed his coat, and followed his brother.

∽∾

Once they were in the truck, waiting for it to warm up, both removed their toboggans. Teddy fumbled, "So, why is Shella coming down? She was not supposed to return until classes were over at graduation."

"She wasn't planning on coming, but I asked her to come. I told her Mom really needed her to come home." Teddy gave him a side-glance of disbelief, as he steered down the powdered streets. "Mom? Mom's not even here. Why did you tell her that?"

"I wanted her to come home, so I could ask her to marry me. Imagine what that would do for Mom, when she comes back home. See, I did not really lie. Mom does need her to come home and marry me."

Teddy was flabbergasted. He had never expected anything like this so fast! Would Shella say 'yes'? Could she actually feel about Tyler like that? He had known the moment would come, but he never thought it would be so soon. He never realized until this very moment, how devastating this would be to him. *He* loved her, not Tyler.

Teddy became quiet for most of the ride. He developed a strong sinking feeling inside that something was horribly wrong. Shella was lost to him forever. Since he had been saved a couple months earlier, God had given him help on his jealousy and destructive rage; however, this would be harder to deal with. Why had God not taken his love for her away? He would have to face every day for the rest of his life alone, watching the only woman he would ever love, happily married to his kid brother. Since God had taken the desire to drink from him, how would he deal with this?

As each mile passed, his heart sank deeper and deeper. Oh how horrid this all was. He fretted so over this news that he almost forgot his quest. It is a good thing Tyler was with him to keep an eye out for Shella's car, because he had failed that mission. He looked sternly ahead, pushing his brother's machine to the limit in the blinding wind and snow.

The four-wheel drive spun and slid quite a bit, as they started to climb Pisgah Mountain. They stopped and put on the chains, which helped the driving tremendously, but they about froze while putting them on. Anybody out in this was bound to freeze to death.

Coming down the backside of Pisgah lay the small older town of Cashiers, which separated Pisgah and Toxaway Mountains. Many tourists loved this quaint dip in the road, because of the magnificent scenery and four waterfalls, which cascaded freely upon the beautiful hillsides around them.

Today though, the place looked anything but beautiful to Teddy. Generally, for him, the snow was white and fluffy, kind of purifying the world, but today, it brought forth doom and despair. They had not passed Shella and Pomalee, which meant they either went back to the college or they were still trying to get down Toxaway.

"God, please let Shella be safe," he prayed silently. He vocalized to Tyler, as he came to the stop light at the junction in Cashiers. They could either go straight, or turn right which would take them to the town. "We can find a phone and call the dorm to see if they are back."

Tyler had been nervously biting his nails. "Yeah, let's pray they did go back." Almost simultaneous with the words in his heart, a snowmobile ambulance passed them at the base of Toxaway, turning into the town of Cashiers. Tyler looked dreadfully at Teddy. "Do you think that was Shella?"

Teddy was already turning the vehicle to follow, "Considering we have not met many other motorists foolish enough to drive in this mess, and it is long enough since the girls left that we should have passed them, I would say it is a good possibility, if not a probability."

"It has been blowing snow pretty hard. Do you think we could have missed them?"

Teddy shook his head grimly. "No." He pondered over the sinking feeling that had grown so intense. He was positive Shella was not safe. Oh, why did Tyler have to be so stupid to make Shella drive in this snow? He was thoughtless and selfish!

It took Teddy driving way too fast for the road conditions to almost catch up with the ambulance, but he did, as it pulled into the local hospital. He left the truck's motor running, as both men jumped from it and ran to the snowmobile.

"Pomalee!" Tyler exclaimed upon seeing her emerge from the back of the vehicle on a stretcher.

"Tyler! Teddy!" she weakly replied from the stretcher. She was pale and bloody. "What are you doing here? Is Shella with you?"

"She isn't with you?" Tyler ran to follow the men that came from within the hospital, as they pushed her through the double doors.

Teddy caught part of another conversation, and found out more information by listening to it. "…call came from the phone down at Harrison's garage. We will go back and start searching for her from there." The two men from the snowmobile were conversing between themselves.

Teddy interrupted, "Are you looking for Shella?"

"Is she the one that called in the accident?" inquired one of the men.

"I do not know. There should have been a girl with the one you just brought in."

The paramedic looked at his watch. "Don't know, but we've got a girl out in this blizzard, and we need to find her, so if you will excuse us."

"I am coming too," Teddy informed.

"Better leave it to those who know these mountains, Son."

Teddy seated himself in the emergency vehicle in spite of the warning. "Shella is out there, and I am going to find her."

The two men did not have time to argue. They had a life to save and time was of the essence. The passenger eyed Teddy curiously for about a minute. Teddy could feel his probing eyes on him, but he refused to look in the direction of the man.

Finally, the driver spoke, "Harold, give the boy an extra blanket. If he is going with us to look for that girl, he will freeze to death wearing that, then we will have two victims." He turned briefly to Teddy. "You said this girl's name is Shell?"

"Shella," he corrected.

"Well, we don't want to lose you trying to find Shella. You stick with Harold. He's got a walkie talkie if you find anything."

"Here, kid." The passenger handed him a whistle. "Even though you are with me, you blow this, if you see anything. I will be able to hear it over the wind."

Teddy took the whistle and put it around his neck, as they came to a stop and a telephone booth at an old service station. The three men immediately hopped out and began a search for the missing girl. Upon scrutiny, no tracks were found. Only shallow hollows every once in a great while could be spotted. It looked as if they followed the road for a while.

They followed the hollows where they thought Shella had started back through the woods, with the assurance they were on the right track, when Teddy spied a broken branch only slightly covered on top of the snow. He had taught her to do that when they were little and went hunting.

"She broke the branches off to find her way back!" he explained, but in the blinding snow and the falling darkness, it was hard to see anything.

Periodically, Harold or the driver would place a flare, in case any got lost, they could see the flares and follow their path, while Teddy kept looking for broken limbs, until the pattern became contradictory. Broken branches went in two different directions. By this time, the driver had gone in another direction, and Harold was left alone with Teddy.

"Maybe she was going in a circle," Harold yelled over the wind. "You go that way, I will go this way. Go fifteen minutes and come back. We will meet back here in thirty minutes, Boy. Blow your whistle if you get in trouble."

Teddy nodded and began in his direction. He grew worried, when he saw a crimson stain on the pure white snow about ten minutes later. His feet automatically began moving quicker, when he realized he must have been going in the right direction. Further along, he found another spot, but he had long forgotten about his whistle. He was just praying for Shella to be all right.

He illuminated his light as far as it would possibly shine in every direction. "Please let me find her in time, Lord." He cried out above the howls. The snow was not falling quite as hard, even though it seemed as if the wind was relentless.

Several times he thought he had caught a glimpse of someone, but it turned out to be a tree. It had been a while, since he had seen a spot of red on the snow, so that he was beginning to believe he had wandered away from her trail again.

Suddenly, his light caught a glimpse of red, but instead of it being stable, on the ground, it was blowing in the wind. He quickened his clumsy step in the deep snow and scramble quickly toward the red. It was a red scarf on the tree limb. It had to be Shella's.

Further, he ran, carrying the knitted yarn with him. Now, he could see more visible indentions in the snow. There was a big hole, where she must have fallen, and there was a larger hole. He was on the right track, as he started stepping into Shella's footprints. She was alive. He could feel it.

Without much further ado, he spied a moving object ahead. He shone his light; yes, it had to be Shella. He hurried as fast as he could.

"Shella!" He yelled to her, but her feet kept stumbling forward, as she did not respond. "Shella! Wait up!" he yelled again.

Still, she made no acknowledgement of having heard him; however, her body was halted in a semi stiff erected stance. He called her name again, but she did not move, until Teddy reached her, and then she began to tilt forward, as it she were a tree hewn at the base. Teddy reached out his arm and barely caught her, as she fell.

"Shella!" he cried again, gently caressing her face.

Her pale white cheeks hosted her closed eyelashes. When she did not respond, he briskly began rubbing her cheeks more vigorously to circulate the blood. As he removed her toboggan, he realized that she had been bleeding. A bit of time must have passed, because it was dried. The fresh bleeding of her hands showed where the soft wet snow had a harsh razor sharp edge to it as she caught herself falling in exhaustion. She looked dead.

"Wake up my love," he pled, as he patted her cheek. "You cannot sleep yet."

He placed his lips on her closed eyelids, her cheek, and then her lips, but each time they touched her skin, it was frigidly cold, deathly cold. Next, he ripped open his coat and pulled her arms underneath his armpits and her face to his chest to get her warm. Pulling the extra blanket from his own shoulders, he placed it around Shella carefully, making sure he did not lose her hands from under his arms. He needed to get her warm.

Briefly, her lashes fluttered open, but quickly fell softly back on her cheeks. She had not recognized him in the glaze of her blank stare. Teddy placed his face against her head to keep the snow from falling on her fragile skin again. Tears came to the man, who thought he would never see another day where he would cry over anything, since the day he found salvation. He would do anything for this to be him instead of Shella. He would make any deal with God, if it would make a difference for her life.

"Wake up, Shella. Please wake up. I love you. Don't you know that, little girl?" He rocked her in his bosom paying no heed to any discomfort he was in. "Do you hear me? I love you. I love the way you laugh, and the way your eyes twinkle, when you get excited. I love the way you smell like flowers when you get close to me. I love your smile, and the way your wrinkle your nose, whenever you dislike something, especially spinach. I love the glory you wear on your beautiful face at any given moment. I love everything about you. Shella, you have to wake up. Please, wake up." His tears fell on her cheek.

He realized she would freeze to death, if he did not get her warm. These temporary measures would not benefit much, if he did not get her out of the cold. He left the torn wet bloody mittens, toboggan, and the red scarf lying on the ground and lifted her body easily in his arms. It was then, that he remembered the whistle, and propping her on his knee, he maneuvered the cold piece of the silver into his mouth and blew shrilly several times consecutively for Harold to hear.

Using his good sense of direction, he began to retrace his steps, to the best of his ability, with an occasional blow on the whistle. He wandered for some time, before he spotted one of the flares that had been placed to mark the way. He waited at the flare for only a couple of minutes, blowing the whistle, until the driver of the snowmobile came toward them.

"You found her?" He yelled over the wind. "I'll radio Harold to come on in." He roared into the walkie-talkie and then turned back to Teddy. "I will relieve you. I'll get her." He reached out his arms.

"Thanks, but I have her. She's not heavy." Again, he tucked his head close to her face and followed the driver.

The driver proved to know the terrain very well. He had no problems following the path of the flares back to safety. To Teddy, it seemed a long while back to the snowmobile, because the going was rough in the high snow. Nonetheless, Teddy trudged on with his precious load cautiously.

The cool temperatures in the cab of the snowmobile felt like Heaven as they waited for Harold to come back. At least it kept the cruel biting wind off of them, even if it were only a few degrees warmer than outside. The driver watched Teddy's loving touch from the front seat.

Teddy pulled off Shella's wet coat. There was a look of death about her. Her skin was so pale and cold. He put his cheek to hers to feel if she were still breathing. Indeed, he could feel soft faint breaths in his ear, so once again he began rubbing her limbs.

"Wake up, sweet love," he whispered to only her.

The paramedic did not need to give much instruction. Teddy appeared to be knowledgeable, and Pete did not want to intrude on what appeared to be a sacred time. There was not much more they could do, until they reached the hospital. He did hand the boy two more blankets to cover her with. Five minutes later, Harold was back, and they were on their way. Teddy kept her close to him for warmth.

ço—ıç

Before long, they were pulling up to the docks where Teddy
followed them up to the hospital the first time. Tyler's truck was still
parked illegally and running full blast, where they had left it, but Teddy
did not notice the vehicle. The same two paramedics that came from
within the hospital to get Pomalee came through the huge steel double
doors again, but this time Teddy followed them, as they took Shella in.

They already had a gurney waiting, because Pete had called them on
the two-way radio as they approached the hospital. Shella's eyes were
opened, but were more glazed and despondent, than the last time she
opened them for him. Her face was blushed brightly, and her lips were
blood red from the fever that had set in. Her skin was hot to the touch.

Teddy was stopped after the second set of doors and directed to a
nurse to show him to the waiting room. He reluctantly watched as they
took Shella in the opposite direction. He wanted to follow her to the
ends of the earth to ensure her safety.

"God, keep her safe," he mumbled half audibly.

Instead of listening to the nurse's reassurance that everything was going to be all right, Teddy sought his reassurance, in silent prayer, from the One who could give complete peace. He followed the nurse, not listening to her chatter, until she showed him into the waiting room, where he found his brother.

"Tyler!" he called out as he came across the floor. "How is Pomalee?" He did not want Tyler to think he had gone out of his way to find Shella, lest it give away his love for her.

"I don't know. They'll not tell me anything, because I am not family," he mocked a woman's voice, giving a funny face.

"I sure wish we could find out something," Teddy complained.

"What is going on with Shella? They didn't bring her in with Pomalee. I thought she was in the ambulance, too, but they did not bring her out, and when I turned around you were gone. I didn't know where you went."

"She left the accident to call for help and was trying to get back. They were able to follow her tracks to find her out in the snow. That is why she wasn't with Pomalee. She is in emergency now. She didn't look good, Tyler."

Tyler shook his head, "Pomalee was beaten up pretty bad, too. I think she will be all right, but I am not sure. Is Shella hurt as bad as Pomalee?"

"She was out in this storm quite a while. It appeared to me that she might have hypothermia. I don't know how long she was out in the cold, but she was deathly cold. She will probably get pneumonia from it."

Tyler mused, "Do you think she will be okay?"

"I hope so. We need to call Christopher, but I would rather wait until we know something to tell him. Do you know what happened? Did you get a chance to talk to Pomalee at all? I heard someone say something about an accident." Teddy inquired.

"No, they took her on back. They wouldn't let me talk to her. You know more than I know about it. All I have are speculations. Nobody here will tell me anything, because I am not family." He slumped in the chair in aggravation.

Teddy was exhausted. He was not aware how strenuous his

escapade in the snow had been on him. Neither of the men had eaten since mid morning, but Teddy didn't care about his own health. Shella looked like death. He was afraid they may have found her too late. He plunked down in a chair thrusting his fingers through his hair in frustration.

"God, please do not let anything happen to her. Please, let us have found her in time," he repeatedly begged inaudibly.

Tyler sat beside him, patting his hand on his brother's shoulder. "Pomalee is going to be okay, Teddy. There was a lot of blood, but her color was good. I really think she will be fine. Quit worrying about it."

Teddy vaguely heard his brother's words. Pomalee was not the one that occupied his mind, and heart. Then, the guilt of his betrayal flooded over him. He knew she hadn't heard, but he had told Shella he loved her. He had told the girl Tyler was getting ready to propose marriage to that *he* loved her.

He couldn't look at Tyler. Heretofore, his feelings were private. No one knew about them, save he and God. He had dared to voice his feelings to another, no matter if she didn't hear him. He no longer was in command of those feelings. Instead of him controlling his feelings, they controlled him.

He must regain his composure about Shella. What would his dear mother think? What would Tyler think about his confession to Shella? Why, oh why did she and Dad give their blessing to Tyler? He had to stop thinking about Shella in that manner.

The hours passed with scarce converse between the two, as neither was aware of the lateness of the hour. They wandered in and out of sleep and restless daze. This long day must finally come to an end at some point. As Tyler sat stretched out uncomfortably in a straight back chair, his head laid back, and eyes half closed, he thought he was dreaming, when Pomalee was being pushed toward him, but it was no dream.

He looked at his watch to find out that it was after six. He looked out the window, and sure enough, the sky was dawning the first signs of light. He nudged Teddy, as if he needed waking, but he was already alert.

Pomalee was gray and was not wearing her noted smile. She was wearing a blue and white hospital gown and was covered in blankets. She gave them a faded smile, a shadow of her normal glee, "I made them let me come out and tell you what is going on." The blanket across her lap veiled any visible injuries to her legs, but her face and neck, the only parts showing, were bruised and scratched. She fingered the blanket sadly, looking down.

Tyler responded first, "Thanks. I have been worried sick. They would not tell us a thing about what was going on. What did they say?"

"They are going to do surgery on my leg in a bit, but you guys are not to worry," Pomalee explained, "because everything is going to be fine."

Her breaking voice knifed Tyler's heart. Something was wrong, really wrong. He had never seen Pomalee, when she was not upbeat and always smiling and confident. "Surgery? What are they going to do to your leg?"

"It all depends on what they find, when they get in there. I had a fight with the emergency brake, and it looks like it won."

Teddy took her hand and patted it tenderly. "What are you not telling us, Pomalee? What else did the doctor say?"

"Whatever do you mean, Teddy?"

"If Shella comes out, and we can't tell her everything, she is going to be mad at us."

"Shella has not come out yet?" she queried. Tyler nodded negatively. Pomalee's eyes filled with tears. "The doctor told me they brought her into the emergency room a while ago, but he would not say if something was seriously wrong with her."

"She is better off than you are, right now, Pomalee," Teddy tried to convince them both. "She may have some frost bite to deal with, but my Father said she will be fine."

Having heard those words, Tyler witnessed behavior from his brother, which caused him to gape in disbelief. Teddy, with Pomalee's hand still in his, took charge and prayed for her surgery with Pomalee and Tyler. It grew a new respect from the younger brother. This was the hero he had grown up always looking up to and wanting to be like. This was the brother he was proud of. He did not know what was going on with him with the drinking and staying out all night before, but he was glad the real Teddy was back.

Pomalee, too, prayed silently for her own reasons. She couldn't tell these friends of Shella's about the personal crisis she was confronting. She must leave this dilemma at the feet of her Savior and bear it alone with Him. She could not tell these wonderful boys what she had overheard. That doctor said it! He did not know she heard, but she heard him say it.

"If it looks as bad in there as I think it is going to look, we might have to take the leg…" he had continued explaining to whomever he was speaking, what damages he diagnosed upon examination. He rattled on with medical jargon that Pomalee did not know, but those words seared her mind.

"We will be waiting out here for you, when it is over." Tyler smiled with reassurance.

"Would you please tell them to let us know what is going on?" Teddy asked in irritation. "They will not tell us anything about either of you."

Pomalee looked at the nurse behind her chair, who, in turn spoke something to the lady behind the desk, but none of the three could hear the words. Then, she turned to Pomalee, "Where is your family, Miss Sorrel?"

"My dad is a missionary in the Philippines. That is where my parents are. That is the only family I have, except these guys and Shella. Please, I would consider it a huge favor, if you would just let them in on what is going on behind the scenes."

"Fine, we will keep in touch." With that, the nurse turned Pomalee away to leave and briefly spoke to the woman behind the desk.

When they had taken her away from Teddy and Tyler, prepped her for surgery, and strapped her on a table, she finally let the tears go, as she fell into darkness.

৸৵

When the two boys had not heard anything about Shella, and the hour was late that following day, Tyler ventured to the front desk to inquire. The red haired lady crisply responded to his question that he was not family. It was not the same woman that was there early that morning, so they were back to square one, but Tyler pressed harder.

"I am her fiancé. Can you give me no information?"

"You will have to hold on. We do not give information to non-family members. I will have to get permission."

With that having been said, she disappeared behind the swinging door. There was a deliberate rudeness in her step. Teddy, realizing what Tyler was doing, stood to join him for her return.

The third shift nurse had been more compliant, since Pomalee had come out and gave permission and requested they keep Teddy and Tyler abreast of her condition, but finding out information about Shella was near impossible. At least this nurse might actually tell them something. Anything was better than this silence.

Upon the nurse's return, "Miss Evans has been admitted. She is in room two fourteen. I am sorry, but that is all I am permitted to disclose."

"Two fourteen?" confirmed Tyler. Over his shoulder, he added, "Thanks."

They found the first elevator available and allowed it to pull them to the second floor. Actually, it was the *only* elevator in the entire hospital, save one used for employees and service. Neither boy spoke as they took long quick strides down the path. Teddy was too worried about what he would find, and Tyler was tired, sleepy, and grumpy.

The sign that came into view as soon as the doors opened told them to go to the right, so they proceeded in that direction, until they heard, "Tyler! Teddy! Guys, wait up."

This time, they followed the voice. Tyler busted excitedly, "Pomalee! How long have you been in a room?"

"Not long."

Pomalee was very pale and her eyes were weak, but the joy in her heart disguised how she was physically feeling. None of that mattered, because God had saved her leg. She still had both legs! How could she be down?

"We just found out that Shella is in a room, too," Tyler continued.

Teddy was glad Pomalee was all right, but he basically wanted to go and see Shella; however, he was afraid of how that would look. It would put too much focus on his behavior, if he pressed it. Tyler should be the one going to her. That thought crushed his heart.

"Have you not seen her, yet? At all?" Pomalee grew concerned.

"That is where we were just now going," Teddy hoped she would release their attentions.

"You should go on then," she confirmed.

"Teddy, why don't you stay here with Pomalee?" Tyler suggested. "We do not want Shella's guest to be alone."

"I am fine really," she protested. "You both go see Shella." Pomalee knew how Teddy felt, no matter how hard he tried to hide it. She knew from the very first time she met him that Shella was the one he loved.

Yet, Teddy could not go. Whether it was because of the guilt he held in his heart or just the fear that his love for Shella would manifest around her, he did not know. All he knew was that he was taking Tyler up on the invitation to stay here.

"I will stay with you, Pomalee, really, I want to. Tyler is right. We cannot leave you by yourself."

Tyler ended his part of the visit with that and left the two alone.

Further down the hall, he turned another right, followed another corridor and the signs directing him to room two fourteen. Upon finding the door, Tyler tapped lightly, and then proceeded into the room.

§∂∂§

"Shella," he called softly, but she was asleep.

He quietly approached her side, touched the sheen of her dark hair, and kissed her temple. She was pale, almost ashen, as if death had taken her. Dark encircled her eyes, all else was colorless, save her lips, which were dark red and chapped. She reminded him of the character of Snow White in the fairy tale.

Quietly, he sat in the chair beside her bed, with intermittences of prayer on Shella's behalf. This had to be the closest to dying she had ever come. He must have been there a couple hours, dozing and praying, before Shella finally opened her eyes.

"Hey, Sleepyhead." He jumped to her side. "It is about time you woke up."

"Teddy?" she mumbled with blurred vision.

"Teddy's with Pomalee, Shella. He is making sure she is being taken care of in your absence."

She tried to push up. "Pomalee? Did they get her? Is she here? Is she okay?"

"Hey, hey, hey! Slow down. Yes, they found and rescued Pomalee. Yes, she is here, and yes, she is going to be okay. She underwent a little bit of surgery, but all is well, now. We have been worried about you."

"It is so cold in here." She pulled her blanket up over her nose. "I am freezing."

"Yes, it is, but I think they have to keep you cool for a while. You like to have frozen to death out there. You should not have left on your own like that."

"If I had not, Pomalee would still be in that car, until the snow thawed, and someone chanced upon her."

"Teddy and I would have found you. Why do you think we are here?" When she did not answer, he continued, "We were concerned that you would not make it in this snow, and we came to look for you."

Shella half listened to his chiding. She was so cold and her feet hurt with sharp needle-like pains shooting through them. She wanted her Mommy. She wanted to hear her precious gentle voice telling her all would be fine. She wanted her mom to kiss her head and give her something to make the pain go away, sing to her like she used to and tell her the story about when she was a little girl and had polio. Her mother had a miraculous healing and the story always made Shella feel better.

"God," she asked in her silence, as tears rolled down her face, which she had turned away from Tyler. "Why did You need Mom and Dad more than me? I miss them so much."

Tyler became nervous. This was one of the few times in his life, where he felt awkward around Shella. As a matter of fact, as he sat recollecting, besides the times she sent him those goofy love notes, and the time her folks died, this was the only time he remembered not knowing what to say. He definitely did not want a repeat of her parents' visitation. In that void of words, he had acted like a goofy little boy

His memory of her love notes made him realize that she loved him once, couldn't she love him again? Maybe she *did* love him, but her sweet lady character would not let her display any affections toward him. Her mom and dad raised her that way, and it was a nice quality.

Maybe, he should just be there for her comfort and let come what may. Her love for him would soon be revealed. It would be enough to begin a marriage, and he would learn to love her like his dad had said. He felt confident he had made the right choice in deciding to propose.

Tyler retreated to the chair, while leaving one hand on Shella's back, which heaved softly beneath the blanket. He could hear an occasional sniff, where she was crying silently. Once again, he stood up, but this time he walked around the bed to face Shella.

"Come here, Shella," he reached for her, as he gently sat beside her on the bed.

She arose, accepting his embrace. Tyler could not understand that he was like a brother to her, and Christopher was not here. At this moment, this was the comfort God had sent her, and she needed a lot of comfort.

"I wish Mom and Dad were here," she confessed.

"I love you, little girl," he was whispering in her hair. "You are not alone."

Through a stopped up nose, she replied, "Thank you for being here."

After a time of comfort, when he knew she was no longer crying, Tyler pushed her back a little to see her face. "Now, tell me what the doctor said about you?"

"Oh," she wiped any remnants of water from her face. "I will be fine. It is just a little frostbite."

Tyler searched her brown eyes to see if his soothing was effective. "My little fawn. You look just like Bambi, when he was caught. You look so scared."

Shella withdrew from the hand that held her face. She didn't like the feeling he was emitting. "Have you called Christopher?"

"You know, I have not. I am sorry. I will call him as soon as I leave here." His tone responded accordingly to the sudden change in the atmosphere.

"Don't!" Shella didn't mean to sound so sharp. "Please do not tell Christopher. He will just think he has to move back home to take care of me again."

Then Tyler spoke the words that would upset Shella, "But you do need someone to take care of you. Why do you think I am here,

Shella?"

Shella was so stunned. She did not even know what to say. She had not the energy to argue with him. "Just please promise me you will not call Christopher."

Receiving the blunt coldness he complied, "Okay, I promise."

He rose from the bed, feeling the unspoken request to leave. He wandered to the door, and in turning, he saw Shella had deliberately turned her back to him, so he soundlessly slipped out of the room to venture back down to Pomalee's room.

Shella lay in the deafening silence of his departure in the depths of loneliness with tears coming once more. She knew she missed her parents, and maybe even Christopher, but this was not in her character to be so blubbery, so she fought it the best she could. Tyler had no business saying that!

As she tried to contemplate the reasons for her moodiness, a face, words spoken, and the strong arms of a rescuer kept interrupting her thought. It was real, wasn't it? Had she dreamed that he loved her as she had loved him? If she had not dreamt it, then why had he not come to see her?

Pomalee was being honored with his visits. It was she who was receiving his attentions. His declaration could not be real. She had hallucinated that Teddy loved her as she was slipping into the grips of eternity. It was the desires of her heart that caused her to hear what was not spoken.

Was that what God was trying to convey to her? Could she have been wrong all this time? Well, if that was the case, she would not be dragged into a relationship with Tyler, just to have a relationship with someone. It was not as if she needed a man, especially, if the only choices were the two Gordon brothers. Dad-blame Christopher for sending Tyler those stupid love letters from her. He was the one to blame for Tyler's attempt to put his claim on her.

Well, she would just have to buck up and face reality. Teddy did not love her. He loved Pomalee, and she would just have to push all these doggone emotions out of her, stop bawling, and be happy for him. "Quit being a sad sap, Shella!" she fussed at herself.

Teddy sat for a couple of hours biting his fingernails, until there was no nail left, while waiting for news on Shella. He was a nervous wreck. Tyler had not come back. He should've come back to give a report.

Pomalee slept for a while, as a result of having just come out of surgery. She was in a lot of pain, but wore a smile and bore it in silence. The medicines given to her made her groggy. When she was awake, she tried to appease Teddy's anxiousness, to no avail.

Finally, she prompted, "Teddy, I don't know why you think you have to stay here with me. Your place is with Shella."

"You are wrong, Pomalee. Tyler is the rightful man to be with her."

"How do you figure that?"

"He is the one everyone sees at the right one for her. You know, he was having her come home this weekend so he could ask her to marry him. I have no place in her life, except as her brother-in-law."

Pomalee's weak smile faded, "But he doesn't love Shella, not like *you* love Shella."

Her words did not register in his mind, as he continued, "Mom and Dad will be thrilled at the news. They have been encouraging him in this matter all along."

Pomalee shifted into a more comfortable position to relieve the pain in her leg. She still did not have the strength to sit up completely. "You are not worried are you? Teddy, she will not say yes."

"How do you know? My brother is very suave, besides they make a handsome couple." He didn't mean to be sounding sorry for himself, but he was.

Pomalee looked at the pitiful creature before her. She had no right to tell him. It was Shella that needed to tell him her feelings. She verbalized only what she felt right to say, "Go see her, Teddy. I know she would want you there."

He did not need anyone to tell him twice. Basically, he was waiting for the opportune moment to see her. He strode out with fingernails still in his mouth. He followed in the same footsteps his brother had trod a while ago, until he came to room two fourteen, but the scene before him stopped him dead in his tracks, forbidding him entrance.

Tyler was holding her close and declaring his love for her. He must not be a witness to this private moment. He didn't *want* to be a witness to this. Confound Tyler! His heart fell from his chest. That was God's answer. Shella's love would not be his.

Boy, what he would not give to have a drink right now, but he knew that was not the answer. God had claimed victory over that demon, and Teddy belonged to God. He could not go back to Pomalee's room and face her constant optimism, so he walked aimlessly, ending in the brisk cold wind.

Outside, the world was a white abyss. The snow had stopped falling, but everything was covered in the white mess. He heard the distant hum of what probably was a truck clearing the roads, but no person was in sight. A few footprints were pressed, sinking about eight or nine inches.

Oh, how he hated this place. He hated this life. He did not stop walking, until he came around the side of the hospital where Tyler's truck was still parked. Oh, how he would like to get in and just drive away. Leave Tyler with his happiness. Leave all memories of Shella or this whole miserable life. The keys were still in the ignitions from where he had left it the day before.

The whole truck was covered in snow, so he climbed back out to scrape the window, after he tried to start it, and it refused to start. Once again, he tried to start it, and this time, he found the culprit. It had run out of gas.

That was certainly the frosting on the cake. That is all he needed! Angry at the world, he set out on foot to get some gas, thinking how much he wanted to sell his house and move far away, so that he would never have to see Shella again. He would politely find a reason not to come to the wedding and never need to come home again. He loved her so much it hurt.

As the next few days passed, the trucks cleared the roads, so that Pomalee, Teddy and Tyler could go home, as soon as she was released. It was decided that Pomalee would go back to Shella's home to recuperate, so that all the Gordon family would be close by for continual assistance.

She would heal much faster in a home rather than in the dorm, besides, the house was already equipped with a ramp from when Shella needed it. The Evans' family doctor was a good one that would be perfect for her care. She would return in June for the graduation ceremony, after everything was normal again.

Shella had to return to school as quickly as she could. The injuries she sustained were considerably less than Pomalee's. Her recuperation period was only a few days. The roads back up Toxaway Mountain were not quite cleared, so after finding out about the accident, Lawrence was glad to agree to come pick Shella up in Cashiers and take her back to school. Tyler and Teddy were not offering, so she took Lawrence up on his offer. She was so close to graduating that she could not afford to miss much at this point. That would mean another year to wait, if she did. Shella was still weak and had come down with pneumonia, but since she was already in the hospital, they had her on antibiotics quickly. She was not well, but well enough to return to school. There was a lot of pain in her feet, but she told no one lest the doctor insist she stay in the hospital longer.

The last year had been so stressful for her. She was just beginning to appreciate Christopher's paternal urges of responsibility. If she had not been so stubborn and childish, when he was trying to make things easier for her, she would be much better off now. Part of her wanted her brother, since her mom couldn't be here, but her pride refused her heart's desire. It was time to start afresh with her home life, without Christopher, without Teddy.

She didn't need either of them, and after graduation, she was not even sure she was going back home at all. She genuinely hoped the best for Teddy and Pomalee, or did she? It was good that she would not be around them for a while. A clean slate. That was her goal. She fought hard to keep jealousy and bitterness from keeping her from her dear friend. One day, she would be able to see the two of them together and be happy, if it killed her.

ৎৡৡৎ

The remainder months of school went smoothly, as Shella did not go back home at all. Her clean slate meant exactly that. She was not going to beat herself up over any of this. Tyler or Georgia was generous enough to call weekly as usual, but it did not seem to be as special as it used to be. Toward the end of the quarter, most calls came from the mom. It seemed that even Tyler had found something to occupy his time, not that Shella minded a bit.

Clean slate, she kept reminding herself, as she sent resumes out to various hospitals in completely different states. Once her job request was accepted, she would look for lodging and be ready to get on with her life in a moment's notice. Maybe she could be near Christopher and Amber. No, she did not particularly want to live around all those people that thought they were better than she. Maine was awfully cold this time of year.

She did interview with a couple hospitals in Washington DC and one in North Carolina, and she received several requests for more interviews. Letters requesting her services began filtering in at the beginning of May. With her grades and working experience, she could pick where she wanted to relocate to satisfy *her*. The world was hers to claim, she just had to choose which one. She weeded out, until she had minimized it to four prospects.

Then came her trip home, which brought all those ideas to a screeching halt. Feeling stronger about her future and about her independence, she felt secure enough to go home and face the things she had tried so hard to forget.

Lawrence and his new girlfriend were generous enough to take her home the last weekend of May, as they were going home too. Graduation was the following Friday night. Her plans were to study hard over the weekend for the last finals she would ever have to take, plus she had to go collect Pomalee for the ceremony.

Shella had decided to take the job in Washington DC, and had returned a letter stating her sincere intent. After graduation, she planned on flying up to find lodging and never come back. She had managed to forget her feelings for Teddy, except whenever she thought about him. In order to never think about him, she would simply never speak to him again.

The air had warmed considerably and spring was in full bloom. Remnants of that cold bitter snow that almost claimed her life were long gone. The old apple tree behind the Gordon house was white with blooms. It didn't matter how long she stayed away or how far she pushed the thoughts from her mind, this old place brought old familiar feelings rushing back. It was memories of her daddy that came back first. She still missed them so much.

Pomalee, who had heard the car pull up, hobbled to open the door in greeting of her best friend. Naturally, she wore a huge grin, "Shella! You are home! I wasn't expecting you. You snuck up on me." Standing on the porch, she waved vigorously at Lawrence, who only emerged the car long enough to get Shella's bag out of the trunk. "Hey Lawrence!"

"Hey Pomalee. See you next weekend," he called back as he returned behind the driver's seat.

Shella hugged Pomalee's neck hard. "How are you? How is your leg?"

"Much better," she sat on the couch and lifted the casted leg up a little. "I will survive. I am so glad you're home. We were wondering if you would make it home before graduation."

Shella distracted, "That was our plans, wasn't it? Are you going to have that cast on, when you hobble across the platform to get your diploma?"

"Get it off Monday." Pomalee showed the colorful drawings and words scripted by everyone around. Tyler had drawn a couple of funny little pictured cartoons, being the comic he was.

"I am glad."

Pomalee sobered, "So is something wrong? I mean you have not been home since the accident." She searched Shella's brown eyes for the truth. Pomalee believed in being straightforward. "I thought you might be angry at me about the accident."

Shella, who was plunked down beside her now, threw her arm over Pomalee's shoulders. "Heaven's no! It *was* an accident. No one can be blamed."

"Then, why have you not called or come home?"

Shella avoided Pomalee's scrutinizing eyes. Her girlfriend could look into her soul and see what Shella didn't want revealed, the truth that secreted her reasons of avoidances.

Just then, a loud knock sounded on the door. Shella motioned to the invalid to stay put, thankful to have gotten out of that pickle so easily. She could never tell Teddy's lover that *she* loved him.

"Hey Shella. I didn't know you were home," Teddy was caught off guard when he saw Shella's face on the other side of the door.

Shella smiled politely and stood aside for him to come in. "Pomalee, I am going upstairs to unpack and hit the shower. See you later, Teddy." She headed to the stairs, grabbing her bag on the way.

"Wait a minute, Shella," Teddy called after her. "I want to ask you something."

Shella stopped, but didn't turn around, at first. "What is it?" Could he hear the anxiety in her voice?

"I came over to see if Pomalee could tell me how to cook some stuff for a dinner, but now that you are here, I can surely use *your* help."

"I am sorry, Teddy, but I don't think I can help you right now. Pomalee is a much better cook than I am."

Pomalee called after her, as she began to climb the stairs. "You should give him the recipe for your chicken casserole, Shella. You know it is delicious."

"Thanks Pomalee, but I am really tired. You go ahead. I may go ahead and turn in early. I have been so swamped with finals and everything. I am truly exhausted"

Pomalee looked sadly at Teddy. Words could not justify the rejection in his pathetic eyes. What was wrong with Shella? Pomalee had never seen her best friend act like that. Was she mad at Teddy, too? Did she not know how much she had hurt him the last three months by not coming home or calling? Teddy would come over every week and the first question out of his mouth was, "Have you heard from Shella?"

"Teddy, I am no replacement for Shella, but I will help you all I can."

He had a hard time taking his eyes from the stairwell. "My folks are coming over to my new house for dinner, and I wanted to fix something nice for them."

"Your new house? You have a new house?" She was stunned.

"Yeah," he shrugged indifferently. It meant nothing to him right now.

"When did you get a new house? Where is it?"

"I have been building it for a couple of years. It is out in Ravenel area."

"That is wonderful! You are certainly full of surprises. Now, let me see. A housewarming meal, let me see…what can we fix?"

Teddy awkwardly eyed the top of the stairs in silence, his hands shoved in his pockets. Shella was mad at him, like the time he kissed her. He knew by her body language and lack of acknowledgement that she was very angry, but why? He had left her alone for Tyler. Possibly, she could have heard his proclamation of love for her and hated him for daring to think that way of her? Tyler hadn't mentioned their engagement. Maybe she had to turn Tyler down, because of those words. She really loved Tyler, and she felt guilty because *he* had proclaimed his love for her.

Pomalee was busy writing a menu, along with directions on how to prepare it, but her mind was not far from her best friend's queer behavior, either. Poor Teddy. He loved Shella so much. Anyone could see that. It could not be Lawrence, because he was serious about this girl he was dating, besides, Shella had plenty of opportunities to have him, if she wanted him. Could it be Tyler? She really didn't think that could be the answer, because he had spent a lot of time with *her* these last couple months, and from the conversations he shared with her, Shella rejected all of his attempts.

No, she thought, Shella loves Teddy. I *know* it. It doesn't take a genius to figure that one out, but what is wrong? "Here you go, Teddy. It may not be the fanciest in the world, but it is easy to prepare."

He pocketed the paper she handed to him and mumbled his, "Thanks."

"Shella really is tired from her trip," Pomalee excused as he headed for the door. "She'll probably be over sometime tomorrow."

"I wouldn't count on it," he grumbled, as the door shut behind him.

Shella went straight to the bath to lose her woes in its hot bubbles. She did not want to think about what Teddy and Pomalee were doing downstairs. She was home all of ten minutes, and already regretting her decision to come home. If she had known that they were going to be rubbing it in her face, she would have stayed at school. She was an intrusion of their romancing. If there was any way to get a hold of

Lawrence, she would have him turn right around and come take her away from here.

She lay back, soaking in the water, until it turned cool. "Clean slate," she repeated softly. The sun was setting, for the light in the window was fading. The fear of walking in on the two downstairs made Shella chose to hop into her pajamas and then the bed.

Of course, sleep did not come easy at first. Shella could not help wondering, dreading, and imagining what was going on in her own living room. Then, came the memory of that kiss of long ago; that kiss that forced her to look at Theodore Patrick Gordon as a man, instead of the little boy she grew up with; that kiss that manifested feelings she never thought of having before; that kiss that stole her breath and heart and gave it a new desire; that kiss...

The morning broke with Pomalee bouncing onto her bed. She jumped from the one good leg as high as she could to land with the heaviest bounce. Shella had not even come back down to talk to her last night, so she was determined to find out what was wrong with her friend this morning.

Shella frowned at being awakened in such a manner as bouncing on the bed. Of course, she should be used to Pomalee waking her up like this. She had only done it for the last four years at college. Shella pulled the covers higher over her head, leaving only a small opening so that she could breathe.

"Shella Esther Evans, do not ignore me. You know very well that you should be awake and dressed at this hour of the day."

"Let me sleep," she mumbled.

"You can't sleep. You have somewhere to be," Pomalee argued.

Shella removed the blankets, which sent her hair flying, so she could see Pomalee, "No, I don't."

"Yes you do!" Pomalee insisted, pulling back the blankets.

Shella sat up grumpily, "No, I do not!"

Pomalee refused to release the blankets as Shella tried to retrieve them. "Yes you do! Now, get up!"

"Okay fine, Miss Smarty Pants, Where do I have to be?"

"You have to help Teddy."

"I told you last night I wasn't going to do that," Shella flopped back down pulling the pillow over her face. "Teddy is *your* problem, not mine."

Pomalee's voice softened, "Are you mad at Teddy, Shella?"

"I do not see how my emotions, or lack thereof, for Teddy should affect the status of your relationship with him."

"Whoa! Whoa! Whoa! What relationship?"

"You know, the relationship between you and Teddy."

"I repeat, what relationship?"

Shella was slightly embarrassed to have to put it into words. "Come on, Pomalee. Are you denying the growing fondness the two of you have?"

"Oh my word! Growing fondness? I cannot believe you just said that. Wait till I tell Teddy we have a growing fondness. He will get a kick out of that." She shook her head in laughter, repeating, "growing fondness?"

Shella flung her pillow at Pomalee. "Don't say anything to Teddy."

Pomalee took Shella's hand in both of her own. "Honey, Teddy's in love with *you*. Don't you know that?"

"No, and how do you know that?"

"How do you not know, Sweetie? His eyes light up the second you walk in a room. That is the only time I see a smile on his face. He walked around like a zombie since you have gone back to school. He mopes around and never goes anywhere. Does that sound like a contented man to you?"

"I just don't know. I wish I could be sure."

Pomalee laughed, "Be assured. He will never believe that the reason you are mad at him is because you think he and I have a growing fondness." Every time she repeated that phrase, she could not help but laugh.

"I am not mad at Teddy," Shella denied.

"He sure thinks so. You didn't see him, after you shot him down last night. He was so pitiful."

"I did not mean to be rude."

Pomalee softened, "Why would you ever think that Teddy had feelings for me?"

Shella squirmed, pulling her hand away. "When we were in the car wreck, he stayed with you the whole time. He did not even come in to see his old friend once."

Pomalee's eyes gleamed with enlightenment, "That is because Tyler told him he was going to ask you to marry him. That was the whole reason he wanted you to come home that weekend. Teddy thought you were engaged to his brother. Of course, he was not going to intrude."

"Marriage! Tyler doesn't love me, nor I him. Everybody knows that. Why should he propose marriage?"

"But did Teddy know that?"

Shella stood in indignation, "Yes, and Tyler never even asked. Thank you God."

"Well Sweetie, he believes you accepted the proposal."

"Well, I'll just get that out of his head right quick and in a hurry."

"Hence, you have somewhere to be," Pomalee nudged.

"What do you mean?"

"His folks are going over to his new house for dinner tonight. He wanted your help preparing a dinner worth eating. You turned him down flat last night."

"I did. I didn't even listen to what he was trying to say. I am so awful."

"So, go help him." Pomalee stood to leave.

"You think I should?"

"Honey, if you had seen his face, when you rejected him last night, you wouldn't ask that."

"I was pretty mean." Shella opened her closet door. "What should I wear?"

Pomalee twirled excitedly almost stumbling over her cast. "It is spring! Wear that yellow sunflower dress."

Shella was becoming excited, too, until a thought struck her. She faced her friend again. "Pomalee, how do *you* feel about Teddy?"

She hobbled to Shella and cupped her hand around her friend's face. "I feel sorry for Teddy. You are breaking his heart."

"So you do not like him a little more than usual?"

"Not that way. I have known from the day I met him that he was crazy over you. I could never feel anything for him in that way. Now, get ready!"

Shella waited until Pomalee left the room and closed the door, before allowing the chill of glee to creep up from her toes to her head.

Could Pomalee be right? She did not want to get her hopes up too high. Was it just wishful thinking to think that she had actually heard Teddy's voice declare his love for her that night in the snow? It had seemed so real.

With shaky hands, she pushed the small wooden stake through the two appropriate holes in the piece of leather to pull back the top half of her hair. "Oh Lord, please do not let me make a fool of myself," she prayed. She took one last critical look in the mirror before returning to Pomalee, who was relaxed on the couch with her leg propped up.

"I was right. That was the perfect choice. Now, go on, get out of here," Pomalee ordered.

"How? Should I go ask Tyler to take me to his brother?"

"I called for a cab while you were upstairs. He is going to meet you over on Willow Street corner, so Tyler will not see you leave."

Shella hugged her neck and ran toward the door, but stopped short. "I have nothing to prepare for a dinner. What if Teddy doesn't have anything in his kitchen?"

"I have taken care of that as well. I called Jimmy, down at the grocer. He has been real good about delivering to me, since I cannot get out. He is filling the bags with all you will need, as we speak. You just have to stop and pick it up."

Shella smiled graciously at her houseguest, "What would I do without you, Pomalee?"

"Don't try and find out," she threatened.

༄∞༅

Little Jimmy Straid had, indeed, packed two bags completely full of supplies, which he brought quickly to the car for Shella, upon seeing the cab pull in the back parking lot. He smiled mischievously at Shella, as if he knew something she did not.

"Your houseguest is mighty pretty." He looked the other way, as he spoke, "Nice too."

Shella held up the money. "Yes, she is. I know she really appreciates your help. It was very kind of you to deliver groceries to my house for her. I don't know any other store that delivers anymore. You are special, Jimmy."

"Oh shucks, Shella Esther. You know Grandpa. He wouldn't let nobody go without, cause they were hurt."

She thanked him again and motioned for the driver to head on over to Teddy's house. The journey gave her a little time to contemplate what she should say to him, once she arrived. She was scared of facing him, all of a sudden. It would be awkward. She tried hard to think about the events of that night in the snow and about the words he had spoken. Were they real, or had it been wishful thinking turned to dreams?

Teddy was not the kind to talk about his feelings to anyone, so it was not possible for him to have confided in Pomalee. No, that was simply romantic notions conjured up by one who had a wild imagination. Pomalee was partial to Shella, and maybe she saw what she wanted to see and not what was really there.

Teddy had put in a driveway that went all the way to the house. It was lined with Bradford pear trees on both sides. It almost did not look like the same place it had back at Christmas. He had been working very hard on this home. The barn was not very big, but it was beautiful. This was something anyone would be proud of.

The door was locked, but when she circled around to the door that led into the kitchen, it was unlocked. Teddy had built an open shed on that side, which housed the lawnmower, a rotor tiller, and a small tractor. It was then that she saw the tree house. She stood in awe at the exactness of the replication. It was *their* tree house! She would have to check it out later.

Preparing a meal was not that hard, as all she needed to do at that moment was put some soup beans on. After that minor task was complete, she was left the rest of the morning and early afternoon to do what she wanted. She did go ahead and make the rolls, so they would have all day to rise and be fluffy.

Her first venture was to the barn, where she found two honey colored quarter horses munching on hay at the gate in front of the barn. Further down, in the field, she spotted a Black Angus cow. She couldn't tell from that distance, but it may have been a bull. There were some yellow baby chicks, about fifty in all, scurrying in the direction of the hay that the horses were munching, which frightened one horse, who took off.

Shella drew near the remaining mare and nuzzled her nose softly. "Hi there pretty girl. What is your name?" The mare reveled in the gentle attention the girl was giving her and appropriately snorted her approval, while the little chicks paid her no mind at all. They were engrossed in finding seeds that fell from the strands of hay.

Before she knew it, Shella had spent all morning out in the refreshing sun brushing, petting, and getting to know the new inhabitants. Where was Teddy? Had she and Pomalee gotten the wrong day and place? Why wasn't he here?

She washed her hands and dug into the preparations, hoping someone would come to eat it. It was a bit early, but she had nothing else to do. Peeling, cutting, baking, and boiling kept her busy for the next two hours, but it was only three thirty.

The bread was rising perfectly and was ready for her to punch and knead and then break into round balls to place on the butter greased bread pan. She carefully covered them with a clean dishtowel to set and rise the second time.

She was not trying to be nosy, but Shella wandered into the living room and watched out the bay window to see if Teddy could be driving down the beautifully rocked driveway. Ten minutes passed and then twenty, but he did not come, so Shella investigated the tree house and all the rooms of the house, save the master bedroom. She wanted to go see that beautiful balcony Teddy built onto it, but it would not be proper to invade his private chamber.

The den, which was located on the side of the kitchen, off to the back of the house, and its sofa, looked inviting. It was not quite what Shella was expecting for Teddy's taste. Had someone else picked this out for him? It was soft plush with brightly colored flowers. She sat down and ooh it felt so comfy. She slipped off her sandals and pulled her legs up, and oh, that felt even better.

It was so soft on her face, as she got lost in a photo album and the oversized cushions. From its pages fell a couple pieces of paper, which Shella immediately picked up to replace. One was Teddy's birth certificate, proving that he weighed eight pounds and fourteen ounces and was twenty-two inches long when he was born. She smiled while reading this. He always had been a cute boy.

The second paper that fell was folded and ragged, and naturally she was tempted to peek. Maybe it was another piece of who Teddy was. She stared at it in amusement. It was a poem written by his hand. She never knew he was a poet. She read the words curiously:

The curve of your lips, the twinkle in your eye

Where God pulled two stars from the sky;

The glory on your face, the beauty of your soul,

Has never yet been told;

The pleasure of your touch, the joy of your kiss

I know of nothing else that makes me feel this.

You're in my dreams while I'm awake and asleep

There is this secret I must keep.

The secret of the love in my heart for you.

Telling you is something I can never do.

Take her from my heart, God, she belongs to another,

I love this girl, yet she belongs to my brother.

She smiled, rubbing the softness of the sofa against her cheek. She carefully replaced the pieces of paper with a smile across her lips.

When the whistle blew at the four o'clock hour, declaring the workday had ended, Teddy sighed in relief. He was glad this day was over. It meant that his set of Saturdays was over, and he would not have to work a Saturday again, for a while.

Now he had to figure out something to fix for supper that was fast and easy. He had worried all day about how he was going to pull this off. In the end, he decided to run by the chicken shack and grab a meal. It was fast and easy, and his mom would not expect more. Yes, he would love to have that fancy meal Pomalee wrote out for his folks, but Pomalee's instructions looked too complicated for him to do in such a short time.

Per his dad's insistence, he had finally grown brave enough to tell his beloved mother about his house and his intentions of leaving the nest for good. His dad was going to bring her to the house, and once Teddy had her eating a decent meal, they would make the announcement.

He operated his old truck down the highway, smelling the box of chicken sitting in the seat next to him. It sure smelled good, anyway. The truck didn't drive straight anymore, since he tried to fly it like a plane into the tree. It was beaten pretty badly, but he refused to get it fixed, because that served as a reminder of what he used to be and what he never wanted to be again.

He really could not blame Shella for hating him. He had hurt her over and over the last year and a half. Sweet beautiful Shella, and to think he almost killed her. Since Christ had saved him, Teddy's feelings for her did not seem so overbearing. He realized he had blamed her for his misery, but it was not his love for Shella that made him be so wicked. Now, his love for her was beautiful and innocent. There was no guilt or shame, only acceptance that she would never love him. He could live with that, as long as Jesus loved him forever. He *could* live with Shella being with Tyler, as long as Christ was with him.

The rocked path to his house brought him to the realization of how lonely he was going to be way out here by himself. It never bothered him until recently. He had been content to spend his life alone with no prospects, or desire for prospects of ever getting married, because he had his family. Now, it just seemed lonely, possibly, because he did not realize how alone he would be with his mom, dad, and Tyler so far away. Maybe he should sell this place.

He noticed something strange was in the air, when he stepped out of his truck. Ginger and Titan, his horses, were not waiting at the gate for him to feed them, like they always were. Generally, they were waiting patiently along with the cows, but today, none were looking for his homecoming. There was a silence about.

The opening of his front door revealed a house full of aromas familiar to his mom's home. Had she come over to cook for him? Now, doggone her! He was supposed to be treating her. Wait a minute, she didn't even know about this place. It could not be his mom, unless dad told her.

There was no sign of a being in the kitchen. A pot was on the stove and a dish in the oven contained a wonderful home cooked feast, but how? No one was in the living room. He took the stairs two at a time to find the upstairs empty as well.

It was not until he started to come down the back steps, which led into the den, that he noticed a yellow lump on the couch. He drew near, holding his breath. Like the porcelain doll his mother gave to his aunt on her birthday, Shella lay, in a peaceful glory, on her stomach right on his very own couch, asleep. Her skin looked as soft as the plush material it was resting on. Teddy's first instinct was to touch her cheek, but at the sight of his hand, he recoiled. He was dirty from work, and touching her would spoil her flawless complexion.

He quietly retreated back up to the second floor to shower and change. His mind raced at the revelation of her presence in his home. She had changed her mind and had come to help him after all! She was beautiful! Her grace toward him was sent from God. She had the most beautiful soul he had ever seen, other than his mom and dad. She was here in the flesh. "Thank You God," he closed his eyes and let the hot water rinse him. "Thank You."

He threw on some clean jeans, a shirt, and shoes so he could hurry back down. He didn't take the time to shave, but quickly ran a comb through his thick wavy hair. He wanted to talk to her and make sure she was not mad at him."

He slipped into the kitchen and retrieved one of the flowers he had bought for his mother and threw the food he had bought at the chicken shack into the refrigerator. The one he grabbed was a white rose, which he took into his den. Squatting on one knee, he indulged in her glory. He still couldn't believe she was here. He hated to awaken her from her angelic slumber. Maybe he should just let her sleep. He placed the rose carefully beside her hand, which supported her cheek, but as careful as he was, the velvet petals accidentally touched her cheek, causing her eyes to flutter open.

"Teddy!" she exclaimed softly.

He noticed the light in her eyes. "Hey." She was glad to see him! "I am sorry, I did not mean to wake you."

She smiled bashfully, "I didn't mean to fall asleep. It is just that your sofa is so comfy."

He was touching her hair softly, trying to move a strand that had fallen from the leather strap. "You are most welcome to fall asleep on my couch any time. I am just glad you are here. Thank you for helping me, Shella."

"Thank you for letting me."

"I can honestly say, I am surprised."

Shella's face became shameful. "I would say so. I have been pretty nasty to you lately. I didn't give you any reason to think that I would come."

"The table, the food, everything is wonderful. You shouldn't have gone to so much trouble."

She returned his touch, with her fingers on his. "Nothing is too good for your sweet momma."

"I can't argue with you there."

Just then, Shella caught a glimpse of his watch and gasped, "Oh my, it is four forty-five!" She bolted up, making sure she took hold of the delicate rose, first. "Why did you let me sleep so late? I have to finish supper."

Teddy followed, "What can I do to help?"

"There is not much left to do. I need to get the bread in the oven."

Shella removed the lid and stirred the beans and then took the roast out of the oven. She pulled a bag of frozen corn on the cob from the freezer and put a pot of water on to boil for it. Lastly, she removed the cloth from the rolls and placed them in the oven.

Teddy took the bunch of mixed flowers to the dining room and placed them beside his mother's seat at the table. Just because he had planned on a fast food meal, didn't mean he should not do something nice for her. He knew she would love the flowers. He took the one white rose, that Shella had lain on the counter, and put it beside her plate. He was just so pleased that she was here.

"What else can I do," he asked, coming back into the kitchen. He stood over the pot and lifted the lid.

Shella shut the oven door. "That's it. Everything is finished, except putting the corn in when that water comes to a boil and taking the rolls out after they're done."

Teddy began timidly, "Shella, you don't know how much I appreciate you coming here today. It means everything to me."

The woman took the three steps to stand behind him. His voice had been husky, which made her slip both of her hands under his arms, clasping them on the muscular shoulders. She dared to rest her chin on his shoulder.

Teddy, surprised at her confidence, hoped that she couldn't hear his heart speeding, as he thought it was going to beat out of his chest. Surely, she could feel it. He closed his eyes as he replaced the lid on the pot, while arguing with himself in thought about what it all meant. He had to wake up from this fantasy. Had he stepped into a surreal world? Yes, he had fallen asleep at work and was dreaming all this.

Shella whispered close to his ear, "I love you, Teddy Gordon. I love the glory you wear on your beautiful face."

He froze mid thought. She had told him many times in life that she loved him, but she never said it like that before. It was different this time. Those were the exact words, which he had spoken to her that night in the snow. She had heard him! Not only that, she affirmed a mutual love. She loved him, a thought that took a few minutes to filter. Turning to face her, he searched her soul through the brown windows to verify that she was genuine.

"You do?" He was not sure if that was audible or if he had thought it in his mind. He was just paralyzed in shock.

"Each and every day since the day in the nursing home..." her voice faded. "Do you remember the day in the nursing home?"

Oh yes, he remembered. Seldom did he ever forget that kiss. So many times he had relived that moment in his mind and in his fantasies. Her soft lips responding to his inexperience. The innocence of young love on the eve of its blossoming, yes he remembered this brand new feeling that crept through his body to make him weak, happy, and scared all at the same time.

His head nodded, as "yes" escaped his lips.

"Oh Teddy! Why do you make me say it? You knew I loved you."

His right eyebrow rose in a perfect upside down v, with a longing in his gaze. "No, I didn't. You got so angry with me for kissing you, that I thought you really resented me for it."

"I was angry because I was thrilled at your kiss, and you repented immediately. I thought you regretted it, because you thought I was Christopher's kid sister and could not love me that way." She was still trying to find answers in his eyes.

"You are definitely no kid." She was almost as tall as he was, which put his lips close to her face, so that she could smell the mint from his toothpaste. "I apologized, because I thought I had taken advantage of your vulnerability, and it was inappropriate. You were standing there in such sorrow. I didn't want you to think I was a jerk for kissing you, when you were going through such tragedy. I didn't know you *wanted* me to kiss you, or trust me, I would have kissed you again and again without apologies."

"I tried to ignore it. I thought I was crazy at first, because you had other girls and didn't act like you loved me. I thought it was wrong to love you."

He lowered his eyes to her lips. The truth was too painful to look into her soul. "I tried to drown you out of my thoughts with beer and other girls, but it never worked. They could never hold a candle to you. Your kiss breathed life into me that only you could energize. I stayed away from you so I wouldn't have to be reminded that you could never love me the way I love you."

"I didn't know what was wrong. I thought you stayed away because you had a lover. I prayed for God to take it from me, because you had another. Then, you accepted Christ as your Savior, and after the accident, it was different. I still loved you, even more, if that is possible. It wasn't just a figment of my imagination. For whatever reasons, God gave me this push, and though I tried to reject it," his fingers barely touched her jaws, as if he were afraid it still was not real, "it grew stronger." She felt a little embarrassed. Why was he looking at her like that? "Say something, please. Am I making a fool of myself,

Teddy?"

His reply was not verbal. All he could think about was that she loved him. It was amazing to think what Shella had said was true. God had prevented this coming together when he was living in sin and full of the devil, but now, his wildest dream had come true. How sweet the grace of God was!

$\wp\!\sim\!\wp$

A knock on his front door finally entered into his subconscious, startling him out of his bliss. Shella pulled back and basically searched for reassurance from him that he really wanted her here in his arms.

"I think we better get that." She pulled on his hand to lead him to the door, but he hesitated, pulling her back to him.

Her smile was precious to him. "I don't want to lose this moment. I wish you knew how much I really love you, but I am afraid I will wake up, none of this will be real, and you won't be here."

"The only place I am going is with you, to open the door."

Again, she pulled his hand to follow, and again, Teddy paused reluctantly. "I love you Shella, but we cannot tell anyone, yet." He lowered his voice, because his guests had entered into the living room.

She smiled at his obvious jest. "Come on," but the somber expression on his face revealed that he was not joking. She quieted to a whisper. "Why not?"

His parents were approaching the door. "I don't have time to tell you this second, please, just do me this favor?" In response to his dad's calling his name, Teddy raised his voice. "I am in the kitchen, Dad. I'll be there in a minute."

The spell was broken. Shella did not understand Teddy. As long as they had wanted to be together, now he was retracting his feelings. Why could they not happily announce their mutual love for one another to his wonderful parents? They, of all people, would be elated for her and Teddy. She had made a fool of herself. He did not feel exactly like she did.

She withdrew her touch from him and moved across the room to accommodate his wishes. Should she leave? Did he not want them to even know she was here? She would have bolted for the door, had

Patrick not walked in at that moment.

The older man glanced from one young person to the other and began, "I hope you do not mind us coming on in, Son, but we knocked for several minutes and didn't hear an answer."

"Of course not, Dad. You are welcome to walk in anytime. I was in the middle of something. I apologize for not letting you and Mom in."

"I am dying to tell your Mother that this is your place. She is asking a blue million questions." He gave his son a masculine embrace of greeting. "Hey, Shella girl. What have you been up to over here? Sure smells like home."

She smiled meekly, accepting his fatherly hug, "Hi, Mr. Gordon. You are looking especially young and handsome, today. What is the special occasion?" She fumbled at putting on the oven mitt to take out the rolls. She wanted to cry again. She was inadequate and foolish and wished she had never come here.

Teddy threw her one last pleading look, before leaving to see his mother. "Thank you."

"This looks like some mighty fine cooking. It was good of you to help Teddy out. You know both of my sons think you are wonderful."

She knew what he was wanting, as he stood there with his arm still around her shoulder. The rolls she had just taken out of the oven were perfectly brown, steaming, soft, and very aromatic. Georgia never let him sample prior to the meal, but Shella grabbed a saucer and placed a roll on it for him. She could not resist his eyes.

He grinned mischievously, which reminded Shella of Teddy's grin. "You know we cannot tell little mother about this? She is set in her ways."

Shella laughed softly, "Your secret is safe with me, Mr. Gordon."

He blew the steam off the roll and took a bite of the soft fluff. He closed his eyes in a gesture that he was in Heaven. "When are you going to start calling me 'Dad', Shella Esther?"

Her laughter turned into confusion, "I beg your pardon?"

"You know you are like the daughter Georgia and I never had. It just seems so informal for you to keep calling me mister all the time." He put his hand on her arm, "If it offends you, please disregard this request. I am not trying to take your own father's place."

"You have a twinkle in your eye, Dad," she accused. "What is going on?"

Georgia carefully pushed open the kitchen door with wide eyes. "This kitchen is huge. Oh look...Patrick, what is that?" She had spied the half eaten roll on the saucer in her husband's hand.

He quickly put the saucer on the counter behind him with a guilty look of surprise. She was not supposed to catch him. Teddy was supposed to take her anywhere, but the kitchen. He looked at Shella for help, which she immediately offered.

"Mrs. Gordon, I tried a new recipe on these rolls, and Mr. Gordon was so kind as to agree to taste test it, before I set them out for consumption. I wouldn't want to serve something inedible."

Georgia knew Shella was covering for her husband, but in light of the joy in her heart, and her love for Shella, she was willing to overlook her husband's minor indiscretion. She went on examining the kitchen. The mother patted Shella's cheek, as she passed her and then followed Teddy back out to tour the rest of the house.

Patrick kissed the girl's head. "You are good for my son. You are good for my family." His husky voice cleared and he moved away with his roll in hand. "What can I carry to that lovely table for you?"

"I need to get the beans in a bowl. Would you care to carve the roast?"

"Show me the knife!"

Shella pulled the roast out of the oven and placed it on a plate, because Teddy did not own a platter. The two had almost as much fun in the kitchen as the other two had exploring the place.

The meal was a wonderful experience, and afterward, Patrick insisted on helping with the clean up process, so that his lovely wife could go outside, and Teddy could show her the grounds and barn. The dad truly was in a different spirit today, but Shella conceded to just bask in his joy.

Still hurt over Teddy's request to keep quiet about loving her, Shella asked her father figure if she could ride home with them, being that she had no other way home. She certainly did not want them to think that she preferred being alone with Teddy. They might get the idea that she *wanted* to be alone with him. Maybe she was being petty, but why did Teddy have to keep it secret? Evidently, he did not love her or he would want to shout it from the mountains. Her pride always overtook her good senses.

It was disappointing, though, when Patrick, with a gleam in his eye, reported that he could not take her home. It was not quite a lie, because, as soon as she asked, he decided to take his wife somewhere else before going home. In fact, he made it up because Shella did ask that particular question.

He was no fool. He knew Teddy loved Shella. That is why he built this house for her. Every minute detail had been catered to please her. The exchanged silence and the way Shella kept *not* looking at Teddy all through the meal confirmed Patrick's suspicions of old. She loved Teddy, too. No, he would let Teddy take her home, so they could work it out.

Maybe his son would come home with some wonderful news of a wedding tonight. That would do beloved Georgia a whole world of good.

They were nearly finished, when the two returned from outside. Shella rewarded her partner a kiss on his handsome old cheek as an offer of thanks, and he returned a kiss on her forehead. "Thank you for helping with the dishes, Dad?"

"Thank *you* for a wonderful evening. Everything was perfect. You served as a lovely hostess." He turned to his wife. "Are you ready, my dear?"

"I sure am. Theodore, I am so very proud of you. You have a magnificent home here. Any young lady would be proud to call this home."

Teddy blushed, "Thanks Mom. I'll see you in a while. I will probably be staying at home tonight."

Georgia concluded with Shella, "Shella Esther, thank you for that delicious meal."

Shella smiled graciously as she often did and then began setting the place mats and linen napkins, which she had made for Teddy a year ago, at their proper places on the table. "I enjoyed it, too. Teddy makes it fun to play house with this gorgeous mansion." Only Teddy detected the hint of sarcasm in her words.

He walked the couple out to their car, returning shortly thereafter, while Shella was placing the last napkin in its ring. She left the room to double check that everything was completed in the kitchen and that she had not left the oven on or anything. Lastly, she took her purse from the cabinet she had put it in and came back into the dining room.

Teddy knew from her coolness toward him all evening that she was less than happy with him. He tried to soothe, "Dad is right, you know? Everything was wonderful. Thank you for all you have done."

Shella Evans's main downfall was her stubborn pride, and right now, Teddy had injured that. She exposed her soul wholly to him and he simply rejected it. Pomalee was wrong. This was wrong. He might have some physical attraction toward her, but he did not really love her, not like that.

"And your mom is right, as well. *Some* girl will be proud to call this home, but it is not to be me." Her voice was cold, as she announced prolifically. "I am ready for you to take me home."

He tried to take her hand, but she pulled it from him. He beseeched with hope, "Shella, I need to explain, please?"

"I don't need you to explain anything to me, Teddy Gordon. I don't need you to tell me you would rather kiss that other girl. I don't need you to tell me you don't love me the way I love you. I don't need you to tell me how I made such a fool of myself today. Don't worry, I will never bother you again. You shouldn't have let me spill all…"

Teddy put his hand over her mouth with care. "Will you please shut up?" He laughed. "Shella, you are the only one I have ever loved. How could you ever think that there is anyone but you?"

She looked like a little girl getting scolded. "Because I am proud to love you and want to tell everyone that I love the most wonderfully incredible, gorgeous, and creatively talented man, and I don't understand why you are so ashamed of m…"

Again, he covered her ramblings with a gentle hand. "Honey, I am not ashamed of you by any means. I would be the proudest person on the face of this earth to show the world you belong to me."

"I don't understand. Why keep it a secret?"

"It's just that not everyone will be as elated about this union as we are." She allowed him to keep his hands on her waist. "Yes, my folks adore you. They want you as a daughter-in-law, as Tyler's wife."

"What?" She frowned in aghast, relocating in front of the couch in her frustration. "I am so sick of hearing that garbage."

"It's true. You should know that. Why do you think I've been so jealous? They implored Tyler to fall in love with and marry you, because you would be the perfect wife. Christopher agrees, too."

"Well I don't agree, and it is *my* choice, not theirs." Did she sound like a bratty child?

"Tyler was supposed to propose the weekend you and Pomalee had the accident? I don't know why he didn't, but he still intends on asking you."

Shella searched his eyes for the truth, "And you were okay with letting him have me? Would you have kept quiet and never said anything?"

"I didn't think you'd ever feel anything for me, except loathe, after everything I have done. How could you love me after I had been a drunken fool and almost killed you?"

"You don't do those things anymore. God saved you and forgave and forgot it all, so have I. As for Tyler, I have no intentions of ever marrying him. He has known that all along."

Teddy couldn't help smiling. He loved her more at this very moment than he thought possible. Then, the remembrance of his sins overwhelmed him. Although God had forgiven and forgotten, Satan hadn't and quickly reminded him of his sins.

"Shella, I love you."

She reached up and kissed the corner of his mouth, "I love you. I love being able to tell you, finally."

"Oh Shella!" He pulled her into his arms as if he would never let her go. "Could you still love me, if you knew all I have done?"

"Teddy, the only thing I need to know is that you have asked my Father into your heart."

"But I have sown seeds that I *will* reap eventually, and if you are my life's partner, you are going to share in that harvest. It is only fair that I forewarn you how bad it is actually going to be."

The girl tightened her arms around his neck. "I don't need to know, any more than you need to know what I have done."

"My love, you could never do anything bad."

"Don't put me on a pedestal, Teddy. I am nowhere as perfect as you choose to believe. In God's eyes, all sin is equal. He has no respect of persons. They are all under the Blood."

He alienated his touch from her innocence. She had seen his unfaithful transgression. He could see how much it had hurt her and repented of his misdeed, but that would never suffice. He would have to pay for his sins.

His voice lowered, as he fought back the shame. "I could live forever and never be sorry enough for what I have done to you. I tried so hard to get you from under my skin. I kissed that girl to hurt you. To my recollection, that was the only time I ever…"

She put her hand on his shoulder to ease his pain, "It doesn't matter.

Theodore, I am in love with the man Christ saved. He found you worth saving, why can't I find you worth loving?"

"I have to show you." Pulling his shirt tail, he exposed his shoulder for her to see. "This is the result of a drunken night I can't even remember. Like my unfaithfulness and almost killing you, this is something I can never take back. I have to live with it and see a reminder of what I have done. You will have to look at it."

"Is it under the Blood, Teddy?" The green blotch on his back made her cringe against her will. She had to remember that Jesus covered it all, and she would have to find a way to never remember it, either.

"Yes." He lowered his shirt.

"Then why do you keep holding on to it? The devil is the one who does not want you to forget. God cast it all into the sea of forgetfulness."

"But…"

She stepped in front of him. "I love you Teddy, flaws and all, as I hope you love me with all mine."

"I adore you, more than you will ever know." He cupped her face in his hands.

She wriggled around until she had the back of her leg exposed. "Do you see that?" She pointed.

"You mean that scar you got when we were running from the old Trumball place, when we were kids?"

"Exactly. This is the mark that I must wear for the rest of my life because of my sin. We'll both have to see that scar as a reminder, and when our children ask about it, I will have to teli them the truth."

"What truth, Shella? We trespassed onto old man Trumball's place to fish and accidentally found his stash of whiskey. That doesn't compare to what I did."

"Says who?"

"You were a kid, plus you were with Christopher, Tyler, and me. You were just following us. We were responsible for you. You didn't do anything really wrong."

"Defined by whom? Are you God to say what is right and what is wrong? Are you so righteous, that you have the ability to set the standards by which we will all be judged?"

"I didn't say that."

"The Bible says that no sin is greater than another sin. It is all evil in God's eyes. There's no difference between telling a little white lie or committing murder. I may have been young, but I knew better. You three didn't twist my arm. I knew it was wrong; therefore, God judged me guilty. I had to take my holy whipping, just like you. Now it is behind us, never to be remembered anymore. Don't you get it?" She put her arms around his neck. "I love you."

He wanted to hold on to this moment forever. He never imagined he could feel this way about any person. "I love you, Shella." He wanted to kiss her, but felt as if it would taint his treasure. Actually, he had wanted to kiss her ever since they were interrupted in the kitchen, but he was glad that God made him wait. "We will have no more misunderstandings, then? We love each other. I don't want to spend another minute apart, because we know that beyond a shadow of a doubt."

"And you are not going to get any more stupid notions about Tyler and me?"

"Does that mean you will help me out for a while, and keep it quiet?"

"I don't like it. I do not like it at all, but I'll play along. How long do we have to keep this up?"

"Will you give me a little time to break this to Tyler and the folks?"

"Yes." She added, "For the time being. Do I have to pretend when no one is around?"

"No. Contrary to what you believe, this is very difficult for me, too."

"I don't believe it's too hard." Her smiling eyes widened at a sudden thought. "If you think I'm going to placate Tyler, think again. I may have to hide my love for you, but I draw the line at pretending to be attracted to him, besides I believe Pomalee has…"

Once again, he quieted her lips with a gentle touch, "Come on, our show is on." Taking her hand, he led her to the bay window where the sun was already setting and settled on the seat with her. "I can't wait until my wife is watching this from the balcony I made for her." He kissed her hand.

ഈൟ

Shella did not have much opportunity to spend any more time with Teddy. On Sunday, they had church, leaving the day to be spent with the family. Since they could not reveal to anyone about their love, except Pomalee, who was sworn to silence, Shella and Teddy went their separate ways, lest someone should tell by the way they looked at each other.

When Tyler found out that Teddy had built a beautiful house, he became somewhat jealous and commanded Shella accompany him to see it, and being that she wanted to be with Teddy, she complied. Of course Pomalee was encouraged to go, making it a foursome, but that didn't stop Shella's attentions from being scrutinized.

Monday, she accompanied Pomalee to the doctor, who took her cast from her leg. Tuesday, she and Pomalee took the insurance check from where the car was totaled and spent the day shopping for a car. Wednesday, they drove back to school for rehearsal, and on Thursday,

Shella had to take her last finals. Friday evening would be the graduation ceremony.

Teddy worked, but thought it best to spend his evenings at his home away from Shella. Pomalee had figured it out, and he did not want to risk anyone else coming to the same conclusions that she had. He had to come up with a plan to tell them all that he had fallen in love with Shella.

It was a good thing that they stayed apart, because what little time they were together on Tuesday, had someone been paying attention, they would have seen the fire in the exchanged glances. Pomalee was a good mediator, but they could not stop the glory that covered them.

He had been praying that God would work a miracle that they may be together. Neither liked sneaking around to steal a kiss or the opportunity to hold hands. What should his strategy be? He loved her so much. He understood how she felt about wanting to tell the whole world. He wanted to openly take her home as his bride with the blessing of his folks, but they did not want her with him. They gave her to Tyler.

He knew she was leaving on Wednesday, yet the need arose to see her, possibly steal a kiss, and reiterate his desire for her to drive extra careful. Tyler was already at her house, but he did not care. He still wanted to see her to tell her of his love one more time. He waited for two hours for his brother to leave and give him the opportunity to sneak over without being seen. Tyler would simply think he went to his house.

He had been watching out his bedroom window, and upon seeing his brother's silhouette emerge from the shadows of the Evans' house, Teddy slipped quietly down the stairs and out the kitchen door. He barely tapped on Shella's kitchen door, which she promptly responded with a smile spread wide.

Taking her hand, he lead her out beneath the big oak on the opposite side of the house from where his was located, so that they would be obscured. He could see her eyes dancing in the moonlight.

"What time are you leaving, tomorrow?" The fragrance of her hair awakened his senses.

"Probably about noon. We have rehearsal at four o'clock."

"Will you drive careful? I don't want any more incidents to keep you from becoming my wife."

"I am always careful." She wrapped her arms around his neck. "You are coming to my graduation?"

"Try and keep me away, Little Girl." He whispered in her hair, "I miss you."

She teased, "How much?"

"Enough to anticipate your return to me on Saturday, and then, I never intend on letting you go again."

She pulled back to look into his loving eyes, "What if I told you I have already accepted a position in another state, and I will not be coming back here?"

His heart fell out. All the strength fled his arms. "You have?"

"I thought you hated me. I couldn't stand the thought of living here, while you loved someone else and gave her your heart."

He was devastated. "Can you change your mind, or are you locked into a commitment?"

"I may be able to get out of it."

He searched her brown eyes for the truth, "Do you *want* to get out of it?"

"Of course I want to get out of it. I don't know what I can and cannot do at this point, but I can try. They may not be pleased, but I have not signed any contract or anything. I really thought it would be best for everyone for me to leave. I thought you and Pomalee were…"

Teddy gently covered her mouth with his hand to quiet her. "Where are we moving to, if you can't dump this job?"

"We? You would really leave your brand new home, your family, your job, and everything?"

"In a heartbeat. My Love, if that is the only way to be with you, I would go to the ends of the earth. We have been through too much for me to ever be separated from you again. When are you going to get that through your head?"

"I love you Theodore Patrick Gordon." She nestled his shoulder.

"Shella Esther Evans, you have the most beautiful glory on your face that I have ever seen." He kissed her goodnight. "I will call you after church tomorrow night. I love you."

Shella didn't let his hand go, "How much longer do we have to keep this a secret?"

"Pray with me that it will not be much longer. Hopefully we can work everything out right after graduation. They'll have to find out before we get married and move away together."

She pressed his hand to finalize the goodbyes, and then retreated to her house. "Be safe yourself, when you come up."

Teddy remained in the shadows as he returned to his own house, thinking about and counting his blessings. God had given him everything he had wanted. There was nothing left to ask for, except for this one miracle. He was in love with a girl that was crazy about him. He knew, beyond a shadow of a doubt, that his future was secured in Heaven, so what more could he ask for?

The next morning, his mom was getting ready for a doctor's

appointment, and Tyler was already gone to work, when Teddy came down for a cup of coffee. His dad was at the kitchen table engrossed in his newspaper, barely noticing Teddy's entrance.

"Morning, Dad," he mumbled happily.

"Mmm." His dad continued to read his article. When he finished, he folded the paper and eyed his son. He had never met a boy that ate ketchup on his eggs before Teddy. There he was smothering his momma's delicious scrambled eggs with the nasty red syrup. That boy was surely strange. "I saw in the paper that they are going to be laying off at the mill." He tried not to look at the nasty ooze on the boy's plate, but was compelled to do so.

"Yes, they told us last week. Over a hundred people, I believe." Teddy placed the revolting looking eggs in his mouth.

The old man grimaced at the sight, "Are you going to get laid off?"

"No sir. They will be keeping me. It does not seem likely that they can get the machines to run without me."

To Teddy's utmost surprise, Patrick inquired, "Boy, when are you going to stop fooling around and ask the girl to marry you, already?"

Teddy dropped his fork, staring at his dad in dismay. "What girl, Dad?"

"Oh come on. Don't act so innocent. Shella's a good girl, but you cannot expect her to wait around for you to get the guts up to ask her forever."

Teddy looked downward. He was used to being ashamed and feeling guilty for these feelings, and here his dad had known for how long? "How long have you known about us?"

"Quite a while, actually." He took another sip of his coffee. "That house you built for her was the first clue."

"I didn't build it for..." He had to stop as not to lie. He really had built it for her, but he did not know she loved him until the other day. How did his dad know? "And just how do you know she loves me?" Was he really going to try and deny it?

"Go ahead and play games, but if you're not careful, she will move on and away, and you will lose her. I figured you would have sense enough to ask her last night. You had the perfect opportunity."

Teddy scraped his plate and washed it quickly. His dad's candor was making him nervous. How could he know? Then, it hit Teddy. He knew! He knew and he was okay with it. His dad had put his approval on him and Shella. He did not want her with Tyler. He started to the door and hesitated briefly.

"Dad, you would not mind if it was I that married Shella?"

Taking his reading glasses from his face, the father followed the steps to where his son was standing. "Why wouldn't you marry her? You are the one she loves. I would mind if you let her get away." He slapped his shoulder.

Teddy smiled. That was one answered prayer. Now, what would his mom say? Had God prepared her heart, as He had his dad's? He was not exactly worried about Tyler's reaction, because Tyler truly did not think of Shella in that way. Tyler would be the easiest of the three, but his mom had the heart attack and could not handle a lot of stress.

That Wednesday night, after Teddy called Shella, like he promised, he found out how wrong he had been. He quickly released his call, when he heard Tyler's truck in the drive, and retired to his room. Tyler had been a little cool toward him at church, or so he thought. Maybe it was just his guilty conscience making him paranoid.

Tyler loudly banged around downstairs for a while, because their mom and dad were not home. When he came up the stairs, he did so with silent steps, because he surprised Teddy by bursting through his door. Taking two steps to stand next to Teddy's dresser, he opened the first drawer and flung its contents on the bed.

"Let me help you pack, Brother," he stated sarcastically.

∞

Teddy threw him a puzzled look. "What is your problem, Tyler?"

"My problem is a two timing girlfriend and a traitor brother, who stabbed me in the back. You can pull the knife out now, Teddy."

By now, three more drawers were joined the others on the bed. Teddy still did not understand. Tyler was gone this morning, when he was talking to Dad, so he did not hear the conversation. That was the only thing he could think of that would make Tyler upset. He and Shella had been extraordinarily careful not to let anyone see them.

Tyler's words infuriated him. His broad shoulders straightened, until he almost stood taller than the younger brother. Whatever Tyler wanted to say about him, he could. Teddy had done many things to hurt Tyler, but when it came to Shella, he best not say anything. She was good and pure.

"What are you talking about, Tyler?" he queried angrily.

"I saw you last night. You didn't know I was there, when you were kissing Shella. You knew she's my girlfriend, but you did not care. What Teddy wanted, Teddy took. How could you do that?" He crammed the empty drawer back into its hull. "Never mind. I know how you could do something like that, but I cannot believe Shella could do something like that."

"Hold it right there, Tyler." Teddy, who was rarely angered by his brother, let the full force of his wrath come through his tone, "Shella is *not* your girlfriend, so she has done nothing of any sort. You know she does not like you that way."

"No thanks to you. You made sure of that." Tyler knew his brother could whip him, even if Teddy was shorter, but that did not matter now. He had gone too far to turn back now.

"Tyler, you don't like her that way, either."

"You did not give me the chance. She would have fallen in love with me, after we were married."

"It doesn't work that way, Tyler, and you know it."

"Are you moving out or what, cause if you don't, I will?" He withdrew the venom of his presence to sulk in his own room. As he left, "It would be better for you, since you have got that new house and all."

Tyler's pride was completely shattered. He could not tell his mom and dad about Teddy and Shella. They had expected *him* to gain Shella's affection.

Teddy had a huge piece of land, a new house, his dream job, and now, a dream girl. Tyler was the prodigal son's brother that believed he should receive the rewards, not the prodigal.

He wanted to confront Shella presently, but she was gone. They were all expected to show up at her graduation. He would deal with her then.

He made up his mind that he was not riding up with Teddy, so if Teddy rode up with their mom and dad, he would go on his own.

He wished Pomalee was still here. He had found her to be a wonderful confidante over the time she stayed at Shella's house. She was fun and whimsical. She was loyal and wise. She always made sense without having judgment. Of course, Shella did not judge him, either, but she had betrayed him. How dare she turn down his affections?

Teddy prayed and enlisted Shella's prayer too. Embarrassment would not allow him to tell her about his altercation with Tyler. He didn't want to bring her goodness into it, and he knew Tyler would eventually get over his anger, when he found someone else to chase after.

He supposed that was God's answer to prayer. Maybe it was not the way he expected God to take care of it, but at least Tyler knew now. That only left his Mom to find out. Would she really be devastated over this? It was only a matter of time, before Tyler told her. He questioned God's plan at this point. Was it really God's answering of prayer, or was it punishment for living such a wicked life?

He was excited about Shella's graduation. In just a couple more days, she would be near him for good. All this leaving and separation would cease. He loved her and wanted to marry her, if she would have him. Maybe they could be married within a month or so, and then she would never have to leave his side again.

Naturally, the devil pointed out his inadequacies which made him anxious. What if she married him and found out he was not the man she thought he was? He knew he was not good enough for her. He had accepted and returned the flirtations of other girls, he had been a drunk, and he had been a shame to his family. These thoughts made him second-guess. What in the world was it that Shella Evans loved about him?

As the day of celebration drew near, excitement spread like a wild fire among all the students that were to graduate, and to their loved ones. On the home front, Teddy was a little anxious to find out what decision Shella had made about their future.

Would she want to stay in the middle of nowhere, USA with him or rather go to a big city that had more to offer? Now that she knew about his tattoo, would she decide she could not love him after all? He determined to get affirmation of Shella's love, one more time before facing his mother that night after graduation.

Tyler drove his own car Friday, mainly because he had to work, and secondly, he did not want to ride with Teddy. As much as he wanted to hate Teddy, it was not in his heart to detest his own brother. His parents had bred him better than that, but he was still hurt over the betrayal. He knew Teddy was right about him and Shella not sharing those feelings, but he had lost the challenge, and that was a slap on his manhood. This gave the wheels in his brain time to spin and plot what he was going to do about his brother and Shella.

Teddy, who had taken the day off at work, rode up with his parents. They arrived early afternoon to find Shella's room swamped with flowers, but no Shella. It seemed like everyone had had the same idea for a gift.

"Where is our girl, Pomalee?" asked Patrick.

"She is down at the Kissing Booth,"

"The Kissing Booth?" questioned Georgia. "Yes, the graduates are putting on a carnival for graduation. They do it every year as a fundraiser. It is a lot of fun. Shella is in charge of the Kissing Booth, again."

"Carnival? Will they have rides and all?" questioned the older man.

"Yes sir. There are only a couple of rides, because it costs so much. We don't think that bigger is always better. We pretty much stick to our booths to make money. Our sorority runs the Ring Toss Booth, also, and our fraternity brothers are in charge of the Dunking Booth and Pie Eating Contest. The chorus runs a Musical Chairs Booth, that sort of thing."

"That sounds like a lot of fun," Georgia smiled at remembering her own college days.

"It is a lot of fun. Mrs. Gordon, please allow me to show you around the house, and then we will explore the carnival. Most of them are closed right now, but that is okay, too." She took the elder lady's arm and giving Teddy a smile, led her up the stairs.

"Dad, I am going to find Shella. I'll catch up with you later. Do you mind?"

"I don't mind. If it had been me, I wouldn't have waited this long," he patted his shoulder.

Shella had been more panicky than Pomalee had ever seen her. She was generally calm under pressure, but this morning she pressed her gown five times. As if graduation was not enough, the two of them were singing with the rest of the senior choir for the ceremony. Shella felt as if she had not enough practice, since she had been disabled after the debacle in the snow. With her sore throat, swollen tonsils, stuffed nose, and everything that comes with pneumonia, she could only practice it in her head, but it was not the same as voicing it. She felt inadequate. She did thank God that she had no solo or duet to sing for the presentation. Maybe she could mouth the words and not ruin it for everyone else.

She put on her white dress and shoes, pulled her hair back into a ponytail, looked at her graduation gown, thinking how she needed to iron it, yet again, when she returned. Meanwhile, she needed to go make the signs for the Kissing Booth, and fix it up for the opening. She grabbed her bag of ribbons, balloons, and other decorations, kissed Pomalee on the cheek, and skipped out the door, trying to forget being nervous.

She passed several friends on their way to fix up their booths, with a song in her heart. Her sweet love would be here in a few hours, and she was going to tell him how she had not accepted the other job. She would be free to go home with him, marry him, and love him forever. God was an awesome God, and His will in her life made her complete.

She had blown up the balloons, made some signs, and was putting up the ribbons, when the sunlight brightened the dark room, where someone had pulled the tarp away to enter.

"We are not opened ye......tttt" Thump!

The chair she was standing on to reach the beam across the top had been placed on the piece of the tarp that dragged on the ground, and when Teddy pulled it back in frustration, it sent the chair over, toppling the girl hard on the ground with a yell.

Teddy charged in. Upon seeing Shella fall, he tried to catch her, but failed. "Are you okay?" He forgot about being angry with her.

"Ow! Ow! Ow!" she cried half laughing, trying to shake it off.

Teddy picked her up easily in his arms and sat her on the wooden shelf. "You are bleeding." He took his handkerchief from his pocket and touched it to her lip. "It's swelling. Let me get some ice."

"They have a snow cone cart down the middle a little way. They will give you a cup of ice."

She watched him close the tarp behind him and then quickly assessed the damage, before he could return. She could feel her lip was already fat. Her ankle hurt a little bit, but it was nothing serious. Her right side hurt. It would probably bruise, where it hit the back of the chair, but nothing major. Upon further searching, she realized her dress was torn in the back. Drat it all! This was the dress she had bought for graduation. What would she wear now? She would have to sing in front of everybody with a fat lip and a dress that did not match. How embarrassing!

Teddy came back shortly with a paper cone full of shaved ice. "Here, put this on your lip. Is it still bleeding?"

"I think it stopped."

"I am so sorry. Are you hurt bad?"

"I will be fine. You know me; always graceful."

He kissed the side of her lip that was not swollen softly. "I am so sorry."

"It was not your fault. I am forever clumsy." She was too happy that Teddy was here to hurt too much. "I am glad you are here. I wasn't expecting you until later. I have so much to tell you."

He put some of the ice in his handkerchief and was handing it to her. "Are you really glad?"

Her dancing eyes faltered, "What do you mean by that? Teddy, what's wrong? Has something happened to your mom or dad?"

Without a word, Teddy reached to the right of her and took the marker she had been writing with to make signs for prices, and began writing on the back of one of her signs. Shella's demeanor changed to amusement as he wrote the words 'sold out' on the paper. Then, he opened the tarp back up and coarsely hung it on a nail that held the closed sign.

"Humph," he grumbled, slapping down two one hundred dollar bills beside her. "Is that enough to buy all your kisses? If not, I can go get some more."

Shella laughed happily, removing a wisp of hair that had fallen on his forehead. "Why Teddy Gordon! If I did not know any better, I would say that you are jealous."

"You better believe I am jealous! How would you like for me to go around kissing a bunch of girls?"

"I didn't know that was an option!" She sported with him. "Thank you so much for volunteering. We will surely earn enough money for next year for sure, now. I know the girls would line up a country mile to kiss that handsome face. Let me have that marker. I'll make the signs right now."

Teddy nuzzled her ear. "You are a dreadful girl. It's not funny. The only lips I want on this ugly mug are yours, Miss Evans."

"You don't want these lips anywhere. They are fat and embarrassing."

"They are beautiful." He kissed them softly, until the sunlight bore in, announcing another intruder.

Patrick Gordon realized what he had interrupted and smiled mischievously at his son, but upon seeing Shella, he declared in alarm, "Teddy, what have you been doing to our Shella. It looks as if she has been beaten."

Teddy eased her down from the shelf to her feet, but as she put her foot to the floor, the heal broke off the rest of the way. This time Teddy secured her from falling.

Shella started laughing. Her philosophy had always been that it is better to laugh than cry. She knew better than to ask what else could go wrong. "I am such a klutz! You should stay away from me."

It was now that they saw the little mother and Pomalee, who wore a smile on her lips. "She fell off the chair," Teddy explained.

"Oh Dear, you are hurt!" cried Georgia, upon seeing her swollen lip.

She was still laughing, "Only my pride." Leaning on her lover's arm, she pulled off the other shoe. Quietly she added only to him, "Um, Teddy, I can't go anywhere."

He frowned in concern, "What is wrong?"

"I ripped my dress," she whispered in mortification.

He promptly slid his coat from his back and placed it around her shoulders, and responded quietly so that no one else would hear. "Do you need me to carry you?"

"I can walk." She was discouraged that everything was falling apart, "I have just ruined everything."

He looked at her pitifully. Pomalee surmised what was going on and came to the rescue. She wrapped her arm around Shella and led her away limping. "Come on. We will have to find you something else to wear. You silly goose. All that ironing you did for naught. Teddy, your folks were coming to get you, so you could go get some dinner. If you will just give us a few minutes, we will be ready to go with you."

ശ‍ൟ

Shella gracefully declined the invitation. She needed to find something else to wear and redo everything. She still needed to finish the booth. She had no time to eat, besides, she was afraid that if she ate something, she might lose it during the ceremony.

She didn't have another white dress, so she had to settle with a pale pink one with white flowers. Her white heels were traded for a pair of shiny silver ones. She would probably be the only one not completely in white, but there was nothing she could do about it at this point.

She tried, yet again, to fix her hair, which refused to do as it was told. She was not one to wear makeup, but today she opted to wear a little lipstick, but after putting it on, she regretted it, because it smeared on her teeth. Now, she was messed up again! Quickly, she grabbed a Kleenex, which caused a chain reaction of everything falling into the floor.

"Stop!" she commanded her trembling. "Breathe. Now, calm down."

She waited a minute, forcing deep breaths to calm her, before picking everything up. This should all have been packed away in the first place. She didn't know why she had procrastinated. She carelessly threw all in her suitcase, except the lipstick. In her frustration, she thrust the little tube in the trash can, where she found an envelope addressed to her in Teddy's handwriting. It must have fallen from her dresser.

Hello Beautiful,

I am very proud of you. Knock them dead up there tonight.

I love you

A smile crossed her pink teeth, as she read the card. It was a precious reminder that helped soothe her nerves. If only she could recognize this love to the whole world. She wanted, so much, to tell his parents how happily in love she was with him.

She quickly finalized readying herself and went on over to finish her booth. She smiled happily at seeing Teddy's 'sold out' sign, before taking it down. He was jealous. That was adorable. She decided not to climb in the chair again, so all her decorating was within her reach.

Next, she journeyed to the banquet hall where Celia, the valedictorian, was practicing her speech. She asked Shella for her evaluation. As she concluded, Shella clapped her hands in excitement in between wiping her eyes.

"Bravo! You should go into journalism. That was excellent. I am going to miss you Celia."

Others were starting to trickle in, and Pomalee came backstage a little later, announcing they had returned. Shella wanted one more chance to see Teddy before it all began. His sweet smile had a calming effect on her that she was in dire need of. Also, she owed it to the family that had so kindly come to see her graduate, to spend more time with them, but as she came out onto the floor, she ran straight into Christopher and Amber.

"Hey there Punk!" Christopher threw his muscular arm around her in a head lock drawing her to him. "Are you too good to talk to your big brother, now that you are a double major graduate?"

Happy to be in his arms, she elated and returned his embrace, "Christopher! When did you get here?"

"About thirty minutes ago."

Shella hugged Amber, "Has my brother been treating you good? If not, I will beat him for you. Trust me, it would be my pleasure."

Christopher touched her fat lip, "Looks like somebody has already been beating on you. Have you been fighting, Punk?"

"Only with inanimate objects."

"Same old Shella. One thing I can always count on is for you to be clumsy." He turned to his wife. "Shella Esther got hurt more than Teddy, Tyler, and me all put together. Definitely, stay away from her, now."

Shella looked at him curiously. "What do you mean, now? I am not a danger to others, just myself." He gave her the raised eyebrow look he was so famous for. "Okay," she laughed, "sometimes I injure others."

"Well, I expect you to learn how to behave in a lady like manner, with grace and agility in the next few months, or I will just have to keep your little niece or nephew from hanging around you."

Shella's mouth dropped open. Christopher had never seen her speechless. Amber glowed happily at her new sister. "We are due in October."

"Hot diggity dog!" Shella jumped up and down in excitement, but quickly stopped, for it hurt her ankle a little. "I am going to be the best aunt you ever saw. You just wait and see. Ooh, I feel sorry for you Amber. If Christopher's children have to pay for Christopher's meanness, I really will pray for you." She grabbed Christopher again in a hug. " I am so glad you guys are here. I have missed you."

"You have? I was not sure if I should come or not, since you made it perfectly clear that you don't want your big brother around."

Shella's brow furrowed, "What are you talking about?"

Amber put her hand on her husband's chest in a gesture for him to behave. "He was furious when he found out about the car wreck and you did not call him to let him know."

"Oh," she looked at him apologetically. "I didn't want you to think you had to come running to take care of me. It really was not that bad. Pomalee was the one really hurt."

"Yes, and you didn't even tell me that much. I should have been here for the both of you. I am responsible to Pomalee's parents for her well being. Shella Esther, that was selfish and wrong."

"I know, and I'm sorry. I should have called. You are right." She kissed his cheek for forgiveness.

"Has anything else happened while I have been gone that you did not want to worry me about? Has any other accidents happened? Any broken bones? What about the house? Did you burn it down? I know the car was totaled."

"You think you are so funny Christopher Aaron. I have news for you. You may be my big brother, but I am perfectly capable of taking care of myself. I didn't call you, and I told you I was wrong. I should have, but I had a lot going on at the time. Furthermore, I had Teddy and Tyler mothering over me, so you didn't really need to be there. While I am on the subject, there has been one change, and you can like it or lump it. I do not really care. It is none of *your* business, but since it is a major change in my life, and you insist on thinking you need to know all about me, I'll tell you. You can whine and gripe all you want, but I am not marrying Tyler. I am in love with Teddy, and he loves me, and I do not care if you or his mom and dad want me with Tyler, it is not going to happen. Teddy is the most wonderful man in the world, and I love him, so you can put that in your pipe and smoke it!"

Christopher was smiling at her tenacity. His kid sister had a good head on her shoulders, after all. "Well, I will declare! Shella Esther, you are full of surprises. I must say that my oldest and dearest friend and my sister getting together is a wonderful idea. What makes you think I would want you with Tyler?"

"Because, you are always pushing me to go out with Tyler, and you sent him those stupid love…"

He interrupted, because he did not want his wife to hear about his childish pranks, "I'm happy for you and Teddy, Shella Esther. You couldn't ask for a better guy. I admit that I had doubts about Teddy, but since he found Jesus, he is a new man. It makes me feel a whole lot better to leave you in his hands. If he loves you, he will take better care of you than I can."

Christopher was doing it again. She didn't need anyone to take care of her! She was an adult. She was about to spout her anger at Christopher when Amber smiled at Shella, while looking over her shoulder. "Speak of the devil."

Across the small crowd of people coming in, Teddy and his parents were approaching. Shella turned quickly to Christopher with pleading eyes. "You cannot say anything about it, yet. Please, Christopher, Teddy needs time to tell his folks and Tyler, before we can say anything. Nobody can know about it."

Greetings incurred hand shaking, hugging, but mostly kissing. Georgia enveloped Shella in another embrace. "You should have come with us, Dear. Are you feeling better?"

"Yes thank you. Did you have a nice dinner?"

"Delicious!" piped in Patrick. "Let me see that lip." He touched his finger to it softly. "It will go down in no time."

Shella laughed, "Unfortunately, not in time for me to have to get in front of everybody." She handed Teddy's coat back to him. "Thank you." He looked curiously at what she held in her hands. "This is for you, Mrs. Gordon. Your son was the first customer at our kissing booth, and he bought you the first kiss."

She handed the woman a large one pound Hershey's chocolate kiss decorated in ribbon and a card, which Shella had filled out for Teddy. Both of the Gordon men smiled coyly. So that was what the Kissing Booth was. Neither one would have guessed that. Shella was not allowed the pleasure of seeing Teddy's reaction for fear his mom and dad might suspect something, but she imagined he was eating crow.

"That was very sweet, Theodore." His mother graced his cheek with a kiss. She could not resist the motherly urge to fix the collar of his coat. "You are such a good boy. All three of my sons are good boys."

Shella smiled at the sight. "I am glad Pomalee kept you company enough. She never gets nervous."

It was Pomalee's turn to laugh, "That is how much you know. I get plenty nervous." She linked her arm in Shella's. "Is it time for us to get ready?"

"It is a few minutes, yet. I brought your cap and gown over with mine." She tried hard not to look at Teddy, lest her face betray her soul. Neither would she look at Christopher, who had that stupid grin on his face, that he had when he was lording something over her, lest he betray her secret.

Patrick took his wife's arm gently, leading her away from the young people. "Come on Momma. We will find a seat. We do not want to get too far back, or we will not be able to see our Shella girl graduate." In truth, he was making an excuse to let Teddy have a few moments with the girl he loved.

"Keep an eye out for your brother, Teddy. He should be here shortly," the mother called back.

ça∽ల

It was all done with so much discretion, that Shella was standing alone with Teddy, before she knew it. Christopher put his arm around Pomalee, and directed her away a couple of steps to fuss at her for not calling him or her parents about the wreck.

"What are your folks going to think about me for not being available to you? I am responsible for you, you know?" Shella heard him chide.

She had only a brief moment to thank Teddy for the card. Shella put her hand on his arm, trying to convey with her smiling eyes, what she could not speak. "Here is your change from your kiss."

"No, I donated it. It is for your sorority." He pushed the money back to her.

"Well, thank you then, and thank you for the card. It was a pleasant surprise."

He blushed, "I meant it."

"You look very nice in your suit. I know how much you hate wearing them."

"I will wear a suit everyday, if it would make you happy," he responded in a low voice.

Pomalee came around his side, and Shella dropped her hand. "Come on Shella. It's time to get ready." She smiled at Teddy, "Next time you see us, we will be college graduates."

Christopher, who had returned, elevated his comment, as they left, "Don't fall on your face, Punk."

Amber elbowed him in the ribs, "You are so terrible to your sister."

He turned and kissed her cheek, "Dear, if I were nice to Shella

Esther, she would think I was mad at her. Right, Teddy?" He nudged his old friend.

Teddy grinned bashfully, "Shella can hold her own, Amber. Trust me, she gives as good as she gets."

Christopher stuck out his hand to his friend. As Teddy reciprocated, he was swallowed in a masculine embrace. Christopher's other hand slapped heartily on his back.

"Thanks for taking care of her, Brother. I couldn't ask for anybody better for my kid sister."

Teddy accepted his approval with enthusiasm. Of course, Shella would have to tell Christopher. He was just glad that Christopher was okay with it. Now, his mom was the only one left to tell, and he was planning on doing that tonight or tomorrow.

ᔥᔥᔐᔐ

They found some seats behind Mr. and Mrs. Gordon for the three of them, while Georgia was doing her best to save at least one seat for Tyler, who came in during the prayer that initiated the ceremony.

Shella was hard to pick out of the multitude of red caps and gowns, but Teddy had no difficulty finding or being mesmerized by her. There was a young man singing the national anthem that sounded as if Heaven had opened its portal and glory came down. After the choral portion came the instrumental portion. Then Celia and Larry Stenbach, the salutatorian gave their speeches, while the singers and musicians worked their way back to their appropriate seats.

So far, the entire service had gone on without a hitch, but Shella's way of thinking was that something humiliating was bound to happen, since everyone she loved was watching. It was not enough that her lip was swollen, and she was the only one in the entire congregation without white shoes on.

Then, it happened. The boy sitting in front of her had been leaning on the back two legs of his chair for most of the ceremony, but when the students on his row stood to get their diplomas, he lost balance, and his chair fell completely backward on Shella's lap, causing at least two other students to trip over him, all of which toppled on Shella and her seat mate. Needless to say, all the ironing she had done was for no purpose. Even her cap was crumpled.

They all scrambled to recover without much shamefacedness, but

Shella could not help breaking out in hysterical laughter. The building anxiety was released, when the object of anticipation happened. It was a good thing she had not worn any makeup, or she would have cried it right back off. This was the graduation she expected.

Fortunately for her, she had managed to stop laughing before they called her name. There was no thunderous applause, because the dean had asked everyone to hold all applause until the end, but naturally, one lone shrill whistle sounded through Christopher's fingers and teeth. She received both pieces of sheepskin with a slightly reddened face, shook the dean's hand, and retreated to her chair.

It seemed like a long time, before all the names were called, and Felicia Zigfried was, once again, in her seat. The graduates were directed to rise, turn their tassels to the other side, and then it was over after the final prayer.

Loud "Hooray's and "No more school!"'s went throughout the crowd, but Pomalee and Shella looked at each other sadly. This was the end of an era in their lives. The simple girlhood dream life was at an end. Tomorrow, they would wake up at new residences to face the cruel real world, responsible, and paying their own way. The fun was over.

"I love you, Pomalee. I am so glad we are still going to be together." Shella hugged her neck.

"Me too. I am so glad we met each other five years ago. Imagine how awful it would be, if we had never come here or met."

"That is a horrid thought dear sister. I am just glad God put you in my life. You are the best. Are you ready to go find our family?"

"Yes, I know you want to be with Teddy." Pomalee was excited. Of course, having completed four years of college was a great feat.

Shella had the offer on the table to go another four years to earn her master's degree or even further to get her doctrine by way of a scholarship, but that was a personal offer she would keep secret. She had no intentions of leaving Teddy for that length of time.

❧

Christopher was the first to pick her up, swinging her around in excitement and then Tyler, followed by huge hugs from Patrick and Georgia. Naturally, Pomalee received the same treatment. After all, she was part of the family.

"Let's celebrate!" Tyler grinned hugely.

"It is getting late, Son. Your mom and I are going to head back home."

"You're right, Dad." Teddy offered, "We will go on, if you don't mind, ladies.

Shella could hardly hide her disappointment, but she understood that was the sacrifice Teddy was willing to make, and she loved him even more for it. "We understand." She hoped she sounded convincing.

"You stay here and enjoy the celebration, Teddy." the father insisted.

"You are not driving home at this hour, Dad. It is a long drive and very late. I am not letting you drive." Besides, he had no other way home.

The father pulled Teddy to the side and spoke in low tones, while Teddy's head was shaking vehemently. Shortly, Christopher stepped over to join them, while Tyler kept the converse in their circle going.

Christopher commanded firmly, "Teddy, Amber and I will take your mom and dad home. We flew down, and have a rental that we have to turn back into the airport. Mr. Gordon, would you and Mrs. Gordon follow us to the airport? I would appreciate the opportunity to drive you two home."

"I really don't mind taking them back home, Christopher." Teddy felt Christopher's hand on his shoulder.

The older man humphed. "I have been driving longer than you two boys have been living. I think I can drive my wife and self home."

"But Sir, in my wife's condition, I think it would be best for her to go home tonight," Christopher kept arguing.

The old man smiled slyly, "Your wife's condition? Well then, by all means, you drive us home. We have to prepare for a grandchild."

Patrick gave in to his request. He wanted Teddy to be able to stay with Shella and ride back with her. Maybe then, he would have some wedding plans to announce. He wouldn't mind having a whole house full of grandchildren.

They all wandered over to the parking lot with the two couples. Meanwhile, Christopher chided Shella about this or that, trying to get her to understand that the choices she made from that moment on would be crucial in her life. The new Shella accepted his overprotective behavior without getting angry with him for babying her. Through the entire trauma she had been in the last year, she had learned to appreciate him in a new light.

Once they were at the car, Georgia gave Pomalee a hug first and then Shella. "Now, you go have fun with my boy. Take care of him for me." Shella's ear was still close to her that she could whisper. "Teddy loves you so."

Shella gave her gracious smile with a kiss on each of the wrinkled cheeks. She worried that they had overstressed themselves over this trip. "I will make sure they both have fun," she assured.

The rest of the farewell hugs and kisses, and duplicate congratulations passed around the crowd, before the two married couples hopped in their cars, leaving the four younger people still standing there. Georgia's acknowledgement did little to ease Shella's nervousness. Tyler had a gleam in his eye, and he was leaving her alone, which was odd. What was he planning on doing?

"Lord, help us to get through this ordeal according to Your plans," she prayed alone.

"To the carnival, we shall go!" Tyler shouted, holding both elbows out for both ladies to take, so he could escort them.

Shella was reluctant, but Pomalee grabbed her arm and Teddy's, leaving Shella no choice, but to grab Tyler's. She lay her head on Pomalee's shoulder, as they entered the banquet hall. "Just think. This is the last time we will come in here."

"Oh, don't make me cry." Each let go of the boy's arm and hugged each other again, trying not to let the tears come.

They found a round table for four, where the underclassmen had decorated so beautifully with crepe paper, flowers, and red and gold tablecloths. It was all gorgeous, leaving the seniors a little sadder about leaving.

Shella promptly excused herself to operate her Kissing Booth. She would have to spend a couple of hours working, before her duty would be fulfilled. Teddy would have followed, but he felt obligated to stay with Pomalee and Tyler. He didn't want a replay of the other night in front of Shella.

Tyler was the only one hungry, but everyone insisted on sampling the food, so as to not offend those that had worked so hard to prepare it. Tyler did not look at his brother, nor did Teddy look at him. Pomalee, on the other hand, noticed everything with curiosity. She chattered incessantly to keep Tyler's mind occupied, so he wouldn't want to go off and chase Shella. She was no idiot. She felt the tension between the two brothers.

Some of the fellow classmates and underclassmen put on a talent show, of sorts, for the entertainment of the banquet. There was singing, joking, and play-acting on the stage, which had most rolling with laughter, but Teddy kept asking himself why he was here. He should have driven his folks home.

After the last act, the lights brightened to an uproarious crowd. Several girls came over asking Pomalee where Shella was. It was the former teammates from her softball team. She had not been able to play this last year, because of her injuries, but they wanted her to get her picture taken with them one last time.

Pomalee directed them to the carnival outside. "Come on fellows. Surely, Shella will be almost finished now."

The whole group, including the ball team chattered and played all the way to the Kissing Booth, where the team mates grabbed Shella, pulling her arm.

"Come on. We want to get our picture taken one last time," one of them insisted.

"Sonya, I was not a part of your team this season."

"So what. We are all a team. You were our captain. We had no team without you."

"Yeah. It is not your fault you couldn't play this year," another chided.

"Come on!" they all blended their voices.

When they dragged her away, Teddy quickly made an excuse to leave, also. Tyler made him uncomfortable all evening. He knew Tyler was up to something and did not want a scene. Did that make him a coward?

Pomalee met up with Shella in the ladies room a little while later, after the pictures had all been snapped. The hour was getting late and both were extremely exhausted from the day's emotional roller coaster. Shella agreed that she was ready to fall into bed. It was nostalgia that made them want to spend one last night, before heading home tomorrow for good.

However, Tyler was not quite ready to call it an evening. He actually wanted to find something else to do, contrary to the girls grumbling at the suggestion. They could see he had something up his sleeve, something mischievous.

∞∞

Teddy had not joined them again, and Shella wanted to be near him. She asked Pomalee to make her excuses to Tyler that she was closing up the Kissing Booth, and would catch up later.

She made a quick chore of closing up the booth, and then took her cap and gown in arm and went to find her lover. Though she did not see him anywhere, she was just relieved to be out in the fresh air to ease the pain that had afflicted her head. The headache was the result of all the stress of the day that had built up and began hurting a couple hours ago.

She was leaning over the fence watching the geese in the moonlight on the campus lake thinking how she wished she was as graceful and beautiful as they were gliding across with ease.

A familiar form approached a little further down the pathway that followed the lake, walking with his hands in his pockets. Shella's face fell under the beams of the moon, and once again, glory came down, appearing in flesh as the most beautifully made of God's creatures.

"Standing all alone like that could be very dangerous, Miss Evans."

She smiled, but remained silent, still looking over the reflection of the water. She was finally going to get a few brief minutes alone with Teddy.

"He is right, you know?" came another voice out of the night from the other direction.

Both turned a startled head. Shella broke the silence, "Lawrence! How does it feel to be a college grad?"

He gave a huge grin. "Absolutely great!" He closed in on them and stuck his hand out for Teddy to shake. "Shella, I was wondering if I could speak to you in private for a few minutes."

Teddy interpolated. "I'll see you tomorrow, Shella." His long strides took him away, until she saw him meet up with Tyler and Pomalee. He wore fatigue and discouragement on his shoulders. Shella wanted to grab and hold him, until he was at peace again. She wanted to tell him that his mother knew he loved her, but even that would have to wait.

"Care to walk?" She suggested, although her mind screamed, "Come back! I don't want to wait until tomorrow to see you again."

"Sure," he agreed and they began a stroll. "I couldn't let this be the last we ever saw each other and not say goodbye. We've had some good years."

"Yes, we have," she confirmed.

"Have you got your plans all set?"

She smiled, "Not quite. I've a few offers, but I am not certain which direction I will be going in."

"You will go far, no matter what you choose to do. You will make a good physical therapist."

"What about you? What are your plans?"

Lawrence put his hand on her back to direct her through the narrow passage first. "Tentative, also. I have an offer in New York I'm strongly considering. It is probably a once in a lifetime opportunity."

"It sounds wonderful! I know you will be great."

Lawrence stopped, as they came to the child care play ground gate. Kicking a rock beneath his foot, he entreated her attention over to the swing, where they had sat so many times before, but he remained standing, as she sat in the wide rubber strap.

"Shella, you'll never know how nice you made my time here. Thank you for all the wonderful days you have graced me with. I know your heart lies elsewhere, but know that I am *always* a phone call away, if you ever get free of him. All it takes is one time for him to not make you happy, and I will be there to snatch you away."

Shella laughed. "I thank you, as well. We were quite a pair for stirring up trouble." She put her feet on the ground to stop the swaying of the swing. "You made college enjoyable for me, too, Lawrence, and I will always love you for it."

"Here, here." He lifted her to her feet by her hand and kissed her cheek softly. "Goodbye, my friend."

She returned his friendly embrace. "Take care of yourself."

He turned and left, so she would not see his remorse. Saying goodbye to her was very hard. He was strongly tempted to kiss her for real for the first time. She had always been reserved about sharing her lips with anyone, and he had never had the pleasure of her kiss. He knew he had no right. A kiss now would taint all they had ever shared.

Shella slid back down into the swing. So much was changing so fast. Her girlhood was officially over. Although a bright, new, and hopeful prospect of a wonderful life with Teddy was dawning, she held dear these precious days of sisterhood.

Teddy, Tyler, and Pomalee came quietly through the gate. They had followed at a distance, like a group of little curious children.

Pomalee stood behind her and placed her arms around Shella's neck, while Tyler plunked into the swing beside her. A still awkward Teddy wandered over to the see saw a little bit away from the others. He was going to leave, but could not without one more goodbye from Shella.

"I am sad," Pomalee cried.

"I know," agreed Shella.

"You two girls are getting me depressed," Tyler accused. "Such sad saps! Cheer up! I command it!"

Pomalee took her hand closest to Tyler and shoved him on the swing. "You hush up. This is a big thing for us."

Tyler's swing swung back mighty close to Shella's. He put his feet down to prevent hitting her and then stood up. Clearing his throat dramatically to make a grand gesture, he began, "I am sick of your girlie bawling. I know just what you two cry babies need. I have something to say, and I would like everyone's attention."

Shella shooed him with her hand, "Oh sit down! We are women, and we have feelings, unlike you heartless men. Just sit down, because nothing you have to say is important."

He jerked his hands to his heart to signify that her words were stabbing him. "I'll have you know, everything I say is very important, Shella Evans. He closed his eyes and puckered his lips in feigned insult. "As I was saying, before I was so rudely interrupted," he turned to Shella and stuck out his tongue. "I have a proposal of marriage for Shella."

A sobering chill fell over Shella and Teddy, and even Pomalee. Shella stood quickly to object, so that Tyler would not make a fool of himself. "Can we please talk about this in private, later, Tyler?"

"No Dearie, let's do it right here and now, in front of our loved ones. Now, sit back down for me." He pushed her shoulders gently back into the swing, "Now, don't interrupt again."

Teddy fidgeted and inched in the opposite direction. He didn't want to hear this garbage. Tyler knew Shella didn't love him, but if he was going to be a glutton for punishment, then he did not want to be a witness to it, even though Tyler deserved it.

Pomalee tried her hand at avoiding this. "Tyler, Teddy and I are going to turn in. We are tired."

"Nope, you can't. This involves you. Please, listen to me. Teddy, hold on for a few minutes. I'll get to the point." In typical Tyler fashion, he waited until he received everyone's undivided attention. "Shella, you are beautiful, audacious, and very gifted, everything any man would consider perfect in a woman. You and I have been through bloody noses, baseball games, and unrequited love notes, yet we remain friends. I love you." There was an effective pause, as no one else dared to breathe. "I know I do not deserve you, but if you will have me, I promise to be the best brother-in-law you could ask for. You see, my big, dumb brother seems to be crazy over you, and, for whatever reasons that I don't even want to know, you are in love with him. It is, quite frankly, getting in the way of my trying to court Miss Pomalee. What do you say, Shella? Will you marry my dumb brother and make us all happy?"